USA TODAY BESTSELL...
DALE MAYER

Whispers
in the
Wisteria

Lovely Lethal Gardens 23

WHISPERS IN THE WISTERIA: LOVELY LETHAL GARDENS,
BOOK 23
Beverly Dale Mayer
Valley Publishing Ltd.

ISBN-13: 978-1-773367-68-2
Print Edition

Books in This Series

About This Book

A new cozy mystery series from *USA Today* best-selling author Dale Mayer. Follow gardener and amateur sleuth Doreen Montgomery—and her amusing and mostly lovable cat, dog, and parrot—as they catch murderers and solve crimes in lovely Kelowna, British Columbia.

Riches to rags. ... Some things stay buried. ... Some things don't, ... and it's chaos once again!

Spending time with Mack is always fun, but, when Doreen overhears a conversation that sounds like a murder confession, he disagrees, ... until a body shows up. Then he's suddenly a whole lot more interested. The deceased young man had planned to attend the local college and had hoped to rekindle a relationship with an ex-girlfriend.

Corporal Mack Moreau knows he can keep Doreen out of this current case, but, when the young man's grandmother calls and says it could be related to the unexplained disappearance of the young man's parents, ... then all bets are off. Doreen and her entourage are smack in the middle again.

When the case suddenly ties to her neighbor, Richard, it comes home in a big way.

Sign up to be notified of all Dale's releases here!
https://geni.us/DaleNews

Chapter 1

Early October …

D OREEN HAD SPENT days giving statements, while the police tried to get things straightened away, lining up flights where Ella had met Bob Small in Vancouver, tracking down hotels where he'd stayed, confirming Bob's story, sorting out where he was staying in town, and finding the apartment that he'd rented under his alias of Troy Little. Days of going through his little black book with names and dates of all his victims. And then Doreen needed some days of recuperation.

When Mack stopped in the following Friday, he sat down on the patio beside her. "The captain wants to know if you're done creating havoc yet."

She winced. "He knows I don't do it on purpose, right?"

"He does know that." Mack smiled. "We're getting quite a bit of notoriety for having closed all these cases. However, the backlog and the number of jurisdictions and all the provinces involved now is insane," he noted. "We have a lot of cases being examined along both sides of the border. Washington and Oregon mostly."

"Oh, ouch," Doreen replied. "Then we get into all those

lovely cross-border niceties too, *huh*?"

"The provincial government's forming a taskforce to go through every one of the Bob Small murders to ensure that everybody he took down gets justice and that every family gets answers to what happened," he murmured. "So, although it won't be an easy job, it will be a thorough one." Mack shook his head, adding, "The fact that Bob Small had a notebook and left you that piece of evidence? That's what blows everybody away. I still don't understand why he didn't kill you."

"I don't either," she admitted calmly. "He intended to. He had a gun with him, pointing it at me. I think that's what he was here for, what he was planning on doing, but then … I don't know. Something about making your birthday cake maybe …"

Mack stared at her.

She shrugged. "I know. It makes no sense."

"No, it doesn't, but then it can be something as simple as ice cream melting in the vehicle that stops a depressed woman from jumping off a bridge and committing suicide. The little things in life can throw a switch and make you do something, right or wrong."

Doreen nodded. "Something about that coffee cake. I cannot remember it all. I told him it was the first one I had ever made and that I was really proud of it, and he's the one who told me how to get it out of the cake pan."

He stared at her, slowly rubbing his face. "Good God," he murmured.

She patted his hand. "Now that you already ate your birthday cake …"

He burst out laughing. "I also didn't get my birthday this year at all, thanks to you," he noted. "Then you tell me that the cake you made for me, first time ever, a serial killer helped you make it …"

"Helped me get it out of the pan," she corrected. "So it wouldn't break or stick to the pan."

"Okay, so with all that craziness, we pushed off my belated celebration until tonight—in case you didn't realize it."

She frowned. "But I made you a cake already."

"You mean, you didn't make me another one?" he asked in mock horror. Then he grinned. "I really enjoyed it. You did a great job on it."

"That was my first coffee cake," she muttered, "and it might very well be the last. So don't hold out hope for more."

"I don't know about that." He laughed. "Maybe it was a fluke, and you should try again."

"*Hmm.* You would say that, just to goad me into baking you another cake." Then she smiled. "Besides I have learned that there's absolutely nothing quite like the joy of seeing other people eat the food you make."

"Exactly," Mack agreed. "That's how I feel when I cook for you."

"Too bad you stopped doing that too," she replied mournfully.

He burst out laughing. "It goes along with that whole, you know, *too much work* thing."

"I'm sorry about that," she said, "but hopefully nothing else will go wrong with your belated birthday dinner, so it can go off without a hitch."

"Yeah, Nick flew in last night. We had dinner together as a family, and now he's coming over today."

"Oh, *great*," she said, with an eye roll. "He won't be terribly happy with me."

"Why? Have you been avoiding him again?" he asked.

"No, I haven't, but my ex keeps trying to get a hold of me."

"And you haven't been answering, right?"

"No, other than that one time, when I thought it was Nan's number, I haven't been answering," she confirmed, with a big fat smile. "And it's making Mathew angrier and angrier."

"And that," Mack noted, a dark cloud over his face, "isn't a good thing."

"No, I understand," she said, a note of worry in her tone. "It is something that I want to talk to Nick about."

Mack nodded. "Nick told me something about he had news, so with any luck …"

"With any luck, my ex signed the papers, and I'm free and clear."

"That's the dream," Mack stated, with a smile.

"So, any other cases?" she asked, looking over at him.

He glared at her. "No—no cases," he snapped, "no cold cases, nothing. That Bob Small case tangentially involved in Ella's death was the big one. And we'll be dealing with the headaches surrounding it for months, if not years."

"It was a big one," she agreed, "and I'm sorry that it turned out to be as rotten as it was."

"Believe me. Everybody is pretty shocked about Ella's and Nelly's personal involvement with Bob Small, not to mention that Nelly killed Ella," he shared. "And it'll still take quite a while to get to the bottom of it all."

WANTING TO GET out before his belated birthday dinner

later today, Doreen and Mack drove down to City Park. As she wandered toward the beautiful pergola encased in wisteria, she smiled in delight as she pointed them out. "The wisteria are so gorgeous."

He looked up at them and smiled. "I don't think I've ever noticed them before."

She laughed, walking under the vine-covered square-shaped structure with some dried purple blossoms still on the ground. "That's because you're always worried about cases." She shook a finger at him. "You've got to have a life outside of crime, you know?"

He rolled his eyes at her. "You're the one telling me that?"

She gave him a fat grin. "Of course I am. Let's sit down over here on the hill." And tucked up on the corner of the wisteria, they sat down on the side and sipped the coffee they had picked up a few minutes earlier while driving through downtown.

"It's a really nice area," she noted, with a sigh of contentment.

He nodded, looked over at her. "Are you worried about my brother tonight?"

"No." She gave an airy wave of her hand. "As long as this divorce is progressing, we're all good."

He nodded. She heard something behind her. As she turned to look, Mack asked, "Is something wrong?"

She shrugged. "No, not necessarily, just hearing people talking."

"It would make sense if people *are* talking," he said in a dry tone. "Look where we are. It's a city park. We're up on a hill where the wisteria are, and you're overlooking one of the most beautiful sections of town," he noted. "People are everywhere."

She chuckled. "I know."

"Besides, … you're supposed to be relaxing and not getting into trouble anymore."

She batted her eyelashes at him. "I thought I did really well last time," she pointed out. "We didn't get into trouble. I didn't get attacked, and nobody got hurt."

He gave her a look.

"Okay, so Nelly died by her own hand, and this guy killed himself, but honestly it's …" She hesitated and then backtracked. "It sounds terrible, but it's not a bad outcome."

"No, it's not a bad outcome," he agreed. "Obviously we had a lot of questions, and it would have been really nice if we had gotten all those answers."

She nodded. "Somehow I don't think you would have gotten him to talk though."

"No, I'm not sure we would have either. He's not the kind to have handed out answers without reason." But then he looked at her and frowned. "Except in your case, where apparently he was quite happy to talk to you."

She shrugged. "I don't know what it was, but he did give me enough for us to sort out a bunch of his cases," she acknowledged.

He nodded. "And we're still puzzled over that too."

She shrugged. "I don't know either. I guess I just said the right things."

"Yeah, that's the problem. It's as if you have a silver tongue, and people spill their guts to you."

In the background behind her, she thought she heard something about *death* or *dead*. She tilted her head to the side, listening intently, even as she sipped her coffee. When she didn't hear anymore, she relaxed. He looked over at her, squeezed her hand, and she smiled. "Sorry, I keep hearing things."

"Hearing things or imagining things?"

"Either. Both. At least I get it right most of the time."

"*Yeah,*" he said, "unfortunately too often. Our workload is showing it. It's almost as if you have your own private police force now."

She burst out laughing. "Now, if that were the case, we could solve a whole pile more."

"I don't want to solve a whole pile more," he argued, groaning. "We need to catch up on what we're doing now."

"Okay," she said. "I'll give you a little bit more time." When he glared at her, she burst out laughing again. "I'm teasing. Don't take it personally."

"Anything to do with you is something that we must take personally," he admitted. "I've never met anybody who can get into the trouble you get into."

In the background she heard more whispers. She turned her head slightly so she could hear more, and then she heard it.

"I don't care. She's dead. We must do something."

She turned to Mack, placed her fingers against her lips, got up, and crept toward where she heard the voices.

"She's dead, I said. I don't know what to do."

She caught sight of a tall, slim man, talking on his phone.

"Don't you understand? When I say dead, I mean dead. As in, we have a body we need to dispose of." And then he froze, turned ever-so-slightly, caught a glimpse of Doreen, and ran in the opposite direction.

Mack was at her side in a heartbeat. "What was that?" he asked, frowning at her. "I thought I heard something about *dead* and *a body to dispose of.*"

"Exactly." She repeated what she'd heard. "But, of course, we didn't get a good look at him, didn't get a chance to talk to him, and we have no idea who's dead."

He stared at her, looked all around at the park. "He's long gone now. You also don't know that they were talking about a human body," he pointed out.

"That's true," she admitted. "He did look a little bit familiar though."

He groaned, closed his eyes, and added, "That won't be good."

With the heavy scent of the wisteria coming down on her, she looked up and chuckled.

He glared at her. "Now what's so funny?"

"*Whispers*," she began. "*Whispers in the Wisteria*." She threw her arms around his neck and gave him a great big hug. "The next mystery for me to solve."

"There is no mystery," he snapped, even as his arms wrapped around her securely. "We don't have a body. We don't have anything."

She gave him a big fat smile and added, "Not yet. But we will soon."

Chapter 2

Sunday Afternoon …

I T WAS SUNDAY afternoon. Doreen was delighted that Mack had stopped in for a quick visit. He'd been called into work on his day off and was, even now, looking tired and worn out. Stretched out beside her, he resembled Mugs who stretched out on the grass beside him. There was no sign of the other two. They'd come to greet him, then disappeared. "You need a holiday," she stated abruptly.

He looked at her and then smiled. "I'm happy that you're concerned about my well-being, *but I'm fine.*"

She rolled her eyes at that. "Of course you're fine."

He sighed. "If somebody would stop bringing in so much work into my department, it wouldn't be so bad."

She just frowned at him.

"I know. You're doing a huge service for everybody," he replied, eyeing her intently. "It has been noticed, though, that you're the one who's solving all these crimes."

"Oops," she muttered.

He nodded. "And it's not so much that you're solving them, but you have had a hand in them."

"Right," she agreed, "and, of course, that is a big difference."

"It's a huge difference," he confirmed. "It's to the point where people trust you. Still, it's a good thing," he added. "The Bob Small stuff won't be on my plate, so that's even better."

She smiled. "Not only that, but it'll also go big, and hopefully a lot of cases will get closed."

He nodded. "That's the plan." He reached an arm over, tucked her up close, and dropped a kiss on her forehead.

She chuckled. "You keep dropping kisses like I'm a two-year-old."

"I would kiss you a little bit differently," he muttered, "but you're the one who keeps holding me back."

She looked up at him. "And your patience, believe me, is very much appreciated."

He gave her an eye roll.

"I gather your patience is wearing thin, isn't it?" she asked frowning. She didn't need something else to worry about.

He shook his head. "I'm not a callow teenager. I know that some things are better when savored."

She raised her eyebrows and then chuckled. "I can get behind that too."

"Good. Speaking of which, have you heard from Nick?"

"I have," she said. "He left a message this morning, saying that he got paperwork back from my soon-to-be ex, and Nick was just now going over it to see what had been changed. He needed time for due diligence, and then he would contact me."

Mack asked her, "As in maybe he signed, and you're in the clear?"

"I don't know yet." Doreen frowned. "I know Nick

mentioned that it has to be filed to make it legal, I guess."

He nodded. "A few things have to happen, but, if he signed, it would mean that he agreed to the conditions. Probably to avoid that upcoming court hearing."

She shrugged. "I, … I don't know. I'm trying to give your brother as much space as he needs to handle this, so that I'm not involved. He doesn't need me breathing down his neck and messing something up."

"No more phone calls from the ex?"

She shook her head. "No, thankfully, and let's not jinx it."

He chuckled. "No, we don't want to do that. He's certainly been a pain in your backside for long enough."

"More than long enough," she murmured. "I hadn't even realized how much, until this whole divorce scenario, not to mention Robin's estate."

"Yeah, once Robin's will is settled, that will be another case of *good riddance*. Plus it seems your ex will have no reason to be bothering you—although distributing an estate can still take a while."

"Which means he'll be around, messing up my world for a while too." Doreen frowned. "Who needs that?"

"He hasn't mentioned Robin's will at all?"

She shook her head. "No, not in a long while."

Goliath suddenly appeared at her side, rubbing up and down her pant legs. She smiled, reaching out a hand to reassure him. He really didn't like it when she brought up her ex. She took a look around for Thaddeus to find him nodding on top of a fence board. She grinned watching him sway gently on his perch.

"And you're expecting him to?"

"He wants her estate as well. Thinks since he had a short

affair with her that Robin would leave everything to him. He forgets that he lied to her too," Doreen added, turning to face him. "I just don't trust him."

"Right," Mack muttered. "That's a good thing. Don't trust him for a minute. Expect him to be a pain in the butt. When and if he crosses the line, we'll deal with it in our own time, if there are any further problems."

"Now, your brother told me that he would handle this for me for free, but do you think I'm supposed to give him some money for it?" she asked worriedly.

Mack shrugged. "Why don't we wait and see how much you get for a settlement? Then you can always find out what Nick's fee would have been, and you can give him a portion, if you want. But he didn't ask for money. He did say he would do this to get you free and clear of Mathew, so you don't have to pay Nick a cent."

"*Not having to,*" she noted, "is one thing. *Wanting to* is an entirely different thing."

He smiled. "I appreciate the fact that, for you, there is a difference. Park that idea for now, and we'll talk to Nick about it later."

She beamed. "Thank you. It's always nice to know that I can bounce things off you."

He nodded. "That's the whole point of being friends—to be there when things get tough. So all is good."

"And not be there when life gets stupidly tough?" she asked, chuckling. When he raised an eyebrow, she shrugged. "No, nothing's wrong. Everything's fine."

He snorted at that. "Says you."

"Yep, says me," she repeated, with a beaming smile. "I just know that sometimes things aren't all that simple." She hesitated and then looked over at him. "So, when I phoned you earlier, you had been called out to work this morning."

"I was," he replied in a noncommittal voice.

"I won't be allowed to ask any questions, *huh?*"

He smiled at her and said, "Nope, sure won't."

She sighed. "Fine, ... but I might be of some help."

"You might, and, if I need any help, I know where to find you."

At that, she burst out laughing. "Nothing personal, but I don't suspect that you'll be asking for help anytime soon."

His grin was wide and infectious, but his tone was serious when he said, "I don't know about that. At times, it's definitely helpful to have you in my corner."

She nodded with satisfaction. "Absolutely. You just need to remember that."

He rolled his eyes. "Sometimes ... it's easier than others."

She asked, "Did you give any more thought to what we heard down at the park?"

He stared at her blankly for a few minutes. "What are you talking about?"

She frowned at him. "It's been on my mind, so I don't know how you could possibly walk away from it quite so easily."

"Walk away from what?" he asked in total surprise.

It was obvious to Doreen that he had completely put it out of his mind. "What we heard down at the wisteria."

He frowned at her, and his smile fell away. "Honey, don't make something out of nothing."

She glared at him. "We heard them talking about a body."

"Yes, we did seem to hear the same thing there, but what kind of a body? It could have been a dog. It could have been a deer somebody hit with their car. It could be all kinds of things."

She frowned, and he just frowned right back. She sighed. "In other words, you're telling me to leave it *alone*." She dragged out the last syllable to emphasize her point.

"Absolutely," he confirmed. "Until a *human* body pops up—"

"A female," Doreen noted.

"I didn't hear that part." Then Mack continued. "I will let you know once a *female* human body pops up that is absolutely connected to what we heard in the park—if that was even real, … which we have no idea that it was. It could be just a game they were playing."

"A game?" she asked, looking at him in astonishment.

"I don't know," Mack admitted. "It was just talk. We don't know who it was on the phone that day. We don't know who he was talking to, and we really don't know for sure what he was talking about."

There was some sense to that, and, as much as she didn't want to believe it, Mack was right.

"I guess now that you've solved our Bob Small mystery," he noted, "you're looking for your next case, *huh*?"

She looked around at her backyard. "I guess I could be doing all kinds of other things," she muttered. "I do have more gardening to do, here and at your mother's. Besides, I have other cases of Solomon's that I could look into. Even a bunch of things for me that I could tie up. For one," she added, "Nan mentioned those safe deposit boxes."

"You mean, she has more than one? And what could she have stashed away in those?" he asked, astonished.

Doreen nodded. "More than one is my understanding."

"Do you know where they are or what's in them? You

might want to check them out before … I'm not saying that she'll pass on anytime soon, but you really do want to have that information available—in case she does."

"I know, and I haven't mentioned it to her lately. I do need to look into that."

"Good enough," he said. "And looking into that should be safe enough." Then he gave her an exaggerated eye roll, with a big cheeky grin.

She smiled at him. "Sometimes you say the nicest things in the worst ways."

He burst out laughing. "Sometimes I have to because *sometimes* you just won't take no for an answer."

"Very true," she muttered. "Very true." She got up and announced, "I'll go make a sandwich. Do you want one?"

He bounded to his feet and asked, "Are you eating anything but sandwiches these days?" When she glared at him, he held up a hand. "Sorry. I just popped in for a little bit. I can't stay."

"Why not?"

This time he glared at her.

She smiled. "Hey, you know I'm just, … just asking a question."

"*Uh-huh,*" he muttered. "Just asking a question."

She chuckled. "You don't have to tell me if you don't want to."

"Okay, good," he replied cheerfully. "I won't." Just then his phone buzzed. He looked down at it, sighed, and muttered, "Okay, I have to go a little earlier than I thought."

"Something's up?"

"Yeah, something weird. Got to go down to the coroner's office."

"Okay then." She gave him a big smile. "If it's anything

I should know about, like a dead woman, like we overheard at the park ..."

He stopped and raised an eyebrow at her. "Like *you* overheard. Just remember. The wind can play tricks with what you hear, making you think it was behind you, when really it was in front of you."

"But the guy I saw *was* on the phone, and he ran off. It had to be him talking, the one I overheard."

"So only one guy can be on his phone at a time in the park? I don't think so. However, I didn't hear all that you heard, so I'll give you the benefit of the doubt."

"You could just trust me on this, you know?"

Mack grinned. "I do trust you in many ways. However, I need evidence in my cases. And it helps to have corroborating evidence. Meaning, two witnesses with the same info to share. Plus this is not your case. Not a cold case. This would be about one of my current cases."

"I wish it was mine. ... It isn't, of course not," she muttered, "but there must be a dead body, if you're heading to the coroner's office."

"It could be about a report on any of my current cases."

She walked with him through the house to the front door, all the animals following in a single file. After he gave the animals a quick goodbye, he gave her a big hug, a goodbye kiss, and whispered, "Hold that thought." With that, he was gone.

"*Hold that thought?*" she muttered to herself. "Easy to say, not quite so easy to do."

With Mack gone, Doreen's train of thought jumped to the vicious love triangle that she, Mack, and Mathew shared. Her soon-to-be ex was dangerous in so many ways. She just wanted her divorce over with already. Was that really asking too much? She knew a lot of people struggled with Doreen's sense of morality and her sense of needing to finish something before moving on to the next relationship, particularly when her divorce seemed to drag on.

In this case she just wanted to know that Mathew was out of her life, before she started something else, with someone else, something new and better for herself. And, of course, that *someone else* was Mack. And as he'd told her earlier, sometimes waiting was well worth it.

She sighed. Just so many things needed to be dealt with that she was hoping her ex would have been long gone out of the equation at this point in time. Her phone rang just then. She looked down to see Nick calling. She answered her phone immediately. "Hey, Nick. You just missed your brother."

"Seems like he lives there these days," he noted cheerfully.

"No, he doesn't, although it does seem like it sometimes."

He chuckled. "I'm glad you two are doing so well together."

"Yeah." She hesitated and then added, "I know he wants more, but not until this divorce is over with."

"Hold that thought," Nick replied.

Repeating what Mack had just said reminded her how much the two brothers were the same.

"Now back to business," Nick began. "I just went over the documents, and your ex appears to have signed off on almost everything."

She stopped and stared blankly around her. "What?"

"You heard me," he said.

"Yeah, I heard you. I just don't believe you." She shook

her head. It was too unbelievable—wasn't it? Mugs woofed gently at her side.

Nick burst out laughing. "I get that a lot. I really do. It's been a long haul, but it's not anywhere near as bad and as ugly as a lot of them. I have seen worse."

"You mean, people have uglier divorces than this?"

"Oh, yes. Sometimes they can get downright nasty."

"This one isn't nasty enough for you?" She shook her head at that. "Can you imagine anything worse? I didn't think this was much fun."

"I didn't say it was fun, but *nasty* is a whole different story. When you deal with the stuff that I have to do, you see a lot more than that. Compared to what I have seen before, Mathew was a walk in the park."

"You've got to be joking, right?"

"No, I am not. There wasn't the he-said, she-said. There weren't the lies. There wasn't the nasty innuendos and the accusations," he muttered. "This was just somebody being greedy and not wanting to share. People do worse than that."

"Okay. Let's just agree to disagree. You were saying he signed? Has he signed everything?"

"He missed a couple pages, so unfortunately it has to go back."

"*Ugh*," she muttered with a heavy groan.

"I know, but I do think that this will be finished soon enough."

"Do you really think so?"

"I do." He asked, "Do you have any concerns about the divorce at all?"

"No, not really. I just want it over with."

"That's good enough for me, and it's understandable. Hopefully, after another day or so, we should be in the clear."

"Do you think he did this as an excuse to extend this process?"

"I don't think so," Nick replied. "No need to sign any of it, if that were the case."

"Okay, good, so this really does show intent."

"It does, indeed. You should be feeling much better about all this."

"I'll feel better when it's signed, sealed, and I don't have to deal with him ever again."

"I get it. This has been a little bit dicey, but we're almost there."

At that, she wished she could see Nick's face, but he sounded pretty happy. "Not there yet," she muttered.

"No, but close enough. ... Okay, we're not done yet, and, until this is locked and loaded, obviously it's not *finished*-finished, but Mathew's come a very long way in a very short time."

"Are you happy with the settlement?" she asked curiously, sagging into the living room chair.

He laughed. "I so am."

"Okay, good. Then I probably will be too."

"Do you want to know?"

"Nope, I do not want to know because none of it is for sure yet."

He went silent for a moment. "You're very unusual."

"Why is that?" she asked, staring down the phone, even as Mugs came over and put his head on her lap.

"Because most women would want to know exactly what they're getting, down to the penny."

"At that point in time I *know* that I'm getting something, I probably will want to know exactly what I'm getting down to the penny, even if it's only to figure out groceries for the next few months."

At that, he burst out laughing so hard, he was almost hysterical.

"Are you okay?" she asked cautiously when he finally calmed down.

"Oh, I'm fine. I don't think you'll have to worry about groceries ever again."

"You say that," she began, "but ..."

"I know. I know. We're not out of danger, and, as a lawyer, I firmly agree with you. We need to make sure this is 100 percent locked and loaded."

"Right, so that's when he signs the last few pages."

"Hopefully he'll get this back to us pretty quickly."

"Is the court date still in effect?"

"It will be until he signs. Yet the hearing date remains set, so he knows how serious I am about this. Plus, depending on where he's at with everything else in his life, I am sure that court hearing was his impetus to sign."

"That would be lovely," she stated, as she beamed. "As long as he's being cooperative, do I still have to hang up on him every time?"

Nick hesitated and then asked, "Do you *want* to talk to him?"

"Goodness no," she replied. "It just feels very strange to have him even in my life. I would prefer he took a walk and didn't call again, but that doesn't mean he will."

"So why did you even ask me that?"

She pondered that. "I don't know. I guess because it was something that I had to consciously sit here and worry about. It's stressful. I would like to not always feel that I'm doing the wrong thing with him," she muttered.

"You don't have to worry about doing something wrong," Nick explained, "as long as you understand why you are worried about hanging up on him."

"The reprisal," she admitted. "To do something like that before meant …"

"You know you're safe, right?" Nick asked.

"He hasn't signed, not completely. Therefore, he hasn't signed. If he hasn't signed, then he hasn't come to terms with the divorce. I'm still legally his wife. So your version of *safe* versus the version of safe that I have seen in my past is very different."

Nick let out a long, slow breath. "Right. No, you're correct. So stay vigilant. I don't think we can take any chanced with Mathew, so hang up on him every time he calls. Got it?"

"Right, got it," she muttered.

They ended the call, and Doreen looked down at Mugs. "Definitely not a phone call that I want to repeat," she muttered. With a loud squawk Thaddeus came hurtling in from the kitchen. That only left one missing and it was the one that tended to get into the most trouble when no one else was looking. Until her gaze landed on a scarf that had fallen to the floor by her coat and found the golden angel sound asleep. "Not much of an opportunist, are you, buddy."

Still, staring down at her phone, she realized how even hearing some of her own issues coming back up so fast had been disconcerting. She was so much further down the road, but to even think how quickly her ex triggered the wrong response when he phoned her did raise red flags. Her fear of saying no and fighting back was a preconditioned response, a response that was still there. Not how she wanted to move forward in life.

Mack was so different. He tolerated so much from her, and sometimes she wondered if she wasn't giving him extra drama to test him, just to see how he would respond. As she sat, she thought about all the times she'd done just that and, with a hard sigh, picked up her phone and sent Mack a quick text. **Sorry for all the times I was difficult.**

And then she got up, went into the kitchen, and made a sandwich.

Chapter 3

LATER THAT AFTERNOON Doreen and her pets sat outside on her deck, a book in her hand, when Mack phoned her.

"What was that all about?"

"What was what all about?" she asked in confusion.

First came silence, then he said, "You sent me an apology text."

"Oh, that."

"Yeah, that," he replied, an odd note in his voice. "What was that all about?"

"Kind of hard to explain."

"Try."

There was that indomitable *you-need-to-explain-this* note to his voice that she knew she would struggle to get out of and never would unscathed. If she told him flat-out that she didn't want to talk about it, he would probably accept it, but was she really ready to have something like that hang around too?

Finally, after he waited without saying anything further, she began, "It's just something that came up in a discussion with Nick."

"Such as?"

Taking a deep breath, she explained it to him.

"Wow," he muttered. "You know you don't have to test me. You know that, right?"

"I know you say that, and I'm sorry that that's how I have been subconsciously looking at a few of these issues. However, after you've been in the situation I've been in"— she struggled to get the words out in a cohesive manner— "you realize that, I think, we test the whole world around us to confirm that nothing surprises us."

"I get that too," he agreed, "which is also why I'm not mad, would never be mad, and would not want you to ever think that I was mad that you were doing something like that."

"And that's also why I wanted to thank you because, at times, I do realize how much I have changed and even recognize it."

She heard the smile in his voice when he asked, "Did my brother say that Mathew signed the settlement?"

"Yes, he signed something, but a few things were left unsigned. So technically he did sign, yet it's still not correctly submitted. I am a little worried that he's still playing games in order to get out of it, and this was like a stopgap."

"And what did Nick say about that?"

"He didn't say a whole lot, but he didn't think that was what it was about. Regardless, Mathew needs to add all his signatures, so we're still not off the hook."

"Right," he muttered. "Hopefully that'll be soon. And, by the way, as to our earlier issue regarding that apology and the reason you tested me, remember that you're always welcome to be you." And, with that, he hung up.

She sat here and smiled at the phone for a long time.

Somehow without noticing it, Goliath had curled up in her lap. She petted him gently. Mugs barked to get her attention. Goliath dug in his claws but didn't raise his head. She bent slightly to reach Mugs. "Hey, buddy. What do you want to do?"

It was obvious he wanted to do something, most likely a walk. She looked down in sudden inspiration and suggested, "Maybe we should go visit Nan, *huh*?" And, with that thought, she picked up the phone and phoned her grandmother.

"Hey, sweetie," Nan greeted her in delight. "You coming down?"

"I was wondering about it," Doreen replied. "It's a nice afternoon."

"You should," Nan agreed. "I'll see if I can come up with a treat."

"You don't have to." Doreen laughed at her grandmother. "I am eating, you know?"

"But are you, though?" Nan asked hesitantly.

"Yes, I am," Doreen stated firmly.

"I'll still see what I can find because I wouldn't mind a little bit of a snack myself."

"That's a different story. I'll grab the animals and come on down."

"Sounds good," Nan replied, "and we can pump you for more information."

"More information? About what?"

"About the body they found," Nan replied.

Doreen stared down at the phone. "What body?" she asked slowly.

At that came silence, and then Nan chuckled. "Did Mack keep it from you?"

"Yes, apparently he did," she muttered. "You want to explain what he kept from me?"

Nan burst out laughing. "Come on down, and I'll tell you when you get here." And, with that, she hung up.

Not sure just what Mack had kept from her, and, of course, he wasn't some crime reporter who was supposed to send her alerts when something came in—although that would be great. Yet he didn't. Then again he would also say, *Current case, his problem, not hers.*

If something had happened, and Doreen didn't know about it, *that* was frustrating. It was especially more so to find out through her grandmother. But then, that Rosemoor retirement home was just a hive of gossip. If someone found one thing out, then they all knew it within minutes.

And, with that, Doreen grabbed the dog leash and announced, "Let's go visit Nan."

Thaddeus even woke up from his spot on his roost long enough to look at her, then crawl up onto her shoulder, sleepily tuck up against her neck, and whisper, "Thaddeus loves Nan. Thaddeus loves Nan."

Doreen chuckled. "I know you do, buddy. I know you do. Let's go down and see her."

And, with all the animals in tow, Doreen headed down to her grandmother's.

Chapter 4

NAN WAS OUT on the patio, waiting for them, as Doreen and her animals walked down to her place. Nan greeted them with her usual affection, letting Thaddeus walk up her arm and settle on her shoulder. She smiled up at Doreen. "You're looking lovely."

Doreen rolled her eyes at her. "Thank you." She gave her grandmother a hug, then sat down at her patio table. "You're looking pretty cheeky too."

"Hey, we're one up on you for a change," she noted, chuckling.

Doreen nodded. "I haven't heard anything," she admitted. "So what's going on? What do you know?"

"They found a body," Nan began.

"A body?" Her mood perked up.

"Yes, a body. Of course that makes it also a current crime and nothing to do with a cold case," she shared in commiseration. "Which is also probably why you probably haven't heard about it."

"I haven't been watching the news much lately, and Mack wouldn't tell me about any dead body if it were tied to an ongoing investigation, or at least he wouldn't want me to interfere," she admitted, shrugging. "We know how touchy he is about that subject."

Nan chuckled once more. "In this matter, it seems to be his case. Not anything to do with you."

"Maybe that's good. Maybe not," Doreen muttered. "I have been restless since this last case, that's for sure. That was a big one."

"You need time to get away from all that drama."

She smiled at her grandmother. "Maybe, and maybe I just need to find something else to do with my life." Nan looked at her in worry. Doreen shrugged. "I'm fine. I'm not having a midlife crisis. Everything's good."

"Glad to hear that," Nan declared tartly. "You can help me pour tea then."

And, with that, Nan took off the tea cozy—one of those little crocheted affairs that covered the whole teapot—and motioned for Doreen to serve. As she did so, Nan bounced off her chair and headed into her kitchen and then quickly came back with a plate. "I almost forgot these. I raided Richie's stash."

She placed a plate of treats down on the small table. Immediately Goliath hopped up to sniff the offerings. Thaddeus didn't appear to care enough to move from his cozy perch. And luckily, at least for the moment, Mugs was sleeping. Goliath was unimpressed and returned to the big plant pot off to the side, curled up and went to sleep.

Doreen frowned at her grandmother. "Richie has a stash?"

"Yes, he always takes a little extra, so he doesn't have to go hungry in the daytime."

"Oh dear," Doreen mumbled, "but then, if you take it, will Richie go hungry?"

"No, I don't think so," Nan stated in a dry tone. "He takes a lot for later. And then, whenever anybody is hungry or wants to share a cup of tea, they go to his place."

"Is it a lure to get people to come and visit?" Doreen asked gently.

"Something like that," Nan noted. "I also know that I can go pick up a little bit of something out of his stash to come and bring to you."

Doreen shook her head at that. "Still doesn't make a whole lot of sense that he would do that."

"Hey, it's Richie. What can you say?" she replied, with a smile.

Doreen wasn't about to get into that discussion. "What's this about a body?"

Nan looked at her blankly for a moment. "Oh, that body," she noted. "It was found down in City Park."

"I was just there this weekend—well, Friday afternoon."

Nan nodded. "I think the body was found on Saturday."

At that, Doreen slowly nodded. "That's possible. I know Mack got called out to some crime scene early this morning. Then he got a call to come to the morgue earlier this afternoon."

"There you go," Nan declared. "He's been a busy man."

"He did make a comment about that." Doreen smirked. "Something about being much busier than he used to be."

Nan's laughter rolled free and easy, and she nodded. "Yep, ever since you came to town, you've been getting things rocking and rolling."

"I wonder if I should have, though," she replied, with a sigh. "He is always so busy now."

"*Ooh*, are you missing him?" Nan asked a bright look in her gaze.

DALE MAYER

"No, that's not why I mentioned that," Doreen replied.

"That's too bad because you should be missing him. If you ask me, he's a good guy, and you don't want to lose that one."

"I wasn't planning on *losing* him," Doreen clarified. "Besides, if I'm in danger of losing him, ... he wasn't mine to begin with."

Nan's eyes widened. "That is a very wise statement. I should have been the one to tell you that myself."

Doreen smiled at her grandmother. "Maybe that's where I heard it from."

"No, you've come a long way," Nan stated. "That's definitely a Doreen statement."

"Is it now? I don't know."

"Oh, don't ruin it. Here I thought you were becoming very wise in your old age."

"I haven't gotten old enough yet," she quipped right back.

Nan burst out laughing. "Now that's true."

"And I'm not in any rush to race ahead in my life," she muttered.

"You should be, but only toward the good things. However, you really do want to let go of all that other stuff."

"Yeah, how does one get to pick and choose?" she asked, staring at Nan. "If you have any insights into how to make life happen the way you want it to happen, I am all ears."

"You have to plan it, for one," Nan stated complacently. "You have to expect to get the good stuff in life and then work for it. You certainly just can't sit back and whine about it." Doreen winced. "Not that I meant that directed at you," Nan pointed out. "You certainly aren't sitting back and doing nothing."

"Sometimes it feels like it."

"Oh, posh," Nan disagreed, with a wave of her hand. "Now, try a treat."

"Treat?" Thaddeus stood up and flapped his wings as if just realizing there was food.

"Yes, human treats," Doreen said in a stern voice. "Not treats for you." Not that her words would make a difference. She looked down at the plate of little fancy cupcakes. "These are lovely," she noted. "Are you sure Richie was happy to have you take them?"

"He was sleeping, so he didn't know."

In the act of taking a bite, Doreen froze and stared at Nan. "You just took them from him, while he was sleeping?"

"Sure, why not?" Nan shrugged, nonplussed. "He sleeps a lot, you know." Doreen didn't even know what to say to that. Nan simply ordered, "Keep eating. Keep eating."

"Sure," Doreen muttered, "but did you ever really consider that maybe he wanted these when he woke up?"

"If he did, then he should have had them already," Nan declared. "Besides, it's not as if he doesn't know where the rest of these are. I didn't take all of them. He still has another ... what? ... Half a dozen?"

"Half dozen?" Doreen repeated astonished. Just then part of her cupcake dropped to the floor. She leaned over to pick it up only to see Mugs staring at her with hopeful eyes and a long slow lick of his tongue. "Wow, you're fast buddy."

He woofed. She broke off another small piece and knowing she shouldn't, gave it to him anyway. Immediately Thaddeus was on the table and eyeing which treat should be his. Nan took the choice away and slowly gave him some of the nuts that had been off to the side of her plate that she'd picked off hers.

"Thaddeus loves Nan," he cooed.

Nan beamed.

Doreen sighed. "Honestly, Thaddeus. You love the one who feeds you."

He immediately snatched up another nut while keeping a gimlet eye on Doreen in case she was going to take it away from him.

Nan laughed in delight before returning to the conversation. "Yep, as I told you. Richie takes a lot these days. He's always hungry."

"H*mm*, are you sure he's always hungry or is he just lonely?"

Nan nodded at her, with a quiet understanding. "See? You do understand."

"I do, and it does bother me to think that he might be lonely in a place like this. There's always people around."

"Sometimes it's too many people," Nan stated. "We may come here because we're lonely, but you can get inundated very, very quickly."

Doreen certainly hadn't had that experience yet, but it made sense. "So what do you know about this body?" she asked, bringing the conversation back around again.

"Not a whole lot," Nan replied. "I was hoping you would have more information."

"No, I don't, but I'm sure Mack or the news will come up with it. At least some of it."

"Yeah, the local website just keeps saying that they'll send an update on it as soon as they get more information."

"Not much choice, is there? They found the body, and, until there's forensics or the police have a chance to investigate, they can't really say much."

"Maybe," Nan conceded, "but it's all so frustrating to the rest of us who want answers."

Doreen stayed studiously quiet at that because answers were what she generally was good at getting. However, this wasn't her case, and she knew that Mack was counting on her to stay out of it. Which she would, given it was something she *could* stay out of it. But that wasn't a guarantee either. "For now, I am not on the case."

Nan studied her granddaughter. "Unless, of course, somebody were to ask you for help."

"Yet they aren't likely to do that," Doreen noted, "because why would they?"

Nan shrugged. "It's happened before."

"Sure, sometimes. Not necessarily for the best reasons though."

"Right. You do have a habit of bringing in some very nefarious creatures into your world."

"Sure, that's all about me, isn't it?" she quipped, with a sigh.

"Maybe not," Nan agreed, with a nod. "I get it. You've definitely got so much going on. Lately your plate has been full of these people just because you have so much success. They just keep coming to you."

"Maybe, but it also makes me feel bad for everybody else because it *seems* that ... I'm the one doing all this, and it has absolutely nothing to do with the police and their efforts, and that's wrong."

"I don't know about *wrong*," Nan clarified cautiously, "but it's *simplistic*, put it that way."

"Fine, whatever you want to call it," Doreen agreed. "Mack puts a ton of work into these cases too."

"I'm sure it makes him feel good to know that you care

about making sure he gets the right amount of acknowledgment."

"Not just him," Doreen added. "All of the police force. They do work hard, you know."

At that, Nan nodded agreeably. "I'm sure they do. And there's only so much any of us can do to make any of this simpler."

"Not sure anybody can make anything simpler when it comes to dead bodies," she muttered, "but hey …"

Just then Richie called out from the front door to Nan's apartment. Nan turned and called back to him, "We're out on the patio."

He came outside, took one look at their goodies, and nodded. "There they are." He smiled. "I was missing a few of those."

"I am so sorry," Doreen murmured. "Do you want them back?" She held out the second one in her hand.

He looked at her and chuckled. "No, I sure don't. Part of the reason I take so many as I do," he explained, "is to make sure people like you get them when you come."

She wanted to believe him yet didn't want him to get in trouble. "It would make me feel terrible to think that you would get into trouble over this," she told him.

"Oh, I won't get into any trouble. Don't you worry about that." He looked over at Nan. "She's always worried about other people, isn't she?"

Nan nodded. "Even when she shouldn't be."

Doreen sighed. "I am standing right here, you know."

"No, technically you're sitting," Nan stated, staring at her. "Now why would you stand when you can sit?"

Doreen opened her mouth and then slowly closed it. "I won't argue with you."

"You can't argue with it, as it's logical." Nan stared at her granddaughter, then turned to Richie, who ignored her stare and looked toward Doreen, who was also staring him down.

Doreen asked him, "Did Darren give you any information on the body?"

He gave her a one-arm shrug. "I did get a little bit of information, but he's not being very forthcoming. It's almost as if he's been warned off," he noted, and such a disgruntled tone filled his voice that Doreen had to laugh.

"Probably has been," Doreen stated. "Just like Mack's not allowed to talk to me. I am sure the captain has made that clear to both of them."

He looked over at her. "Since when did you ever care about that?" he scoffed.

"Every once in a while, I do have to," Doreen explained. "I can't always be in Mack's face, bugging him for information that he's not allowed to give."

"No, that's why we have to find information on our own," Richie stated. "You up for this one?"

"It's an ongoing investigation, a current case," Doreen replied. "Given that it's not a cold case, Mack won't let me in on it."

He frowned. "Do we need Mack's permission?"

Doreen hesitated. "It's one of those unspoken agreements between friends. I'll stay out of his way if he stays out of mine, and then I can do what I need to do on my own cases."

His shoulders slumped. "And here I was hoping we had another case to work on. You know how life is very boring if we don't."

She looked at him. "I thought life was very busy around

Rosemoor."

"It is," Richie agreed. "It's always busy, but that doesn't mean *busy* can't be boring too."

She pondered that. "I guess if you're always so busy, that can be a stress too."

"Which is one of the reasons why I like to pick up all my treats, take them back to my room, and have them to myself," he shared, with a smile.

At that, Doreen looked down at her plate and frowned. Nan had stacked more cupcakes there.

"No, no, no," Nan said, patting her granddaughter's hand. "Richie didn't mean that he didn't want to share. He just didn't want to have to go back into the melee in the kitchen and see all those people sitting around, having coffee and gossiping," she muttered. "You have no idea how long those people can keep it up."

Considering Nan was really good at keeping all that up herself, Doreen had a very good idea. She looked over at Richie. "I appreciate it today, but please don't think you have to always pick up something for me."

"Oh, I don't," he said, with a wave of his hand. "I pick it up for a lot of people. Some don't want to go back to the kitchen all the time. Besides, you should know. Darren did say something about this body."

"What did he say?" Nan asked, pumping him for information.

"Something about …" he started off in the distance as if pondering the memory, "it wasn't local."

"Oh, good," Nan replied, "meaning, the victim wasn't local, I presume."

He nodded. "I think it was somebody visiting."

Doreen looked at him. "That's sad. This town runs on

tourist dollars. You would think that something like that would attract too much bad press."

"But, if they're into drugs and stuff," Richie noted, "what will you do? That element is always here, even when we don't want it to be here. … Yet you know it's here."

Doreen pondered that and shrugged. "I think drugs are everywhere, doesn't matter what town you go to. They'll be there, and it's a matter of trying to keep it in control."

He smiled. "How about you run for office?" he suggested. "I would vote for you."

Nan looked at Doreen in delight. "Oh my, you should run for mayor."

Doreen stared at her in shock. "Why on earth would anybody give me a mayoral position? And why on earth would you want me to get involved in politics? That would be terrible."

"No." Nan chuckled. "You're honest, and that already means you'll do well."

"Why?" she asked. "Everybody else will eat me for breakfast."

Richie burst out laughing. "She's got a point, you know. She's too honest. Everybody will come up against her and cheat her out of everything. Not to mention they will tear her apart. She doesn't have a diplomatic bone in her body."

"Not unless she surrounds herself with a good team," Nan offered, warming up to the idea.

Something that Doreen needed to put a kibosh on immediately. "No politics," she stated firmly.

Nan stared at her in dismay. "It would be a good job. You could work from home. You could still do things like this on the side, and think about it, you would get insider information all the time."

She stared at her. "Do you really think being a mayor will get me any more information than I get now? Or that I'll have time to do any of these cases?"

Nan pondered that for a few minutes, looking over at Richie and adding, "I guess she has a point."

And thankfully that discussion was shelved.

Chapter 5

As Doreen walked home over an hour later, she pondered what would force somebody like Nan to even bring up politics as a career for Doreen? Was it something that she could do? She didn't think she had the right personality. She couldn't lie. She couldn't hide anything. She would completely blurt out absolutely everything on her mind. She didn't understand even how that had become a thing for her to consider. When she was married, she'd been really good at keeping her own counsel and not saying anything. But, of course, the fear of reprisal was always there. Although her husband had just thought she'd become very good at being submissive.

Now, with all those restraints taken down again, she had nothing holding her back. As she walked back home, she stopped at the creek several times to let the animals play. Of course Mugs was soaked in minutes. Laughing at his antics, she finally convinced all three to go home and just as she neared her house, she heard Richard in his backyard.

"No, no, and no." He repeated it over and over.

She waited, wondering if he would say anything else. Who was he even talking to? Finally, unable to resist, she asked, "You talking to me?"

His head popped over the top of the fence, and he glared at her. "Does it look like I'm talking to you?"

She pondered that, and then in a cheeky voice replied, "Actually it does."

His glare turned thunderous. "You're just being a nosy busybody."

"No, I was just wondering if you needed any help."

He frowned at her. "Why would I need help, particularly from you? Nobody's been murdered." And, with that, he dropped back behind the fence again and didn't say another word.

She walked around Richard's fence to her house, wondering if that's all people thought she was good for. And then, of course, why would they think anything else? It's not as if she had much in the way of skills, and she certainly didn't have much in the way of credentials or education. On paper it looked like she had nothing to offer.

Back home, she was too depressed to even think of tea and didn't want any more coffee either, but picked up her weeding tools and her gardening gloves and headed out to do a little bit of work. Almost immediately, as she stepped out her back door, her phone rang. Not knowing the number, she answered it cautiously. She'd had just enough bad experiences with people lately to worry.

Hearing someone older, their voice creaky and somewhat tremulous, Doreen asked, "Can I help you? This is Doreen."

"Are you the lady who solves all those murders?"

She winced. "Well, I've been lucky enough to assist the police in closing a few cases," she replied cautiously.

The other woman let out a sigh. "I'm glad to hear it. I've

made several phone calls trying to find you."

Doreen stared down at her phone. "What's the matter?"

"It's my grandson. He just died in Kelowna. I'm Bessie Owens."

"Oh, I am so sorry to hear that."

"There were a lot of good things about him, but there were also a lot of difficult things about him," she shared. "Still, he's family, and I need answers."

"Did he die recently?

"Yes, I guess you may have heard about the body that they found there."

"Oh dear," she muttered, staring across her yard. "You do know the police are on it, right?"

"Yeah, I do know. I'm also dying, and I don't have time for the police to park this case and to bring it up in another year or two. I'm ninety-two years old, you know? And my grandson had a lot of trouble over the years, but I thought he'd finally gone straight," Bessie explained. "He promised me ... He told me that he was out of the drugs, the bad deals, and doing well again."

"So now you're afraid that he got back in bed with the wrong crowd, is that it?"

Bessie hesitated. "Actually I know he was murdered, although the police haven't told me that."

"So how do you know he was murdered?" Doreen asked.

"Because he was out of the drugs, so, other than that element, I don't know who might have killed him."

"If he had an unpleasant health history, all kinds of things could have killed him," Doreen suggested.

Bessie snapped, "I'm not a fool, I know what this is about, and I'm telling you that he didn't kill himself. He was murdered."

DALE MAYER —

"If he has been murdered, do you have anybody in mind who could have done this?" Doreen stepped back into her kitchen and grabbed a notebook and a pen and sat outside at her patio table. The animals immediately took up positions around her, with Thaddeus on the table waiting for her to open up her book.

"He had *friends*," Bessie replied in disgust. "The kind of *friends* who'll lead you down the wrong pathway and leave you there to hold the bag."

"Right, and what was he doing in Kelowna?"

"He was attending a course on becoming an arborist," she replied. "It was part of his new future."

"Oh, nice," Doreen exclaimed.

"Yeah, it would have been, if he'd had a chance to finish it and to have that life," Bessie declared, reminding Doreen that her comment was hardly appropriate, considering somebody could no longer live their dream.

"I am sorry," she murmured. "Okay, so he was here to be an arborist, and what else?" She flipped open her book to a blank page and jotted down a few notes. As soon as she put the pen down, Thaddeus grabbed it and imitated her movements, managing to scribble on the left side page. She snatched the pen out of his foot, trying to stay focused on the conversation, but Thaddeus wasn't having it.

He snatched it out of her grasp and backed away triumphantly.

Doreen glared at him but managed to hear the rest of the conversation. "He had an ex-girlfriend, was hoping to get back in touch with her again. Her new boyfriend used to be his best friend."

"Okay, so they were together, they split, and then she's been going out with his best friend?" If she had the pen she could write this down, but …

"Yes."

"And do you think that they had something to do with this?"

"It's possible. I don't know." Bessie hesitated. "I raised my grandson. I tried hard to do a decent job, but I'll tell you flat-out. I'm old, and being old is not the easiest time to have a toddler to look after. I know that the internet is a bad place, and, in my day, we had all kinds of bad places, but they were nothing like what you could find out from the internet now. *Still* I firmly believe that he got straight and clear, and he wouldn't have been into drugs anymore."

"And you know for sure he wasn't using?"

"Yes, he went to rehab," Bessie declared, her voice breaking up. "I feel responsible for him, and, as I said, I'm dying. I don't have more than six months to go, and I really want to see this closed."

Doreen sat here for a long moment.

"Did you hear me?" Bessie asked in that same querulous tone.

"I hear you," Doreen replied gently. "Yet, so far, you haven't given me anything that the police won't have already found out. So, without more, it won't get this case any further along the line."

"No, you'll have to talk to his ex-girlfriend and his best friend."

"Hang on a minute," Doreen said. "Why did you raise him?"

Bessie sighed. "See? That's the thing. I wondered if you would pick up on that."

"If you would tell me flat-out what's going on maybe I wouldn't need you to test me." At her curt tone, even

Doreen winced because, of course, testing was what people did, particularly when they had something to share but they were worried about it.

"His parents disappeared. My daughter disappeared some twenty-four, twenty-five-odd years ago," Bessie shared. "From one moment to the next they disappeared. They were on the way up to Kelowna to visit some friends of theirs. Then they planned to go camping together for a long weekend. As far I know, they wanted some special time to help their marriage because they were struggling together. I suggested they go off and spend some time to figure out what they really wanted, and I would keep the boy while they were off dealing with their issues."

"And they never came back?" Thaddeus tired of playing with his pen, took a few steps forward and dropped it on her book. Doreen snatched it up and moved the book closer.

"No," Bessie muttered, her voice breaking. "They never came back."

"Oh my, that would be terrible."

"We opened a police file. We talked to everybody. We had everybody go up and down the roads to see if they had gone off the highway. There was just … nothing." She hesitated. "It was the worst time of my life."

"I am so sorry, and, of course, you blamed yourself."

"How could I not?" Bessie asked. "I'm the one who suggested they go away."

"Yes, I understand," Doreen muttered. "I still don't think that you were necessarily to blame."

"No, I'm not to blame, but, at the same time, it was my suggestion. So I felt responsible, and I ended up with Edwin, as nobody else was willing to take him."

"Okay, and Edwin was how old now?"

"He had just turned twenty-seven," Bessie replied. "Old enough to have done better with his world, old enough to know better definitely, and old enough to have gotten into trouble, and yet was already on his way back out," she explained. "So now I feel like I failed my daughter and my grandson."

Not a whole lot Doreen could say about that. "I am so sorry," she muttered. "Do you have anything written down about his parents' disappearance?"

Bessie hesitated. "What would that have to do with Edwin's murder?"

"It might give me an in for getting information from the police," she shared. "I presume the file's just been left open. Technically that is a cold case."

"Yes, missing, presumed dead. We went through the process to have them declared legally dead, so that we could deal with the estate, and that wasn't much fun either," she muttered.

"Right, no such thing as fun when it comes to something like that," Doreen noted. "I am so sorry for your loss."

"I have a few things to send you," she noted. "My granddaughter, Sylvee, will help me do that."

"Oh, good, can she email all that to me then?"

"Does that mean you'll take on the case?"

Doreen hesitated at the wording. "I'm not saying I can do anything with this, but I can talk to the police, and, if there's anything I can do to help you find answers, I will." She added, "I am not in any way legally capable of doing any of this, but I will do what I can."

Bessie asked, "You're not a PI?"

"No, I'm not. I'm what's known as an amateur sleuth, and apparently, so far, that has done me well."

"In that case, keep doing you. I just need you to find out what happened to my grandson. Edwin deserves that much at least."

"Will do," Doreen said.

And, with that, Bessie gave her contact info to Doreen, along with Sylvee's, and then hung up.

Chapter 6

DOREEN SAT FOR a long moment. She didn't really want to involve herself in Mack's current case, and wouldn't, if there was any way out of it. But two people were missing, a missing family, who'd been stitched into Mack's current case, made this a whole different story.

That was something she could look into. Twenty-five years was a long time, and, unless they had any particular reason to disappear, there was no reason that they would have gone away without their child, particularly when they only had the one, even to make a new life for themselves. It happened, but it wasn't very often that they would leave without their child.

If they went camping and never showed up for their jobs again, then what was their means of income and support? Plus something like that took a lot of planning to just disappear off the face of the Earth and to relocate as new people somewhere else. Chances were, they were deceased, but Doreen couldn't say that for sure because, of course, without bodies, how did anybody know what was going on? Looking down at her notes, she pondered whether she should phone Mack, or maybe do some research first.

And, with that, she got up, walked to her laptop sitting at the kitchen table, and sat down. Goliath, stretched out on the table, opened his eyes to watch her but closed them again as she opened her laptop. Thaddeus was snoozing on his living room roost and Mugs, well, he followed her step for step. There was something so very comforting about having him at her side. She reached down to scratch his neck before turning her attention to her laptop.

She had the names of the parents who had gone missing, and she had Edwin's name. She quickly typed that into Google and brought up a local news site and found an article on Edwin's death. Absolutely no way had Edwin committed suicide. He'd been shot in the back of the head, according to the article published merely hours ago. She winced at that. That was too much like execution style, which could bring in the drug element again, no matter what Bessie said.

Chances were, Mack would come down hard on her if she interfered. She pondered that for a long moment and then realized the best thing she could do was to be honest and upfront. And, with that, she checked the time. He may or may not be busy. At least she had something for him. She quickly dialed him, and, when he answered, his voice was fatigued.

"Hey. What's up?"

"I got a very strange phone call," she began cautiously.

First came silence. "Oh good God, not again."

"Yeah," she whispered. "It's not my *Whispers in the Wisteria* case because the dead body is male. However, in this particular case, there's also potentially a cold case to go with your murder case."

"Who are you talking about?"

She added, "Your morgue victim is Edwin, right?"

He sighed. "Yep."

"His grandmother called me just now," she shared.

"Yes, I have talked to her. We contacted her to make next-of-kin notifications, and I had to inform her of his passing," Mack noted. "I think she's ninety-something."

"Yeah, ninety-two to be exact. She has less than six months to live."

"Ouch. At that age, you know that could be true for anybody, just due to old age, not disease or anything."

She smiled at that. "I know, but she's asked me to look into Edwin's death."

He snorted at that. "It's nice that everybody has so much confidence in the police to do the job." He was clearly frustrated at that.

"I think she's afraid that Edwin got back into drugs. Plus his parents disappeared twenty-five-odd years ago," Doreen told him. "This poor woman was tasked with the job of raising Edwin, and she feels terribly guilty."

"I would agree with you there," Mack muttered. "And it's unfortunate that somebody of her age—even back then, she would have been sixty-something—taking on this toddler. I didn't know that she had raised him."

"She did, and apparently Edwin came here to take a course at the community college to become an arborist. And he was hoping to reconnect with his ex-girlfriend, who's going out with his former best friend now."

"Former best friend?" Mack repeated.

"Yeah, his girlfriend broke up with Edwin, and then his best friend moved right in. Maybe a little too quickly, as far as Bessie knew anyway. She didn't really have a ton of information about it. However, I do have some names for you." She quickly gave him the girlfriend's and her current boyfriend's names. "What I don't have," Doreen added, "is any contact information on any of these people. Where did you find Edwin's body?"

"I'm not sure I can give you anything either," he muttered, obviously caught up in thought.

"That's fine. I'll get it myself." She chuckled. "I know you probably already have this, or, if you don't, you would have gotten this info very quickly. However, since I had it, I'm giving it to you."

"Appreciate it," he replied cheerfully.

And, with that, they ended the call, and she headed back outside to make notes of what questions she wanted to ask of the girlfriend and her boyfriend. And should probably start with the Kelowna phone book to see if they were listed. If not, head to Google. While sitting there, she received another phone call from an unknown number. Surprised, and a little worried at this becoming commonplace, she answered cautiously.

When she realized it was the granddaughter Sylvee, Doreen smiled. "Hey, I presume you have some information for me from Bessie."

"Yes, I would send emails to you first, then mail the rest," Sylvee clarified, "but I realized that my grandmother didn't get your email address."

Doreen laughed. "That's true." She quickly gave it to her and asked, "I don't suppose you have any contact information for Edwin's ex-girlfriend or her current boyfriend, do you?"

"I have their phone number." She quickly gave it to Doreen. "I wanted to contact them myself, but I know there's an investigation going on, and I didn't want to get in the way of any of that. That can complicate things."

"That's a good idea," Doreen replied. "Did the cops tell your grandmother where they found Edwin's body?"

"Yeah, it was at some city park."

"What day was it found?" Doreen asked, frowning.

"I'm not sure. Possibly this weekend. Why don't you check with the cops?"

"I know the police much prefer if I stay out of their way too," Doreen shared, with a note of humor.

"Yet you appear to be okay with it?" she asked cautiously.

"No, I've just worked with them enough that they know me," she explained.

"I hope you can get to the bottom of this. I know my grandmother is pretty upset."

"With good reason too," Doreen agreed. "Why was she the one who was elected to look after Edwin?"

"I think she felt guilty. I don't know my cousin all that well. When he started going down the drug route, I avoided him because his friends were all of the same ilk, and they weren't the people you necessarily wanted to meet in the dark of night or in cold corners," she murmured. "Once we realized where Edwin was going and who he was hanging out with it, it just became a problem in so many ways."

"Of course it did," Doreen said. "And everybody wants to help, but nobody knows what to do."

"Exactly," Sylvee confirmed. "You do understand."

"I understand a lot in life," Doreen muttered, "and sometimes there are just no easy answers for helping out."

"My grandmother went pretty much off the rails when she realized where Edwin was heading, and I guess she just didn't know how to handle him for some time."

"I don't imagine she would. I can't imagine trying to do

something like that myself," Doreen admitted. "What are you supposed to do? They don't listen at that age, and, when they're with their friends, their friends know everything, and their friends are the best people in the world. There's only so much you can do to dissuade them."

"And, in this case, there wasn't anything she could do, and Edwin was intent on making all these decisions on his own. He was reaching for all the forbidden fruits and none the wiser. Grandma felt like there was no way of getting to him, although she tried so hard."

"I'm sure she did. What was their relationship like?"

"It was lovely, yet hot and cold all the time. He was fairly tolerant of all her *interfering*, as he would call it, understanding that she was a few generations older than the rest of the people around him. I think honestly he did a pretty good job, and so did she. He wasn't into anything until he left her house, and it's almost as if all those heavy restraints that he'd been raised up under fell away. Then he had to try everything and got into trouble constantly and eventually came back to her, saying she was right, and he needed a hand to get straightened back out again."

"Oh, good for him," Doreen declared. "It's not often that you see young people capable of making those kinds of steps forward and understanding who was right and how wrong the path was that they went down."

"Edwin knew that he was in trouble, and he knew that, of everybody, she was the one who would give him a hand straightening him back out. She paid for rehab. She sent him back up for a second one, when he came to her and admitted that he was slipping and was desperately hanging on to his sobriety and did not wanna slide."

"In other words, she has a real strong reason to believe

drugs had nothing to do with this. She thinks there has to be another reason."

"He was going back to school to become an arborist."

"Good for him," Doreen said.

"It would have been," the cousin replied, "except he didn't make it. I don't know any of the details either as to what happened. I think I heard something about he was shot. At least that's what the news is saying. I'm not sure anybody's told my grandmother that."

"Generally they would have told her, but then maybe she wasn't in any shape to hear it."

Silence came on the other end. Sylvee added in a quiet voice, "You could be right. She's pretty interested in only hearing what she wants to hear at this stage of her life. It would be nice if what she heard were good things, but, too often, the reality of what we're coming up against is just the opposite. Edwin was a good person," Sylvee shared. "I know he had his problems, but he certainly didn't deserve to get killed."

"Do you have any idea what he was doing in Kelowna?"

"Sure, he went to make peace with his ex and see if they could rekindle something. He also wanted to know if she was still with his best friend and was happy. That's the gist of it, I guess. What I gathered, if she was happy, Edwin would leave it alone. However, if she wasn't happy, … he would try and woo her back again."

The old-fashioned term made Doreen smile. "I like to hear that too. Obviously he recognized something that the two of them had."

"He did. Doesn't mean that anybody would appreciate his methods though."

"Ouch. Was he the type to use a hammer when a

thumbtack would have done the job?"

"Oh, yeah, and he was nothing if not forceful and adamant about how he was right. And, when he was wrong, he was also good about admitting that he was wrong. Just not everybody would even listen by then."

"Of course not. Chances are he was surrounded by strong-minded individuals at the same time."

"Our grandmother is very much like that, not a whole lot of give in her. There's an awful lot of love, but there's not a lot of give."

"And that can make it difficult too," Doreen noted, with a sigh. "My grandmother's got an awful lot of spirit in her, but she's not hard. She's very soft and full of love. ... I can't imagine what my life would be like if she was any other way."

"That's the thing," Sylvee noted. "You think that people are easy, that you understand them, and that you can do so much for them, but, even when you try to explain things, it doesn't mean that they get it. Not many people can understand it."

"Are you talking about your cousin or your grandmother?"

"Yes," she replied, "and yes."

Doreen laughed. "In other words, they were both very much alike."

"Very much alike, both stubborn, both were right, the other was wrong, they came to loggerheads a lot. He left at what? Seventeen, I think. He made it through school, which had been his promise to her. He kept at it, and then he buggered off, and it went downhill from there."

"Yet he learned his lesson," Doreen pointed out, "so not downhill totally."

"No, but definitely not into the avenue that we would have liked to see him go. At least at this point in time we don't think this was drug-related."

"I'm hoping not," Doreen replied. "For all I know, his ex-best friend decided to pop him one because he was coming after his girlfriend."

"That's possible too."

Doreen asked her, "Were either of these two friends involved in drugs, do you know?"

"I don't know. I know the girlfriend wasn't. Back then, she was always angry at Edwin for doing anything related to drugs. But she did like her booze pretty well. She drank a bottle of wine pretty steadily."

Doreen nodded. "I've met a lot of people who didn't consider themselves to have an alcohol problem because they just had a little bit of wine in the evening."

"Yeah, but a little bit of wine turns into a bottle of wine very quickly for that gal," Sylvee noted, with a laugh.

"Very often, yes." Doreen smiled. "Okay, if you have any other information, email it to me, and I'll contact these people—even though I know the cops will do it as well. Still, maybe I can glean something from them."

"If some personal effects are here, I don't know yet. I have to go through it all still."

"If you find anything interesting, anything that pertains to where he was going, what he was doing, anything that was bothering him, send it my way," Doreen suggested.

With Sylvee promising to take a look and would do so, they ended the call.

Quickly, without giving Mack a chance to say anything, Doreen picked up the phone and contacted the girlfriend. The other woman answered, but her voice was teary, as if she'd been crying a lot. Doreen introduced herself.

Gina snapped, "Oh my gosh, are you a reporter? The last thing I want are reporters hounding me up and down. Isn't it enough that we're all grieving?"

"I'm sorry. I'm not a reporter. I am somebody who's looking into the circumstances surrounding Edwin's death."

"Are you a cop?" Gina asked suspiciously.

"No, I'm not a cop. Edwin's grandmother phoned me and asked me to try and find out what happened."

At first came silence on the other end. "That sounds like the old lady. She was not one to trust the police, and she always thought she knew more than everybody else."

"Did she though?" Doreen asked. "Was she the person who knew stuff, or just the one who made you think that she did, and, when push came to shove, she didn't?"

Gina snorted. "She was both. She tried to convince you that she knew everything, and, when you believed it, something would happen that made you realize that she didn't know everything. She just knew a lot of things, and, what she didn't know, she just pulled the wool over your eyes to make you think that she did."

It was a bit convoluted, but Doreen thought she got it. "Okay. Did you see Edwin when he came up to Kelowna?"

"Yes, I did. And believe me. That cost me in other ways that I don't want to think about at the moment."

"Your boyfriend was upset, I gather."

"Yeah, he was. You see? Edwin was always a bit of a problem between the two of us because I'm the one who broke up with Edwin because of his drug problems. So, with all that bad blood, and Edwin going back to rehab and all that mess, I didn't want to deal with him. So I broke up with him. Now my current boyfriend, who was Edwin's best friend, is always reminded that Edwin was trying to go straight, making all these healthy decisions and straightening his life, maybe I was still connected to Edwin in some way. Or emotionally at least."

"You would be," Doreen noted. "You don't spend a certain amount of time with somebody and walk away because you think they're on a destructive path and stop your emotions. You'll always wonder what they're doing, if they've done something good, or you look back on it with anger because emotionally you were there for him, but he wasn't there for you."

Gina went really quiet. "He was different this time," she shared. "He was excited about something. I wanted to hear him, to see him, but I also knew it would be something that made for a very unpleasant visit at home."

"Of course. I get that. Are you engaged to be married, or how strong is your relationship right now?"

"I would have said it was very strong," she replied. "I now have to redefine that because, ever since Edwin contacted me, I haven't been able to stop thinking about him. Now that he's dead, I feel that I've done him a disservice, and then Oscar …"

Doreen nodded. "He is not dealing with it any better, I guess. I'm sorry for that. Nothing like a death to shake things up."

"Not in a good way," Gina muttered. "I am not grieving Edwin because I didn't have that relationship with him. Obviously I would grieve who he could have been and all that good stuff, but I wasn't as emotionally attached … or at least I didn't think I was. And now, after having seen him, after that rough patch, and talking to him and seeing how different he was? Well, it just brought it all back again."

"You mean, the emotions?"

"Yeah, the emotions," she cried out. "I didn't want to still feel that way. I didn't want to still care, but I do. I ..." And then she corrected herself. "I *did.*"

"No, you still do," Doreen noted. "And just because he's gone now doesn't mean that you still don't. He deserves that much. You have to honor that aspect too."

"How?" she asked in bewilderment. "He just came into my life, blasted the security and sense of well-being I had with Oscar, and now Edwin's gone, and that future that had been so tantalizing close again ... is also gone. I wish he had never contacted me," she muttered. "It would have been so much easier."

"I'm sorry. I can't imagine."

"I didn't think I still cared," she whispered. "I just thought that it was all over with and that I was much better off without him."

"And instead you found out that, because he had changed, it brought up all that hope that you had had before."

"Exactly," Gina whispered.

"How long did you talk with him?"

"We went for coffee, and we ended up talking for about three hours," she said. "It was just like old times. It was great."

"Did your partner know?"

"Not until afterward," she replied. "Oscar was really angry about it. But he'd gotten a call from Edwin as well und wanted to talk to me about it. I also got Edwin's phone call to me, and, at the time, I didn't overthink it. It wasn't a date or anything, so I didn't bother asking Oscar. We didn't discuss it, and I just went and talked to Edwin. So, of course, it seemed like a betrayal for Oscar. He was, … *is* mad."

"Of course."

"And even now, Edwin's dead, and I don't even get a chance to find closure in any way. Neither does Oscar."

"What do you mean?"

"Because Edwin's dead, Oscar can't tell if I cared about Edwin. There is all that bad blood. Oscar is wondering which of them I cared about more. He is rethinking all of it. Whether I would leave him to return to Edwin, and now Oscar has to always wonder because, while we're still together, he wonders if I still preferred to stay with Edwin," she cried out. "It's just so messed up."

"I am sorry. When you said Edwin was really excited, did he say anything about it? Did he mention anything? … Give you any idea why he might have been killed?"

"No," she muttered. "Not at all. He was excited though. He was excited about something going on in his world, told me that he was close to solving it."

"Solving what?" Doreen asked curiously.

"He didn't say. But I tell you the one thing that he was obsessed with was his parents' deaths."

Doreen straightened. "That makes sense. He lost his family to whatever was going on at the time, so I'm sure it's gripped him all his life. His parents just disappeared. No one knows whether they are dead or what happened to them. That means no closure for anyone."

"Exactly," Gina agreed, "even though it was probably better off that he didn't know or didn't get involved."

"Why is that?" Doreen asked.

"If there are no answers after all this time, there won't be any answers now. What's he supposed to do? Spend his entire life turning around and looking backward?"

Doreen didn't say anything.

"I guess that sounds pretty harsh. After all, I've got my parents and siblings, and I certainly didn't have to go through something like that. It makes me sound like I'm a terrible person now." And she started to cry again.

Doreen winced. "I know you are hurting, but you need to let some of that guilt go because beating yourself up like that doesn't help. All you're doing right now is turning yourself inside out, upside down over this. Yet it won't bring Edwin back."

"Sure," she muttered. "If I hadn't met him that night, would he still be alive?"

Doreen frowned. "Why would you even ask that?"

"Because he died that night. I don't even know who killed him and what happened. I don't know where he was going after talking to me. He told me that he would go meet somebody else, but he didn't tell me who."

Hearing the odd note in Gina's voice, Doreen asked, "You were afraid that he would meet your boyfriend, aren't you?"

She hesitated. "Why would you even ask that?"

"Because it's natural. You know that some jealousy is possibly between them, and you're afraid that a fight might have broken out and that Oscar might have done something."

"I don't know. I don't know what to say." And then she started to bawl again.

"Maybe you should talk to Oscar. Let him know that you're … hurt. You need to talk to Oscar and find out what he was doing all that time. So that you can at least put it to rest."

"But, if I let him know that's what I was even thinking,

he'll get mad and say that I didn't trust him and how could I even think such a thing. It'll just drive a wedge even further between us."

At that, Doreen had to agree; it would make things harder. "I'm sorry. I can see that too. I don't know what to suggest then. If that had been me, I would have confronted the hurt."

"There's nothing anybody can suggest to help right now," she muttered. "Just to know that Edwin was here and so close and so much different fromRoscoe what he had been before and then to have that ripped away from me?" she sobbed. "It's not fair. He finally became the man I always wanted him to become, and now I'm terribly jealous of whoever was there for him."

"His grandmother," Doreen replied. "His grandmother was there for him."

Gina gasped. "Only his grandmother? Did he not have any other relationships?"

"I don't know that," Doreen said. "I'll have to talk to his cousin Sylvee and see if there was anybody else. However, as far as I know, his grandmother helped him to get straightened up again. She helped him to sort out the mess that was his life."

"And, for that, I have to give that old lady kudos. She was tough to be around. She had no filters. None, all the time. But she pulled through in the end." With that, Gina ended the call.

Chapter 7

DOREEN PONDERED THE sensibility of phoning Oscar, Gina's boyfriend. And then decided to hold off. Doreen should have asked for an address as to where they were. She quickly phoned Gina back and got a busy signal. Frowning at that, Doreen then picked up the phone again and contacted the boyfriend.

When he found out who she was, he snapped, "I don't need any busybodies getting in the way of my personal business here. The guy's dead. Leave him alone, for goodness' sake."

"I'm sure you understand that his grandmother's very upset."

"She's always upset," he snapped again. "She was forever nagging him about one thing or another."

Doreen's eyebrows shot up. "Considering she took on raising somebody of that age and did her best, maybe we need to give her some credit. Maybe a little bit more generosity in this instance, given that she raised him and straightened him out at the end."

Oscar snorted. "You don't know what she's like. She probably could have killed him herself. If she could have driven up this far and done the job herself, then she would have. She was more than mad at him for most of his life."

Doreen pondered that long after their phone call had ended. Oscar had refused to answer any other questions, which, considering his state of mind, appeared to be due to anger and frustration. Oscar was no good to her. She decided that she would call him later and see if he was more receptive. Not that he was in any way guaranteed to be more cooperative, but she could hope.

When Nan called, and Doreen answered, Nan was all over her. "What are you up to?"

"Why do you always think I'm up to something?" Doreen asked cautiously.

"I don't know. Something in your voice. It just felt like it."

"Yeah, well, maybe things have gotten a little bit more complicated than I expected."

"Ooh, did you get a case?" Nan asked in delight.

"Somebody asked me to take another look into the body that was found. Trouble is, not everybody is terribly interested in talking to me." She talked with Nan for a little bit, giving her what she had for information, and then Doreen decided to phone the boyfriend back again.

When he heard her voice again, he barked, "What's the matter? Don't you take no for an answer?"

"No, I really don't. I need to know if you met Edwin that night, and I need to know if you have any idea what he was so excited about."

There was silence on the other end. "I talked to him that night. I didn't meet him," Oscar said finally.

"Have you told that to the police?"

"Not yet. Will they call me?"

"Oh, yeah, they'll be calling you," she stated in that definitive tone.

"*Great*," Oscar muttered. "Here I was hoping this guy would finally be out of my life. Good riddance and all that, but you have to muck it up."

"It's tough. Especially when he was your girlfriend's ex-partner."

"Yeah, but she's the one who ditched him," Oscar declared, "so Edwin should not be coming back looking for forgiveness or wanting to get back together with her. He was also my friend, but he torched all the bridges when he tried to take away my girlfriend."

"My understanding is that might have been part of his thought process," Doreen admitted, "but I don't know for sure."

"Of course not, and then you're just spreading rumors and lies. She wouldn't have left me for him."

"Good. Do you have any idea why he was so excited?"

"Yeah, he had a breakthrough in his parents' case," he muttered. "I didn't believe him. It's typical, the stuff he used to always spread around."

"Is that so?"

"Yes, now you need to stop contacting me," Oscar demanded. "The next time you do, you'd better have a lawyer." And, with that, he hung up on her.

Such an interesting response, particularly for somebody who argued how he hadn't done anything.

She pondered for a long moment why the current boyfriend would be threatening to send attorneys after Doreen. She looked over at Thaddeus. "What do you think, Thaddeus? Is Oscar guilty?"

"He's guilty," he cried out. "He's guilty, guilty, guilty."

She chuckled. "Great, so now you've got new words." At that, he bobbed his head up and down, cackling.

She added, "If you could talk like a normal person, we might have a conversation. As it is, I feel that I'm always guessing what you're up to." Trouble was, even guessing, she was pretty clear on some things.

What she needed now was any case files on the couple who went missing twenty-five-years ago. If Edwin had caught a break in the cold case, what the heck did that mean? Did he suspect foul play in his parents' disappearance? Doreen was sure everybody had gone the gambit from both sides of that problem. How could you not, when two people disappeared without a trace and left a young boy behind? That wasn't normal. Of course not much was normal in Doreen's world either.

When Mack phoned a little bit later, he shared, "I've got the files from the missing couple way back when. I went through them, but nothing is really suspicious about it."

"Nothing suspicious except that they just up and disappeared one day."

He chuckled. "Yeah, outside of that."

"I talked to both the girlfriend and the boyfriend," she shared, "more like his BFF turned frenemy."

"Did you get any more information off Gina than I did?" There was no rancor in his voice, just curiosity. "I haven't connected with the boyfriend yet."

"The boyfriend's definitely angry, didn't like me talking to him, didn't like me calling him at all," she stated. "Basically told me that I better have a lawyer the next time I bother him."

"Oh, interesting. I wonder what he's so pissed off about."

WHISPERS IN THE WISTERIA

"He's pissed off at the idea that Edwin came back, supposedly trying to get back with Gina."

"Ah, that's kinda lovely, a love triangle."

"Yep, that," Doreen muttered. "The girlfriend, on the other hand, is thinking that she just lost the love of her life all over again."

"What?" When she explained it further, Mack replied, "Oh, that's tough."

"It's tough for everybody. Apparently Edwin made some poor decisions, headed down an ugly path, got a lot of people upset and angry with him, so his girlfriend split, or more likely left him and cut her losses. Edwin finally smartened up and went back to see if his old girlfriend was still receptive, and, of course, that set off her current boyfriend. In the meantime, Gina may be confused about her current relationship. Oscar, on the other hand, is so angry and says he didn't see Edwin that night. Yet he talked to him on the phone."

"You don't believe him?" Mack asked, his voice sharp.

"I don't know, but something in his voice I didn't like."

"I have his alibi, which is that he was home alone."

"Great, where was Gina?"

"Out with Edwin for three hours."

"Yeah, that's what she told me, *three hours*, but then he didn't die during those three hours obviously. If he did, you would have picked up the girlfriend by now, so where was Edwin afterward? She told me that Edwin was supposed to go meet somebody else. She secretly worried that it was her current boyfriend, Oscar, who would meet up with Edwin, and that her current boyfriend did something."

"Of course she does now"—Mack sighed—"but one of the detectives talked to him. Oscar says he was home alone all evening."

"Until Gina got home?"

"Yes," Mack confirmed. "She came home right after the meeting, and they went to bed."

"That's pretty standard, I guess, isn't it?" she asked.

"Yeah, unfortunately it's way too standard."

"I know. It's, … it's almost too pat, too complete, too nice and neat."

"Yet that's what people do. They go home, and they go to bed," he noted in a dry tone. "So it really doesn't matter."

"Except somebody, somewhere along the line, met up with Edwin, and things went bad. And he was shot in the back of the head, or so the newspaper said although if that was a reporting of the facts or just something they made up I don't know."

"Yep."

"What if Edwin just saw something?"

"It could be. Edwin could have seen something. He could have interfered in something. He could have stopped to help somebody. We don't know for sure." Mack sighed again. "We're on it. You stay out of it."

"Yeah, as much as I can," she replied, with a dry tone. "One more thing I want to ask you. Any chance I can read that cold case file?" He hesitated. "You don't really think it's connected to Edwin's death, do you?" she asked.

"No, I don't, but, if Edwin was making inquiries and found a breakthrough about it, then how can I not wonder?"

"I'm glad you're wondering at least," she replied. "We don't want to close off any avenues just yet. There are too many things to sort out."

"We're not closing any avenues," Mack stated. "Remember? This is what we do."

"I know. I know. I know," she said in an appeasing tone of voice. "It would just help if I had a little bit of information."

"I'll send you what I can."

"Hey, before you hang up, did you ever find the dead woman's body?"

"*Doreen*," he warned her, and, with that, he ended the call.

"Well, at least I have Edwin and his parents' case." She sat here, then pondered if anybody she knew would have known anything about the missing persons. Just then she heard Richard out in his backyard. She rapped on the fence, and he poked his head over and glared at her.

"Hey," she greeted him, "great way to communicate."

He shook his head. "No, it isn't a great way to communicate. We don't want to communicate with you."

That was one of the first times that he'd ever used a plural pronoun. She nodded slowly. "Right, I guess you're pretty fed up with me, aren't you?"

He nodded. "Yep, sure am."

She shrugged. "Okay, I won't bother you then." Except that she really wanted answers. As he went to step back down, hidden by his fence again, she added, "Unless you know something."

"Know what?" he asked in exasperation, as he poked his head over the top of his fence again. "What are you interfering in now?"

"Somebody contacted me to look into a case from a long time ago that's related to a recent murder investigation right here in town," she explained.

He frowned. "What case?"

"A couple who disappeared on their way to Kelowna,

Zeus and Rosalina Kinderline."

He stared at her.

She stared right back, then slowly nodded. "Yeah. Did you know them?"

"No, but my brother did. They were planning on meeting up when they arrived, but they didn't make it here."

"And nobody heard anything in all these years?" Doreen asked.

Richard shook his head. "No sign of them anywhere."

And such a disgruntled tone filled his voice that she wondered whether it was Richard or his brother who had tried to find them. "Were you involved in the search at all?"

"Everybody was," he stated. "Kelowna wasn't all that big twenty-five years ago. It's not a place where somebody just disappears off the face of the Earth without a trace."

She frowned at him. "What do you think happened?"

He shook his head. "I don't have a clue, and I won't speculate."

"Even not that they are alive somewhere?"

At her suggestion, he gave a sarcastic *harrumph.* "Except that they're not alive. I can guarantee you that. They were really close with my brother. If they were alive, they would have contacted him." And then Richard went to disappear on the other side of the fence, yet he poked his head back out again. "But if you find out anything ..."

"I'll tell you," she replied. "It's quite possible that they just drove off the road."

He nodded. "The locals here spent a lot of hours driving up and down various roads, trying to find them, so it's not as simple as just driving off the road. We could find no signs of them."

"Maybe their bodies are still there. Maybe they died

twenty-five years ago. Maybe they took off, starting a new life."

Richard shook his head. "I don't think they would have tried to disappear, and there was an awful lot of talk back then. You could get some people pretty upset if you start acting like you think they took off, ... looking for a new life."

"Did you hear about the body they found in City Park?"

He nodded. "Yeah, I heard something about it on the news. Who was it?"

She hesitated and then replied, "It's Zeus and Rosalina's son."

He stared at her, his jaw dropping. "What?"

She nodded. "That's why I'm looking into it. Nobody knows if Edwin's death is related to his parents' disappearance. Nobody knows whether it's just bad luck or something else is going on here. His grandmother called me, asked for my help."

Richard remained in shock, then shrugged out of his trance. "I have to tell my brother." He appeared to be seriously upset, and he quickly dropped behind his fence.

She called out to him, "Hey, Richard."

"Yeah, what?" he muttered, his voice impatient. "What now?"

"Can I talk to your brother too? Maybe ask him if he'll talk to me about the circumstances?"

"Yeah, sure," Richard said. "I'll talk to him." And, with that, he raced inside, and the door slammed behind him.

Doreen heard the satisfying *thunk*, only this time she knew it was not him being angry with her or disgusted at the scenario going on around them but more at the circumstances of the news he'd just heard.

She pondered that, as she headed to her garden and found her work gloves again. What she really needed to do was to get a better idea of the circumstances surrounding the Kinderlines' life back then. The mother had mentioned something about marital problems and needing a break away and time off to sort it out, potentially why she had been feeling as guilty as anybody.

Doreen had to find out what those problems were between Zeus and Rosalina.

Should she contact the old woman and ask or would the mother just get mad at Doreen? Still, it really didn't matter if she got mad or not. These were questions that needed to be asked to get answers.

She pulled out her phone, and, when Bessie answered, she said, "It's Doreen."

"Have you got something?" she barked into the phone.

"No, still looking, but apparently ..." She hesitated.

"Come on. Speak up," Bessie snapped. "I don't have time to wait for you to get your thoughts together. Better you phone me when they are together." Before Doreen could get the next word out, Bessie had already slammed down her phone.

Doreen stared at her cell. That explained some of the behavior that Oscar had mentioned; even Gina had intimated that the grandma wasn't the easiest to get along with. Yet who could blame Bessie right now, what with her life at a premium? So, if somebody needed anything done, they really did need to stop wasting time. Doreen quickly phoned her back.

When Bessie again barked into the phone, Doreen explained, "I was trying to find a nice way to say it."

"I don't care much for niceties," she muttered. "Just say

it."

"Your grandson implied before his death that he had a breakthrough regarding his parents' disappearance."

Shock was evident in her voice when she asked, "Edwin said that?"

"He told his ex-best friend, Oscar," she replied, hating the way that came out so awkwardly, "Edwin figured he had found something out about his parents' disappearance."

"You think it's related to Edwin's death?" Bessie asked slowly.

"It's quite possible, yes."

"Good God." She went quiet for a long moment. "Now you're tasked with two jobs. You need to find out answers on both of those cases."

Doreen stared into her phone. "I don't know that I can find answers for something that happened twenty-five years ago."

"According to all the gossip, you've done more than that already," Bessie corrected, "so this is just right up your alley. What's one more time?"

"Depends on the information that's available and not available," Doreen noted. "Not everybody is willing to talk or to share things that happened back then."

"Especially if any nefarious goings-on were around that time," she agreed. "Then you can bet nobody'll want to talk at all."

"That's part of the problem," Doreen stated. "As soon as people find out what you're after, they don't always tell you the truth."

Bessie pondered that. "I don't know what Edwin could possibly have found," she shared in confusion.

"So that's what I'll ask you about. Would Edwin have

seen anything that might have given him an idea? Do you have boxes of stuff from them? Anything of Zeus's or Rosalina's, or Edwin's for that matter?"

"I do, but they're up in the attic."

"Was Edwin up there?"

"He might have been. It's as if like I watch where he goes. Plus I'm hard of hearing," she admitted. "He could have gone anywhere, and I wouldn't have known."

"He didn't say anything to you about it?"

"No, he didn't. I would have told him to shut down that line of thought right fast."

"Why is that?"

"Because we've been over and over and over it," Bessie explained. "Absolutely nothing to be gained by bringing up all that pain again."

"Except it's still unsolved, and, maybe for Edwin, that pain would never quit, not until he got some answers."

"There are no answers," Bessie wailed. "You think I didn't try all these years? That was my daughter," she snapped. "I would have done anything to have answers on what happened to her. If I could have saved her, I would have cheerfully taken her place, wherever she is. She's surely gone on to heaven but that husband of hers? Well, as far as I'm concerned, he would end up in Hades."

Doreen immediately nabbed on to that. "Why?"

"Because he was bad news."

"And yet you wanted them to stay together."

"Sure, because of the boy's sake, Edwin needed both parents, not just one. Besides, my girl would have been good for Edwin, had she been around when Edwin was growing up. But Zeus? He had a long way to go."

"So maybe he had connections that were much less than

good."

"Absolutely, especially that ne'er-do-well in Kelowna he wanted to go see."

"What ne'er-do-well was that?"

"Roscoe," Bessie snapped. "They were friends for a long time, but he was one of those iffy people."

"In what way?"

"Always into get-rich-quick business dealings," she muttered, an odd tone in her voice. "They were more like scams, if you ask me. Planning big scores."

"Does he have a criminal record?"

"No, I don't think so, but then what do I know," she replied. "Nobody talks to me about any of that stuff anymore. It's seems the minute you grow old and you lose somebody, people think you've lost all your faculties too, and nobody thinks that you could stand to talk about any of it anymore," she snapped and started rambling. "Once you lose somebody, they talk loud around you, as if you're hard of hearing all of a sudden. The talk is all kinds of nasty."

Doreen remembered hearing various things like that from other people over the years, concerning her own marriage. She had heard a lot of comments on how she had been duped and how well she could have done in a healthier marriage. "I'm sorry that happened to you, all of it," Doreen said. "Obviously you're definitely of sound mind."

"Thanks for that," Bessie noted grudgingly. "It's really irritating when everybody thinks they know more than you do."

Doreen winced there. "Oh, I agree there," she confirmed, with feeling.

Bessie cackled. "I gather you've got somebody in your life who thinks they know more than you."

"I did have, just trying to get the paperwork signed to get rid of him. Hopefully that will be over soon."

Bessie cackled again. "Best thing you can ever do is drop those men. Yet I still believe one special male is in that whole sea of them, but finding him? Well, that's not easy."

"No, sure isn't. What about your husband?" she asked.

"Dead and gone for many years. And the world's a much better place for it, if you ask me."

"Oh?"

Bessie laughed. "He was also bad news. And that's how I know, from firsthand knowledge. When you start to see them, you recognize them all around the world."

"I see. So what was Zeus and Rosalina's relationship like? You said that they needed some time away to sort their issues."

"Yeah, the baby Edwin had wreaked all kinds of havoc. Rosalina couldn't sleep. She couldn't rest. She was getting cranky and miserable. Babies sense all that angst in their mothers, so Edwin was getting upset because his mother was cranky and miserable. And Zeus was having none of it. You know just no good was to be had from any of it, so I wanted the parents to take a few days to just go and spend some time alone, just the two of them."

"That sounds like a very generous offer on your part."

"Maybe," she grumped. "They didn't take it that way though. I think there were some hard feelings."

"You mean, like you were ordering them around?"

"Why don't people do what they're supposed to do?" Bessie asked. "All Zeus had to do was to take Rosalina away for a few days. Was that so much to ask?"

Doreen grimaced. "I guess it depends on who's asking."

"That's the problem," Bessie declared. "I admit it. I was

more of an ordering person."

"*Was?*" Doreen asked, with a note of humor.

Silence came first on the other end, and then Bessie broke up in laughter. "Oh, I do like talking to you," she admitted. "You don't pull your punches, do you?"

"I try to be honest," Doreen replied, "without being unnecessarily hurtful."

"Sometimes that doesn't work out so well."

"Maybe not, but there's also a good possibility that, when people are given a chance, they become better people."

"If you're hoping that for me, you're chasing a lost cause," Bessie stated. "I'm facing my maker pretty-darn fast. I just want to find out what happened to my daughter."

"And your grandson too, I presume."

"Him too, although I'm afraid of what I'll hear there."

"Why is that?"

"Because he told me that he was heading down the straight path. Straight and narrow, but that doesn't mean he really was. Again, along with that hard-of-hearing aspect, a lot of times people treat an older person like they're stupid. I'm not stupid," she declared, her tone turning harsh. "And just because Edwin denied that he was heading down that path doesn't mean he wasn't." Bessie took a moment to compose herself, and, with an audible sigh, she added, "Now don't bother me again until you got something more." Then, without warning, she hung up.

Chapter 8

Monday Morning …

DOREEN WOKE UP the next morning, exhausted, as if she'd been running all night. She knew it was basically her mind going over and over this case. *Or cases*, she thought inwardly. It had been a quiet evening, and all she'd done was sit and sort out notes. Still, that did not get her anywhere because she didn't have enough information. She had a bunch of half-baked ideas and a loose timeline of it all. She needed to go for a long walk to clear her head.

With that thought, she wondered about contacting Richard and asking him about his brother. She could only imagine what his reaction to that would be. She got up and dressed, headed down to the kitchen, opened up the back door for the animals, and stepped out onto her deck. When the coffee was done dripping, she quickly walked back inside, poured herself a cup, and then stepped back outside to enjoy the fresh air and the sunshine. She'd barely sat down when Richard poked his head over the fence.

"There you are," he grumped.

She nodded. "Yes, here I am." Doreen wasn't sure where else she was expected to be, considering it was 7:30 in the morning. Checking her watch, she realized it really was already past eight o'clock.

"A little bit later in the morning for you." Richard studied her intently.

"Yep," she agreed. "Didn't sleep all that well."

"Yeah, feeling guilty much?" he asked, and then he cackled.

She shook her head. "Got nothing to be guilty for. Now, what can I do for you?"

"My brother says he'll talk to you," Richard confirmed reluctantly. "I'm not sure it's a good idea, but, hey, maybe, if anybody can solve this, you can."

At that faint praise comment she frowned at him.

He ignored her and continued. "His name's Roscoe. He lives not too far from here."

"Good," she replied, that name resonating on the inside. "What time do you think he would want to talk to me?"

"He's hoping to talk to you this morning. He suggested 9:00 a.m., but I've been waiting to see if you wake up in time or not."

"It's eight now," she noted. "So is his place near? Within walking distance?"

Richard nodded. "It is. Head down across Lakeshore. There's a nice walkway through to the Rec Center, and he backs up onto that."

"If you give me his address, I'll look him up on the map and see if I can walk there in time."

He quickly reeled off the address. "There. I've done my job." And, with that, Richard disappeared.

Thankfully she'd written down the address, as he wasn't around to repeat it. She quickly popped it into Google on her phone and brought up a map, showing where she was going. Luckily it wasn't all that far. Then it made sense that, as brothers, they would choose to live close to each other— although Doreen wasn't sure they shared much of a relationship. However, Richard had certainly been eager to talk to Roscoe, once he found out who had died recently.

And, with that uppermost in her mind, Doreen made toast with quince jelly, smiling as she dished out some for herself because it really was good. She would have to stop by Esther's and tell her how much she appreciated it. But then again Esther might take that as Doreen requesting more, and that wouldn't go over too well with Esther. Although, since Doreen had shared the reward money with Esther on the return of the real yellow diamond, Doreen wondered if she'd get a better reception. Still, it was lovely jelly, and Doreen really appreciated it. However, maybe Esther didn't want to sell any more. Still, everybody liked to be appreciated for the work they do.

With the animals on leashes, and Goliath being difficult but wanting to come, Doreen took the leash off the big Maine Coon cat and told him, "Now you behave yourself." With that done, they set off.

Google noted it was a thirty-minute walk to Roscoe's house from hers, and that was fine with her. She needed to get out and about and just clear her head. A rough night was not the easiest way to start the day. The walk, however, was lovely, and it did a lot to make for a beautiful morning. As she headed to Roscoe's, she pondered the questions to ask him.

By the time she got closer, she noted they would be a few minutes late but not too bad. Providing Roscoe wasn't as grumpy as his brother, it would all be good. She walked up to the front door, and, even as she went to knock, it opened under her hand. And there, if it wasn't a twin of her neighbor, she didn't know what to think.

She nodded. "Hey, I'm—"

"Doreen," he supplied, with a bark.

She winced. "Yes, that's correct."

He nodded. "Come in. Come in. Come in."

She wasn't sure how to respond but stepped inside. "I hope it's okay if I have the animals."

"Richard warned me that you would come with them." He stared down at them, frowning.

"We can sit outside, if you want."

He took a minute, but waved them on. "That's fine. Come through. We'll sit out back."

She followed him through a really nice-looking living room, furnished with beautiful furniture, something she hadn't had since her marriage and couldn't even imagine now because the animals would destroy it in a heartbeat. She followed him outdoors, where he had a nice table set up and ready.

He pointed at a chair and said, "Sit."

She held back a smile at the order. She noted an awful lot of similarities between him and his brother. "Thank you for talking with me," she said, still a bit unsure of him.

He nodded. "I would have called you anyway," Roscoe shared, "so this just made it easier."

She stared at him. "Why would you call me?"

"I want answers," he growled. "I want answers on what happened."

She nodded. "I'm working on it, but that doesn't mean I'll get there."

"We didn't get there back then," he stated, "and you seem to be getting where nobody else is managing to get to over all kinds of cases. So I suspect you'll get further than any of us. That's why I wanted to call."

"That's a vote of confidence," she noted, "and I much appreciate it." He waved his hand, as if to say that was of no account. "Now what can you tell me about what happened back then?"

"They left, drove away, and disappeared. They had called us the previous night, saying they would be leaving early in the morning, to expect them around noon, and they never showed. I phoned them again and again and again, got no answer, and we realized there must have been some sort of accident. We looked for them all that weekend, and, not finding anything, we put in a missing persons' report that they never showed up. Before we could do that, we contacted Rosalina's mother to see if she had heard from them. Then me and a bunch of my buddies all got in vehicles, and we started driving the roads, all the way back to where they started from—Vancouver."

"So you searched?"

"We drove all the way back down to Chilliwack, found out that they had filled up with fuel basically at the turn, off the roadside, just before coming up the Coquihalla Highway. They were recognized. Their vehicle was recognized. People remembered them, which is a good thing."

"Why is that?"

"Because they were fighting," he admitted in a hard voice. "Something they did a lot of back then."

"That's not a good start to a holiday, is it?"

"No, but it was them," he snapped.

He glared at her, but she didn't take it personally, assuming it was just about the memories coming up. So much must be going on in his mind, with all this coming back up again. "Go ahead. Then what?"

"We drove all the way back to Vancouver. We stopped everywhere along the way. We looked down ravines, ... checked hospitals locally. We looked everywhere. Then we drove all the way back here, again looking everywhere."

She nodded. "But, with hundreds of miles to cover, it would be so easy to miss a vehicle, if it had driven off the highway."

"It wouldn't have been easy," he corrected, "but it certainly could have happened. With all the overgrowth along that route, you never quite know how far down somebody may have driven. By that time, the police took action, as we had helicopters, search and rescue, the whole nine yards. We had everything, and we did all that we could think of."

"What did you find?"

"Nothing. A whole lot of nothing. They disappeared without a trace."

"So it's like a five-hour drive from Vancouver to Kelowna, right?"

He nodded. "They were at the Chilliwack turn about 8:15 a.m., I believe," Roscoe shared. "They were expected up here noon*ish*."

"So Chilliwack is only some ninety minutes from Vancouver. So they left around 6:45 a.m. from home?"

He nodded. "Somewhere around there, yes."

"Okay, and you have to factor in meals along the way, hunting for bathrooms, getting gas, and whatnot," she muttered, thinking about that. "An awful lot of territory to cover."

"Too much," Roscoe said, "and that was our problem. I spent weekends upon weekends driving up and down that stretch of highway, until my wife finally got me to stop. I was so obsessed with finding them."

She looked over at him. "Are you still married?"

"No."

He was so harsh when he said that that she had to wonder.

Then he frowned at her. "What difference does that make?"

"None, I just wondered how long her tolerance lasted."

"Much less than mine, but then she didn't particularly like Zeus to begin with, and he was one of my best mates," he explained. "When you lose a best friend like that, and you don't have any answers, you do everything you can to find them."

"I know," she replied gently. "I'll do the best I can to find out what happened now too."

He sat back, glared at her for a moment, and then his shoulders sagged. "It was really heartbreaking. They absolutely loved that baby of theirs." And then his glare ramped up again. "Now, your turn. What's this about that baby? I hear he was the one who died just a few days ago."

She nodded. "Yes, apparently. I have no way to ID him, but the news came from the police. I have spoken to the grandmother and to his cousin, Sylvee."

"It's just terrible." Roscoe nodded. "Just terrible."

"Did you have any contact with Edwin back then?"

"No, not at all," he declared, with his distinctive bark. "I knew his father, and, once his parents were gone, ... none of us really knew what to do or to say in order to keep in touch with the family. That mother was crazy. I mean, seriously crazy."

"I've spoken to her," Doreen acknowledged. "I guess she wasn't the easiest."

He snorted. "There's *easy*, there's *hard*, and then there's her. She was more than a hound." He shook his head. "She definitely fit that last category."

"Do you know what family problems the couple were having?"

He frowned at her. "Who said they were having family problems?"

She stared right back at him. "The mother."

He snorted. "I wouldn't listen to anything that old bat says."

Almost immediately Thaddeus, who'd been quiet up until then, poked his head out of her hair and cried out loud, flapping his wings, "Old bat. Old bat. Old bat."

Roscoe stared in shock. "I didn't know he was there."

"Sorry, he tends to blend in."

"Yeah, you're not kidding."

For the first time, she saw Roscoe relax, and then he burst out laughing. "But you got it right, buddy. She's an old bat."

Thaddeus went off again. "Old bat. Old bat. Old bat."

She finally managed to get him shushed down, but Roscoe was enjoying Thaddeus too much. "What can you tell me about her that would make you say that?" she asked Roscoe.

"They fought all the time," he began. "My buddy told me that his wife would never tell her mother to stay in her place. That old woman was always interfering, getting in the way, just being a general pain in the butt," he snapped. "Like why, why does anyone have to interfere in what should have been somebody else's relationship?"

"Okay, yet, at the gas station, apparently they were arguing too."

"Sure." Roscoe shrugged. "Couples argue."

"So you don't think that their relationship was in trouble."

"Nope, sure don't," he muttered. "That's the old bat again."

Thaddeus started to rant, "Old bat. Old bat. Old bat." She pinched his beak closed, and he went "*he-he-he-he-he.*"

Roscoe stared at the bird in fascination. "He would be quite a party trick."

"Oh, yeah, *quite* a party trick." She couldn't say much to that and just rolled her eyes.

He laughed at her and added, "No wonder you don't like to go to parties."

"Can't say I've been invited to very many," she replied, with a shrug. "I have a tendency to piss people off. *Big-time.* People just don't like me."

He nodded. "Like my brother," he confirmed, with a certain smack of satisfaction. "He's pretty annoyed with you too."

She nodded. "I'm not sure what in particular bothers him though."

"You started to rattle his cage with the media attention and the cops and all the strangers. Then you bring in a cop lover and, after that, of course"—he burst out laughing—"I think the Japanese tour buses completed the process."

She winced. "I don't think anybody's happy about those for sure." She sighed. "Now think about Zeus. What was he like as a person? Was he the kind to drive straight through to Kelowna? Was he the kind to stop and visit and look at all the sights? Was he the kind to tuck in behind a semi and just pull up in his backdraft and drive straight through?"

Roscoe contemplated that. "Most of the time I would

have said the last part of that, … but I know, with his wife, she often liked to sightsee. Thus, if they were spending time together, I imagine that they would have stopped a few places."

"Would they have taken any side roads or gone down a dirt road just to explore it? Is that even a possibility?"

"They did say that they would be here at a certain hour," Roscoe noted, "so I wouldn't have thought so. However, that was always a consideration for us, as we searched for them. We just don't know why they would have."

Doreen suggested, "It could be anything, from having pulled over on the roadside to change a tire and coming up on somebody doing something nefarious, or maybe someone out there forced them off the road. Maybe someone offered them one million dollars to never go home again. I mean, who's to say what happened?"

He frowned at her. "I can't say any of us thought of something like that."

"No, but *something* happened," she stated, "and, as long as something happened, only so many suggestions work. Obviously lots of variables are involved, but generally it'll be a contest between whether they decided to disappear themselves, somebody decided for them that they should disappear, or they had one of those terrible accidents, and their bodies may not show up for another fifty years."

He sat back and looked at her. "That sums it up, doesn't it?" There was a hard tone to his voice, and the glint of fury in his eyes scared her.

She nodded. "Unless you can think about another situation."

"We didn't mention aliens," he stated in a matter-of-fact manner.

Startled, she looked at him. "What?"

He smiled. "No, I'm not crazy, but plenty of people back then wondered if maybe the aliens had something to do with their disappearance."

"Why the aliens?" she asked hesitantly.

"Your guess is as good as mine. Maybe it was all the rave back then," he said, with a shrug. "When you start talking conspiracies, you can bring out all kinds of crazies in this world. Especially here."

"I won't get into a discussion on whether aliens exist or not," she noted, "because I haven't a clue, but I highly doubt, given all the other things that can go wrong with people, that aliens had anything to do with this."

"It would be nice if I did have some answer," Roscoe shared, "even if it's not necessarily the right one. Still, it would be reassuring to hear anything that was reasonable. The idea that somebody else could have killed them … wasn't really one that we entertained, but it's not impossible."

"Do you know if maybe Zeus met anybody else? Were they traveling in a convoy? Was he the type of person to meet somebody at the gas station and help them out? What if a woman was in trouble? Would he have stopped to give her a hand? You know? What was this Zeus person like?"

Roscoe considered that for a moment. "Honestly, there was a lot to like about him, but he did have a few shortcomings," he admitted hesitantly.

"Such as?"

"He would have definitely stopped to help out a woman, but not while his wife was there because he probably would have had something else on his mind. Zeus was nothing short of a dog, who jumped the bone he saw from afar,"

Roscoe explained, giving her a sideways look.

"Ah, so he wasn't the kind to be faithful."

"Not really. He wasn't really sure that the rules of marriage were something he should have to abide by. We had to restrain him time and time again, when we were out together."

"Ah, so marriage was more like a life sentence instead of a joyous time, is that it?"

"Something like that. He was …" Roscoe stopped and then shrugged. "I don't really know how to say it other than he was a man's man."

She pondered that. "Meaning? That he got along well with men, and women were more or less a tool to him?"

"Yeah, something like that," Roscoe agreed slowly. "It's just he liked women. He really liked women. And he really loved Rosalina, but I'm not sure that he was faithful to her. Nothing I can say for sure there."

Doreen nodded slowly. "Okay, that's good to know."

"But it has no bearing on this," he declared. "What possible bearing could it have? So what if he was flirting right and left, correct?"

"I don't know," she replied. "Until we get to the bottom of it, no way to know."

"I don't think it has anything to do with it," he repeated, with a wave of his hand. "He made a lot of mistakes in his young life, but he was a good guy."

And Doreen presumed that's what it meant to be a man's man. Mistakes were easily glossed over, and nobody cared, as long as everybody got to have a good time. "Would he have left his wife?"

"No, I don't think so. He liked having her." Roscoe stopped and winced.

"Having her there and available, by any chance?" Doreen asked.

He sighed. "That makes him sound like a heel."

"Yep, sure does." Doreen stared at him. "Like you said, a man's man. A guy would understand that, but a woman wouldn't."

"No, I don't know too many women who would be okay with it."

"No, I sure don't either." She stared off in the distance. "So maybe there were some marital problems."

"And again it has nothing to do with it," he stated bluntly. "I doubt she would have pulled the steering wheel and sent them careening off a cliff, particularly one that would be so far from the road that we would never get to see them again."

"And even then," Doreen added, "I doubt she would have done that on purpose, unless she was afraid in some way. Or in a fury. She doesn't sound anything like that."

"You mean, like afraid for her life?" Roscoe asked. "Don't get me wrong. Zeus wasn't the kind to kill anybody. He was very much loved by everybody, and that was probably the problem. He wanted to love too many *everybodys*."

She didn't know quite what to say to that. "And I don't think, given that she had a child at home, that Rosalina would have been looking at killing herself."

"No, I don't think so."

"What about her temper? Did she have one?"

"According to Zeus, she did," he replied cautiously. "I didn't know her anywhere near as well as I knew him."

"Did he have a temper?"

He nodded. "Yep, sure did. Zeus would blow like a volcano," he declared, with a big fat grin.

"Ah, and again that's a man's man thing, right?"

"What do you mean?"

"For a woman to have a guy blow like that isn't exactly a fun time, but, for you guys, it's something to be proud of?"

"I don't know about *proud of.*" Roscoe looked uncomfortable at that. "I don't want you putting words in my mouth."

"No, not trying to put words in your mouth, just trying to understand what Zeus was like."

"Anyway, he wasn't the kind to lose it very often."

Still, Roscoe looked uncomfortable at that statement. "But, when he did, it was phenomenal, right?"

"Yeah," he agreed reluctantly. "When he did, it was pretty impressive."

And again, on that whole concept of being a man's man, she deliberately stayed quiet. She didn't want to give off mixed vibes and shut down this flow of information. "Okay, so what else? What did he do for a job?"

"He was a bank clerk."

"Oh, and is that the job he thought he would do?"

"Heavens, no." Roscoe laughed. "I never would have thought he would settle for something like that."

"Settle?"

"Yep, *settle.* Zeus always had big dreams," Roscoe remembered, with a big smirk. "He would go places, would be seen at places, would be somebody."

"Not just somebody's husband and somebody's father, I presume."

"No, he was okay to be that too, but he would be *somebody.* He had larger-than-life dreams, if you get what I mean."

Considering it was a common theme running through this conversation, it wasn't hard to. "Got it," she murmured. "How long had he worked there?"

Roscoe shook his head. "Maybe six months, maybe a little bit longer." Roscoe frowned. "I'm not really sure." He turned to her. "What difference does it make?"

"Just an idea whether he was happy, not happy, was it something that he wanted to do, something he didn't want to do?"

"I don't know if he wanted to do it or not, but he was trying to accept responsibility for his family. He wanted to provide for them."

"And that's always a good thing."

"You see? Now that's a woman thing for you," he pointed out. "I don't see that as a guy thing at all."

"It might not be, but it is something that women generally appreciate when a guy accepts responsibility and helps pay the bills." She nodded, as she considered him. "I'm just trying to get an idea of his mind-set."

"He didn't like the idea of working for a living. He would be *somebody*. Remember that part?"

She nodded. "Yeah, I remember that part. It's just often in direct contrast to a lot of other parts, such as paying bills."

Roscoe snorted. "That's true."

"Was he happy at the bank?"

"Not the last time I talked to him. He was looking for something else, looking for the next *best deal*."

"Right. And Rosalina?"

"She wasn't working at the time. He mentioned something about her planning on going back to work. She wanted to stay home and look after the baby, but they couldn't afford to. Zeus wasn't flush, and no way they could afford regular daycare, but with her mother there for easy childcare, they just decided to get away."

"Right, so then sometimes it's easier for the mother to stay home."

"Not in this case. Rosalina made just as much money as Zeus. She needed to go back to work and help pitch in."

The bitter tone to his comment made her want to keep well out of that discussion because definitely something personal was involved there. "Okay, so what else can you tell me about them? How long were they married?"

"Eighteen months."

She stopped. "Then the baby ..."

"Yeah, she was pregnant with the baby when they got married."

"Shotgun wedding," she muttered, with a nod.

"And yet it shouldn't have to be a shotgun wedding," he stated angrily.

"Don't shoot the messenger," she replied. "I'm just trying to get an idea of who they were to the people around them."

He sighed. "I didn't realize how much all this was pissing me right off."

"Apparently it's pissing you off pretty well," she pointed out, with a smile.

He nodded. "Isn't that the truth. Whatever. I just want to get answers." He stared off in the distance. "Their disappearance didn't kill my marriage, but it sure put mine through a bad patch because I just couldn't understand what happened to them."

"I'm sorry. It's hard for everybody when something like this happens."

He just nodded, not saying anything.

"Did he have friends with …" She wasn't sure how to phrase it. "Did he have any friends who had criminal records or anything that could have come back to bite him in the butt?"

He slowly shook his head. "Not that I know of."

She didn't say anything, just stayed quiet.

He frowned, as he thought more about it. "I really don't think so."

"Okay, again, I'm just asking questions. Did somebody in his history have a criminal record or in some way may have wanted Zeus to go back into whatever it was that they might have been doing together?"

"I don't think so," he repeated. "We were both bad back then. I had a juvie record. I went straight and cleaned up my act," he admitted, "but Zeus's mother-in-law never believed that. Neither did Rosalina."

Doreen nodded. "No, I don't imagine Bessie would. I think she's pretty much black and white."

"Ya think? That woman is just hard on everybody."

"Particularly herself, I presume."

"Maybe, doesn't really matter though. None of this will bring them back."

"No, it won't." Doreen pondered a bunch of options and then said, "That's all that's coming to mind at the moment."

"It's still more questions than anybody else asked," he noted, looking at her with a renewed respect.

"I'm sure they asked it back then or at least a version of it. *Did he have any dreams? Was there anything he wanted to do or to be when he grew up?*" she said, for lack of a better way to say it.

"No, I don't think so, except that he would be a big

shot. He never really was much for specifics. Not a thinker, if you ask me."

She nodded. "So many people want to be big shots. You almost want to tell them all to stop trying to be a big shot and just try to be you."

"And that's a really good lesson to learn," Roscoe agreed. "Most people don't learn it though."

She gave a sad smile. "No, they sure don't."

Chapter 9

DOREEN STOOD AND held out a slip of paper to Roscoe. "Here's my phone number. Call me if you think of anything else, anything at all." She turned, heading for the door, then looked back at him, thinking how to better put it. "Also, when you were looking for these guys, and I know a lot of people were looking with you, was anybody a little *too* interested in getting answers?"

"A lot of people were looking. It seemed to really hit people's hearts that this had happened. A couple gone without a trace, their baby left behind? I don't know what you mean, though."

She sighed. "Obviously we don't know whether a crime was committed or this was just a really bad accident. Sometimes, though, people involved in a crime like to watch the cops the same way arsonists like to watch the fires they set. They become very eager, energetic, involved—after the fact—and some tend to volunteer to help find their victims." She studied Roscoe's face. "So I just wondered if anybody in the search crowd stood out, someone who was a little too eager."

He nodded. "Yeah, there was one guy, but he'd already

lost his son, who never came home again. Thus he wanted to make sure it didn't happen to anybody else."

"And do you know who that was?" she asked him.

He shrugged. "Yeah, his name was … Let me just think about that for a moment." He went quiet for a moment. "Something like … I think *Stanley*, but the search and rescue guys knew him from his son's case, so he checks out."

"I guess you don't have a last name, do you?"

"I don't. Never was any good with first names, and last ones totally defeat me."

"Anybody else stand out?"

He shook his head. "No, people helped that first weekend, but, after that, it was a bit much for most people. Not me though. I'm still looking."

"Seems to be an endless search for nothing," she noted, "so not everybody can manage to keep it up. Nobody searches forever, not without something giving them hope."

"I get that," Roscoe said. "It was hard. It was really hard because I didn't want to give up, and yet everybody else did, and that got me angrier and even more determined to find answers."

"And maybe it wasn't that they seemed to give up but that they just didn't have the same understanding as you did. Zeus was your best friend, and you were trying hard to keep him alive in your mind."

His voice caught when he replied, "That's for sure, but we never saw them again."

"Got it. Do you mind giving me your phone number in case I have any other questions?"

He shrugged. "Sure, whatever. Although Richard warned me that you can be a nag," he stated, narrowing his gaze at her.

She looked at him. "I promise I won't bother you unnecessarily. I may have questions, as soon as I leave here. So it would bother me that I didn't ask you something."

He nodded. "Isn't that frustrating?"

"It's very frustrating," she admitted, smiling. "And I wouldn't want to feel that I couldn't ask more questions, just because I forgot to say something the first time."

"Whatever," Roscoe said. "I'm not a lightweight like my brother. If you're bugging me too much, believe me. I'll tell you."

"Great." She gave him a bright smile, trying hard not to wince at that. The last thing she wanted was more people thinking she was a pain in the butt. Apparently Richard had warned a lot of people that that's what she was already. She walked back to the front door with the animals in tow. "Thank you for speaking with me."

"You're welcome. Now I sure hope you can go do your thing. I really want to get this wrapped up." He looked at his watch, frowned, and added, "Hopefully you'll have it done by the weekend."

She turned and asked, "*This* weekend?"

He nodded. "We're having a memorial this weekend."

"Why is that?"

"What do you mean, why is that?" he asked in affront. "It's been twenty-five years."

"You mean, a memorial for Zeus, for his family?"

"Yes, he disappeared twenty-five years ago yesterday." And, with that, he closed the door in her face.

Chapter 10

NOT ONLY WAS Doreen now expected to find answers by a deadline, but it brought up something completely unrelated and yet quite possibly related in a big way. She got outside of Roscoe's small yard and walked toward home. The animals had been beyond quiet. She wasn't even sure why. Sometimes Mugs got to be quite chaotic, and other times he was just really, really quiet. She didn't know when or why, but, at this point in time, she would rather have her animals be more lively. "What's the matter, Mugs?"

He looked up at her and woofed.

"Yeah? What was that *woof* about? Or are you just thinking?"

He woofed again.

"Thinking is fine. We just need to come up with a little bit more than just thinking."

As she wandered home, she dialed Mack.

His voice was frustrated and fed up. "Doreen, is it important?"

"Maybe not. I'll talk to you later."

"No, wait. Sorry. Look it's just been one of those days."

"I get it. I just came from Roscoe's place."

"And who's Roscoe?" he asked. "I haven't heard you mention that name before."

"No, he was the guy who your missing couple were coming up to see twenty-five years ago. And did you know that Edwin, the couple's son, was killed twenty-five years later to the day? They are planning a memorial."

"What are you talking about?" Mack asked, suddenly coming on board to what the conversation was about.

"The couple who went missing, went missing twenty-five years ago yesterday," she repeated. "And their son was killed twenty-five years later to the day. There's a memorial for the couple this weekend in town."

"What? Surely that's a coincidence."

She waited for him to catch up to her.

"I know. I know. I know. I'm not a big fan of coincidences."

"Neither am I. At least not now. I used to be. I used to think it was great, until I met you," she stated, with a note of humor.

"Oh, so I'm now to blame, am I?" he teased.

"Not necessarily to blame, but definitely part of that whole not-sure-how-this-fits-in-my-life conundrum. And—before you hang up on me—I know that Edwin is the dead body the guy in the park was talking about because we have no dead women showing up. So I must have misheard the *he* as *she*, and you've been all too happy to have me sidetracked, haven't you? Thought this would keep me out of your current case for a little longer, didn't you? Don't even bother arguing about it. The jig is up. And be forewarned. I'll be watching for this trick again." And, with that, she ended the call.

He phoned almost a minute later and avoided that last

issue she brought up, going back to their earlier subject of conversation. "I'm not even thinking apparently. What else did Roscoe tell you?"

"Apparently Zeus was a *man's man*," she repeated in a dry tone. "He liked the ladies a little too much. He worked at a bank and had only been there a few months, but he was looking for a big score, a big way to be a big man. He got Rosalina pregnant, and they had a wedding soon afterward. When they got married, it was pretty-well a shotgun wedding, and you can blame Rosalina's mother for that."

"Right." Mack chuckled. "Twenty-five years ago wasn't all that long ago."

"Might not have been all that long ago for Mother, but she's old-school."

"She definitely is. Okay. I'll have to talk to you later. We can get into that Roscoe conversation when I have more time and can focus on that." And he rang off.

On the way home, she passed the Chinese food place, her favorite one, and she pondered whether she could afford to pick up something or not.

As it happened, Mr. Wu was outside washing windows. He recognized her and asked, "You come order food?"

She shrugged. "I was just wondering about it."

"No, you come order food," he said, a note of insistence in his voice.

She hesitated, as something was odd about this conversation. "Okay," she muttered, "but just one dish."

"Just one dish," he said. "Just one dish." And he went inside and came back with a to-go order for her.

She looked at it. "But I didn't order this."

"Other customer order," he explained, "but no-show. It's for you." And, with that, he went back inside and disappeared behind the counter.

She stared down at the to-go bag, knowing that a part of her should just say, *Thank you*, and another part of her should argue, *Ah, this is so weird*. She decided to take it home and not look a gift in the face, realizing that, of all the things that had happened, this was one of the good ones.

By the time Doreen got home, she was quite tired and a little bit worn out. How does that happen when she hadn't done a whole lot yet? It was just that sinking feeling, probably more of a case of her brain moving around at lightning speed and coming up with nothing to really gnaw on. Her mind worked so much better when she had things in there to rattle around. Of course she'd rattled it around as much as she could, but still some things just wouldn't cooperate. She disarmed the alarm, stepped inside, carried the food to the kitchen table, and then unhooked everybody.

She opened up the back door to let Mugs out but said, "I'll feed you first, okay?"

Mugs barked at her, but he still seemed a little off. She wondered if something was wrong or ... He was her best friend. She didn't want anything to happen to him. She bent down and gave him a cuddle. "Are you okay, buddy? What's the matter?"

He just woofed again and walked outside, where he flumped down on the deck. She was worried enough that she ate outside, trying to figure out if something was seriously wrong with him. However, he just seemed out of sorts.

"Maybe you're just bored. Maybe you need another mystery to keep you occupied," she muttered.

Of course nobody would think that was a good idea. She had plenty of things to keep her busy and plenty of things to keep her mind rattling around. Yet, right now, she was worried about Mugs.

She sighed, stretched out beside him on the deck and again asked, "You okay, buddy?"

He woofed at her, rolled over, so he was up against her arms, and cuddled in.

With her heart gently breaking, she cuddled him close and whispered, "I can't have anything happen to you. You know that, right? You're way too special."

He woofed at her again and this time closed his eyes, as if he were content.

She thought about all the times that he had saved her life and had jumped into the fray to ensure that she was okay. And she started to worry that she'd missed a sign of something. She checked him over while he dozed but couldn't find any injury or any soreness. He didn't walk with a limp. There just didn't seem to be anything. Yet something was off. She'd noticed it a couple weeks ago, and then things had gone crazy, and she had forgotten about it again.

She chastised herself for that because there was no point in having pets like this and then forgetting if something could be wrong. It's not that she'd wanted to forget, but, well, life had gotten busy. For the rest of the day, every time he turned over or rolled over, Doreen jumped up and checked him, and still nothing appeared to be obviously wrong. He ate dinner just fine, and, if anything, it just set her off a little bit more.

When Mack phoned later, he asked, "What's the matter?"

"How do you know there's even *a matter*?" she asked distractedly.

"Because you sound like something is wrong."

"I'm just worried about Mugs," she admitted, with a

sigh. "I noticed it a couple weeks ago, and then today he was just, I don't know. He wasn't showing very much enthusiasm for the life around him."

"Meaning?"

"I don't know," she cried out. "I don't … I don't know what I mean. Just that he's … He's been off."

"Maybe he's tired. He's certainly been chasing after bad guys with you for a long time."

"I know, but I didn't think it was a problem," she muttered.

"Nobody said it is a problem. Nobody said it's a problem at all. Maybe you're thinking it's a problem. Don't lean into it too much."

"*Sure,*" she grumbled. "You can say that, but it seems to be a problem."

"Maybe just relax. Maybe he's picking up on your mood or something. If he's eating, pooping and sleeping, it's all good."

"Maybe," she conceded. "I'll keep an eye on him."

"You do that, and, if you're really worried, you can take him to the vet—but just consider this. You can't tell me what's wrong with Mugs, so what do you think a vet will say about that?"

On that note, he hung up, leaving her staring down at the phone because he was right. She couldn't describe what was going on easily to Mack, of all people. She was hoping that somebody would just take a look at the dog and would figure it out. But the only person who really knew Mugs the way she did was her. So if there was any figuring out to be done, well, it would be up to her.

For the rest of the day, he seemed perfectly normal, and slowly some of her panic eased.

When she crawled into bed that night, she told him, "Be sure you tell me if something is wrong."

He just woofed and curled up in bed.

She remembered all the times she had had *off* days and thought, *Well, maybe that's all it is.* Lord knows, Mugs had a right to them, the same as everybody else did. More so, Mugs was always a busy boy, always ready for the next adventure at any time.

Maybe that's all it was. Maybe he just needed something else to do. And yet on that walk to Roscoe's, Mugs didn't really seem to care. Maybe because absolutely nothing held Mugs's interest at Roscoe's place. She had to ponder a name like Roscoe too. Richard and Roscoe.

As she was nodding off, she got a text from Roscoe of all people. She looked at it.

Just remembered the name. Stanley Gupta.

The name of the too-interested guy in the searchers, that Roscoe said he would find for Doreen.

She sent back a thumbs-up, determined that in the morning she would find out more about this guy. But she took the name into her dream state and found herself walking and walking and walking, forever looking for this name on a road sign.

Chapter 11

Tuesday Morning...

B Y THE TIME Doreen woke the next morning, she was tired and worn out. Nan called almost immediately, while Doreen was still trying to get clothes on after a hot shower.

"Are you all right?" Nan asked.

"I am fine," Doreen mumbled. "Just really tired, another bad night."

"Oh dear," Nan replied, "you're not supposed to have those."

"Somebody needs to tell my subconscious then," Doreen noted, with a note of humor.

But Nan wasn't to be put off. "Maybe you should go see a doctor."

Doreen knew being sick was unacceptable to her grandmother, who fretted. "Nope, I don't need to see a doctor," Doreen argued. "I'm fine, Nan."

But Nan wasn't so sure. "You know it's pretty easy for you to get sick, and you've been overdoing it a lot."

"I'm not exactly overdoing it right now though, am I?"

"I don't know. What are you doing?" Nan asked.

Doreen groaned. "I'm about to go put on coffee."

"What? You're not even up yet?"

Nan sounded so horrified that Doreen sighed and chuckled lightly. "Nope, I'm not downstairs yet. I'm just getting up and around now."

"It's almost eight o'clock," Nan pointed out in amazement.

"I know. As I mentioned, I had a bad night, and I'm just heading out of the shower."

"Fine," Nan huffed. "Have your coffee and then call me, and we'll talk about it later here, in person."

"Talk about what?" Doreen asked.

"I found some information. Didn't I tell you? Of course I told you. You see? You really need to wake up in the early morning, dear." She added, "I'll touch base with you again in an hour." And, with that, Nan hung up.

Doreen frowned at her phone. "She did not say anything about any information," she muttered.

But then she wondered if maybe she had been so tired that she hadn't heard whatever Nan had been saying. She misheard a *she* for a *he* in the park the past weekend too. But, no, she wouldn't go down that rabbit hole. And, boy, those were rabbit holes with Nan. Doreen drank down her first cup of coffee, knowing she would need a double dose for today, just with the way that it'd started.

Then she pushed open the back door and let Mugs out. He raced outside, barking, and she raced outside behind him. "What's the matter, buddy?"

Almost immediately he stopped. He sniffed around the backyard and headed toward the river. She walked down beside him. She didn't call out to him; she just wanted to see what he was doing and where he was going. He was very knowledgeable about the area. She just didn't know what may have set him off.

With the other animals dawdling nearby, Doreen glanced back at Thaddeus, who was walking down the pathway, looking around, as if he hadn't seen anything yet this morning. He slept almost as much as she did. She didn't know how that worked, but that bird had a serious capacity for sleep.

As Doreen made it to the river, Mugs was heading into the water. She watched in astonishment as he raced in and splashed around, acting as if he hadn't had a bath in forever. "You okay, buddy?"

He woofed at her, wagged his tail, and barked and jumped around. She picked up a stick and threw it for him. And, with that, she saw the old Mugs again, playful and full of life. She shook her head. "Did you just need a day to snooze or something?" she muttered to herself, still watching him.

Because that's what it seemed he was doing now, just having fun. Maybe they had too much work and not enough play. For that, she felt guilty because that was probably her fault. It seemed as if everything was always so much work these days that they never quite got in the same amount of playtime. Or even just rest time. It often became something else.

Determined to do better, she picked up the stick and spent a good twenty minutes playing with Mugs, until he was done. He came out of the river and flumped down at her feet. Then he was panting, happily rolling around on his back, just enjoying himself.

She bent down and gave him a big cuddle. "You seem to be so much better. I was worried about you for a while, buddy."

He woofed at her and bounded to his feet and started to walk up to the house. She watched in astonishment as he went across the patio and up the steps to stretch out full length on the deck and fell back asleep again.

"Maybe that's all it was," she muttered to herself. "Maybe he just wanted some special playtime. Maybe he just wanted some exercise. I don't know."

She went inside, refilled her coffee cup, and stepped back outside again. Mugs remained where he was, happily splayed out on the deck. He didn't even lift his head when she sat down beside him. She rubbed his belly, and he grunted once, and that was it. She smiled. "You, my dear sir, are quite the character."

Thaddeus landed beside her, with an awkward thud. "Character. Character. Character."

She laughed. "You, my crazy friend, are the biggest character of all."

And didn't he preen as if he understood. She marveled at the antics of all her pets. Even Goliath. Especially right now, as he'd found a patch of catnip in her garden—maybe Richard had dropped the seeds over the fence? Goliath was stretched out on his back in the middle of the plants, dreaming sweet dreams.

They were all so different and yet so much fun. They filled the empty holes in her world. Then being close to Nan and Mack had done a lot to lighten the dark shadows of her world too.

By the time she had her second cup, she was starting to feel better again herself. Nan phoned her back right on the hour. "I thought I was supposed to phone you," Doreen said drily.

"I couldn't wait," Nan replied. "You should come down."

"You mean, now that I'm awake?"

"Yes," Nan agreed, "as long as your brain's turned on and it's safe to talk to you, you should come down."

"Okay. Why?"

"We have news. Haven't I said that already?" And, with that, Nan hung up.

Doreen groaned at her grandmother's antics, yet she still asked, "Mugs, you want to go see Nan?"

He bounded to his feet and barked.

Even Thaddeus perked up beside her. "Thaddeus loves Nan. Thaddeus loves Nan."

"I know you do, buddy. Let's go see your favorite person. You want to walk?" Thaddeus hopped onto the table and looked up at her. "So you want to go for a ride?"

He cawed several times and then hopped onto her arm. He walked up to her shoulder, then cried out, "Giddyup, giddyup, giddyup."

She glared at him. "That's not funny."

"*He-he-he-he-he.*"

"It's not," she scolded. "You should be nice when you're getting a ride."

All she got in return was another "*He-he-he-he,*" and she sighed. "It's a good thing I love you." At that, she got an immediate response.

"Good thing I love you."

And danged if he didn't get the accent right on the *you* part.

She groaned. "You're too smart for your own britches."

"Too smart for your own britches. Too smart for your own britches."

She glared at him. "That's not what we say to people."

"That's not what we say to people. That's not what we say to people. That's not—"

"Okay, stop," Doreen cried out in frustration.

Instead Thaddeus just laughed at her some more, and then he subsided into quiet mode and tucked up against her shoulder.

"You are all nuts today," she muttered.

She turned to look for Goliath, who was lying on the pathway behind them. "Come on, Goliath. Let's go see Nan, buddy."

He just stared at her.

"Oh no, not you too," Doreen muttered. "I'm not sure what everybody's problem is right now, but wow."

When they were almost too far away from Goliath for Doreen's comfort, the cat finally jumped up to his feet and raced toward her. As he skated by her, he jumped over Mugs's back—a move that had Doreen gasping in astonishment—then dropped down in front of Mugs, almost tripping him up.

"Good Lord," Doreen noted, "you're all playful."

Maybe they were just bored. Maybe they needed something extra in life. And yet who would have thought that there wasn't enough activity going on for all of them? Before long, keeping an eye on all the animals' antics, Doreen arrived at Nan's in good shape. Nan was sitting outside, and so were her cronies, Richie at the forefront, and Maisie had joined them today. Nan must have forgiven her for dating one of Nan's old boyfriends.

Doreen smiled at them all, as she walked toward them. "Hey, all."

Then came a shout at her from the other side. She froze

WHISPERS IN THE WISTERIA

and looked, and there was a gardener, shaking his fist at her.

She raised her hand and called out, "Good morning."

"It's not a good morning, you fool. Get those animals on a leash."

She groaned, looked down at them, and quickly put Goliath on Nan's patio. "We're just visiting," Doreen called out.

He continued to glare at her.

She winced and turned toward Nan. "Wow, you got yet another new gardener?"

Nan nodded. "And this one's cranky," she announced.

"Yeah, I think I found that out for myself." Doreen shook her head, sat down, and looked at the trio, all grinning with some expectation, as if waiting to hit the jackpot. "Wow, I don't know what you guys are up to," Doreen said, "but it seems to be big enough."

"Oh, it's really big," Richie declared, beaming.

"Yeah? And what is this all about?" Doreen asked.

"We decided we should tell you first, and then you can decide if we should tell Darren and Mack."

"*Right*." Doreen's heart sank. "Is it one of our cases, or is it something else entirely?"

"We're not sure," Richie stated, with that same air of importance.

"Okay, … so you want to tell me what it is then?"

"We're not sure again," Maisie added.

"Okay." Doreen smiled at Nan and suggested, "I really could use a cup of tea."

Nan beamed and told Doreen, "Go put on the kettle."

Surprised, Doreen got up and walked into the kitchen, as she heard them all muttering behind her. She put on the teakettle and waited and waited.

Finally Nan called to her, "You can come back out, you know."

Doreen rejoined them. "I wasn't sure if you guys had enough time for your confidential discussion." Doreen shook her head. "You all sure were busy chattering, doing just fine without me out here."

"We are," Nan confirmed, "but that doesn't mean that you can't be here too."

"If you say so," Doreen muttered. "Didn't seem you were ready for me yet."

Nan looked at her and then nodded. "Very insightful, dear. And you're right. We should have had this hashed out before we hauled you down here."

"That's all right," Doreen replied, with an airy wave of her hand. "What did you decide?"

"We decided we'll tell you," Richie stated, with that air of self-importance.

She turned to him and slowly nodded. "Okay, and what is it you'll tell me?"

Nonplussed, he looked at her, then over at Nan.

"Oh, for heaven's sake, Richie, you couldn't have forgotten already."

He popped up with an injured air and argued with her. "Of course not. I just wasn't expecting Doreen to get so direct about it."

"Richie, when have you ever known me *not* to be direct?" Doreen asked. "Obviously you guys are up to something, so why don't you fill me in. Better do it quickly."

Maisie jumped the gun and took the lead. "We know who killed Edwin," she cried out triumphantly.

Doreen stared at her. "What?"

Nan nodded carefully. "At least we think we do."

"Okay," Doreen began. "Are you sure you didn't want to bring Mack in on this?"

"Nope, because, if we're wrong, … he'll get mad at us, so we'll tell you, and then you'll go tell him."

"So, if you're wrong, he can get mad at me?" Doreen asked, with a note of humor.

Surprise, surprise, they all nodded. Maisie and Richie even said, "Exactly," at the same time.

Chapter 12

DOREEN'S JAW DROPPED, and she stared at the three seniors, all beaming at her. Just then her phone rang. She glanced down to see it was Mack. She held up a finger to hold off their responses and asked, "Mack, what's up?"

"I need to talk to you," he stated. "Are you at home?"

"No." She frowned at his tone. "I'm down at Nan's."

He hesitated. "Can you go home? I need to talk to you."

She continued to frown. "Yes, of course I can. I'll meet you there in a few minutes."

"Okay." And he hung up.

She glanced back at the three in front of her. "So do you want to tell me who you think killed Edwin?" she asked.

Maisie burst out with the news. "It was the boyfriend."

She stared at her. "Whose boyfriend?"

"The ex-girlfriend's new boyfriend, Oscar," Maisie declared. "He was the best friend of poor Edwin, until Gina and Edwin broke up. Word is, Oscar hooked up with Gina before she broke up with Edwin," she added in a hoarse whisper.

Doreen stared at her. "You know this how?"

She chuckled. "Because Edwin's aunt works for the hospital and is one of the nurses who comes by Rosemoor all the time."

Doreen stared at Maisie. "She told you that the couple got together before the girlfriend broke up with Edwin?"

At that, all three of them nodded.

Nan explained further. "Now Edwin comes back into town, upsetting the current boyfriend, and *boom*. Just like that Edwin is dead." Nan beamed. "Simple."

"But you don't know that he did it, not to mention there's a time gap here."

"Sure, but who else did it?" Nan asked reasonably. "You know it's always a love triangle."

"It's *often* a love triangle," Doreen corrected. She looked down at her phone and added, "That was Mack. He needs to talk to me, and he wants to meet me at home."

"Oh, go, go, go," Nan said. "Now it's up to you whether you want to tell him yourself or to report that the information came from us."

"I'll definitely tell him that the information came from you," Doreen replied. "Don't worry about that." As she went to leave, they all looked at each other, probably imagining Mack's response to their meddling. Doreen added, "I'll talk to you in a little bit. Let me think about your idea."

"Not a whole lot to think about, dear." Nan sniffed.

Doreen winced. "Got it." She went to nudge Mugs toward the parking lot, but he was lying down, showing no interest in moving. She frowned. "I'm not sure what's wrong with him these days. He's not himself."

"Maybe it's time to get him a friend," Maisie suggested.

She looked over at her. "A friend? He's got Goliath and Thaddeus, not to mention me."

"But he's also tired out," Nan noted.

"Possibly, yet he really enjoyed playing in the river today. I don't know what is up with him. Maybe he's just worn out from this morning." She managed to get him to his feet, and he waddled toward the grass.

As she looked on, Nan smirked. "He needs to be on a diet. That's what it is."

Doreen stared at her grandmother in shock. "Is he fat?"

"He's definitely gained weight these last few months."

"Oh dear." Doreen stared at Mugs, noticing his belly and his waddle. "At least that's fixable."

At that, Richie chuckled. "Not everybody gets to eat whatever they want and not have it go to their belly," he patted his flat stomach. "Honestly it would drive me crazy to have my food curtailed. No way."

Doreen sighed. "Come on, Mugs. We'll get more exercise. That'll fix this."

Mugs wagged his tail and started to dance around.

"Good," Doreen said. "Keep it up. Come on, buddy. Let's go. We'll do lots more walking over the next bit, just so you can drop a pound or two."

They had done a ton of walking when they first arrived in town, just so Doreen could see what there was to offer here. Even in several of these cold cases they had been moving around pretty steadily, and she thought she'd kept it up, but maybe they'd been complacent.

Vowing to do better and to cut back on the treats somewhat—although Mugs certainly wouldn't like that—she headed home at a much faster pace than normal. Plus she knew Mack was waiting on her. Still she picked up sticks and threw them for Mugs, and, by the time he got home, he was panting heavily. She came up the back walkway and found Mack standing on her deck, his hands on his hips, waiting for her.

She smiled up at him. "Hey," she greeted him, and she threw another stick for Mugs.

Mugs raced forward, grabbed the stick, took it to Mack, and dropped it at his feet, before lying down, panting beside him.

"Wow, he's had a workout, hasn't he?" he asked, studying Mugs.

"On purpose, as it seems he's gained some weight," Doreen explained. "I feel so guilty."

He looked over at her and smiled. "It's not disastrous. He's not horribly overweight. Maybe a pound or two but not much more."

"He's been in a slump lately," she muttered. "I mentioned it to you too. I didn't know what was wrong, and then Nan and her cronies pointed out that he's getting a little chunky."

"As in *chonky*," he misquoted.

She sighed. "Right? I feel terrible."

"I'm sure it won't take much to wear off and maybe just cut back on some of the treats."

"I was thinking that too, but I really didn't think I was giving him too much."

"Maybe not, but you know sometimes they can get too much of a good thing, and they won't stop or say no either."

"True. Anyway, what was the matter that you wanted me to meet you right now?"

He shrugged. "Remember when we were in City Park on the weekend?"

"Yeah, of course I do. I overheard that conversation about a dead body."

He nodded, stared at her intently, and asked, "You remember *exactly* what went on in that conversation?"

She stopped and stared. "Now you want to know?" He glared at her. She threw up her hands. "Yeah, it was something about we have to get rid of the body."

"Was it *we* have to get rid of the body?"

"It was something along that line, I have to think about it. Why?" He hesitated. "So Edwin *is* connected to that?" she asked in excitement. "I knew it. I told you that earlier. You can't keep denying it."

He sighed and shook his head.

"Right, I'm not supposed to get excited about bodies," she muttered, "but it's hard."

"For you, it is." He nodded, with a smile. "And something came up that might connect the body to the park."

"What's that?"

"They found a leaf."

"A leaf from?"

"From a wisteria plant."

She nodded. "Now that would be good forensic evidence."

"Sure, but there's forensics and then this wisteria, which grows in many places in town."

"I wonder if they can match it to those particular plants at the park."

He shrugged. "That's why I wanted to ask you more about what we heard that day."

"So not just your take on it but mine too," she noted, with a smile.

"Doreen, we both heard pieces and parts. You more than me. And I've already told about the wind distortion element. That's why we prefer to have corroborating witnesses, not just relying on one person."

Doreen smirked, still so happy he was asking for her help on one of his current cases. "By the way, Richie, Nan, and Maisie are all of the opinion that they've got Edwin's murder all solved. They told me that I could tell you and claim it as my idea or give them credit for it," she added, with an eye roll.

"Oh do they?" Mack crossed his arms and leaned against the railing on her deck. "I just can't wait to hear this one."

She chuckled. "They're convinced it's the boyfriend."

"Boyfriend?"

She nodded. "Yeah, *boyfriend*, as in Edwin's old best friend, Oscar, who became Edwin's ex-girlfriend's new partner."

He sighed. "Of course they think it would be him."

She nodded. "And there's not a whole lot I can convince them of otherwise at the moment, not until we have something to tell them."

"I hope you're not telling them anything." Mack glared at her.

"I'm not trying to tell them anything, but you know what the gossip mill around Rosemoor is like."

"It's terrible. Isn't it?"

"It's quite fascinating. It's a whole microsociety all on its own."

"Sure, but not necessarily one that we all need to have as active as it is."

Mack bent down and patted Mugs on the shoulder. Mugs woofed and raced around, barking madly. Mack picked up the stick and threw it for him several more times. "Do this a few times a day, and any extra pounds will melt away."

"He's also happier. I wonder if my downtime has just

bored him."

"Maybe, or maybe it's just your downtime needs to include playtime for him."

She nodded. "I wouldn't want anything to happen to him."

Mack looked over at her and smiled. "Hey, it's okay, you know. He's fine."

"None of that's ever really been on me before," she muttered. "Sometimes I think there are huge gaps in my education."

"But he was always your dog, wasn't he?" Mack asked.

"Sure, but it's not like I looked after him, not during my marriage. I wasn't responsible for his walks, his diet, anything like that," she muttered. "So now I feel it's all on me, and I'm screwing up." She stared at Mugs, frowning, unsure of herself.

"You're doing a wonderful job with him," Mack stated. "Don't even go down that pathway."

"But what if I'm screwing it up? What if I'm ruining him? Maybe he needs to see a doggy shrink."

He stared at her for a long moment and then groaned. "Seriously? Is that even a real thing?"

Grinning, she laughed. "Of course it is. I'm sure my girlfriend took hers in to see a shrink because he was having some behavioral problems."

"A doggy shrink," Mack repeated. "Seriously?"

She shrugged. "That's what she called it. Why would I doubt it?"

And he just shook his head. "No, you wouldn't have any reason to doubt it, I'm sure."

She glared at him. "Are you laughing at me again?"

"Never." Then he smiled and clarified, "I'm laughing

with you."

"But I'm not laughing," she noted, frowning.

"You could, if you wanted to."

She sighed. "I guess it sounds funny, doesn't it?"

"It does sound funny, but we have certainly heard funnier things in life. I don't belong to the world of the rich, where things like shrinks for dogs are commonplace, but that doesn't mean it doesn't happen. If you had said that somebody was working on her dog's behavioral problems, that would have made sense to me but ..."

"But a doggy shrink is not the same thing, is it?" she asked, looking at him.

"I don't know," he replied, getting confused, yet amused.

She shrugged. "It doesn't matter what we call them, I guess. However, the bottom line is, I think Mugs has been a little depressed, and I haven't been giving him enough exercise, and I think they probably have the same serotonin issues that we do." Then she frowned, tapping her jawbone. "I'll have to research it."

"Yeah, you do that," he replied. "While you check out Google, I'll go back to work."

"I thought you were off duty now," she said, looking down at her cell phone. "Don't you get lunch?"

"While we've got this case that's hot," Mack explained, "we're trying to run down all these leads. We're all eating on the run, if we get to eat at all."

"Right, and not getting very far, I'm sure."

"The forensics helps a lot, and yet, at the same time, it just confuses everything."

"That's because wisterias are all over town. However, there won't be very many people who were talking about dead bodies in town, especially while near wisterias—both the dead body or the guy on the phone."

"But we didn't get a description. You saw him better than I did. I just caught the back of him, running, and nothing stood out."

"Right," she muttered. "Any cameras around that corner?"

Mack nodded. "Chester is checking that. There are a bunch in various places, so it's a matter of trying to track down where the phone guy went."

"All those condos are around that park area too. You might check those security cameras."

He looked over at her and smiled.

She sighed, raising her hands. "I get it. I get it. *It's fine. It's all under control. You know what you're doing.* I'm just *shocked* that your brain is functioning and working so well," she teased.

He laughed. "If you come up with anything else, you can let me know."

"Right, because, of course, that's *your* case."

"Exactly," he confirmed. "And, if you find out anything on the cold case and what happened to that couple …"

She lowered her voice. "Yeah, it involves …" And she pointed to Richard's place, next door.

Mack stared at her, then over at Richard's fence. "You want to explain that? How is Richard involved in all this?"

She whispered, "We better head inside for this."

He walked up to the kitchen door, waited for her to open it and to turn off the alarm. When she stepped inside, she turned to him and further explained the Richard and Roscoe information.

"So the missing couple were coming to see Richard's

brother?" Mack asked in astonishment.

"Yeah, his name is Roscoe, and I spoke with him earlier. Edwin's grandmother, Bessie, told me that Roscoe was a loser and basically just trouble, and he, ... Roscoe, told me that she was the same. As I remember it, he used curse words to describe her."

"Of course."

"Whatever they think of each other is just noise at this point. However, he did give me an interesting insight into Zeus, calling him a man's man."

At that, Mack smiled. "It is a commonplace term."

"Does that make you a man's man?" she asked suspiciously.

His lips twitched. "I would like to think that men respect me, yet I wouldn't necessarily call myself a man's man."

She frowned at him. "So, if you're not a man's man, does that make you a ladies' man?"

He blinked at her several times. "Is this a trick question?" he asked cautiously.

"I don't know," she admitted. "I'm confused on those terms."

"Good," Mack noted. "Stay confused but don't get too hung up on it. Now, what else did you find out?"

She shrugged. "Not a whole lot. Not if you consider that Roscoe and the locals, including the police and search and rescue, spent a lot of weekends trying to find the vehicle, and nobody ever found anything. Not a sign of the couple or their vehicle anywhere around here."

"The fact that no credit cards or even a passport were ever used again is always suspicious. Either they went to ground or somebody helped them *into* the ground." He smiled. "Or ..." And he waited for her, looking at her expectantly.

"Or it was an accident, and they drove off into a lake or into a crevice or a ravine. I mean, who knows?"

"Exactly. And because they did the driving twenty-five years ago, it doesn't necessarily mean that the ground and the layout looks the same as now."

"How would that work?" she asked. "If anything, it would have much heavier overgrowth."

"Except for all the fires we've had, and that has cleaned out an awful lot of the old bush and debris."

"Oh." She pondered that. "That's a really good point. It could all look very different now, couldn't it?"

He nodded. "If we had a weekend to spare, we could go take a look. You might want to remind Roscoe that what wouldn't have been seen might come to light now. Although I'd rather get this investigation completed before everyone goes crazy and we're inundated with calls of what else people see."

"Yeah, he's counting on me to solve this."

At that, Mack turned and stared at her. "You know you have got to stop overpromising, right?"

"I didn't promise anything," she replied, chewing on her bottom lip, "but nobody listens to me. He also reminded me that I did solve very old cold cases, *past expiration date* cases, so to speak."

Mack smiled, walked over, and gave her a hug. "That you very well did. I would suggest dinner later, but I have to go now, and I might not get away even then."

"I know. You go on," she replied. "I'll just make a sandwich."

At that, he stopped and asked, "Have you eaten anything but a sandwich in the last few days?"

She frowned. "I was taking a holiday from cooking," she announced. When his lips twitched, she glared at him. "That looks an awful lot like you're making fun of me," she noted, her hands on her hips.

"Never." He smiled broadly at her. "Besides, I don't like to make fun of people. I'll laugh *with* them, but I don't want to make fun of them."

"That sounds good," she declared, "yet it feels remarkably like you are making fun of me."

"Nope," he disagreed cheerfully. "We'll get more food into your diet plan though. How do you feel about pierogies?"

She frowned at him. "*Pierogies?*"

He stopped and frowned back at her. "Smokies, sauerkraut, pierogies? Any of that mean anything to you?"

She slowly shook her head. "I've heard of sauerkraut, but isn't that rotten cabbage?"

He rolled his eyes and whispered something under his breath. "*Nooo*, it's fermented."

She nodded. "And things that are fermented are bad, right?"

"*Nooo*, they're not bad," he replied. "Where did you get that from?"

She frowned. "Don't they wait until it turns bad?"

He scrubbed the back of his head and added, "I guess that's a perception issue. They wait until it *sours*, so is that what you call *bad?*"

"Turns? Ferments?" she repeated. "Isn't it *bad?*"

"Some things, when they're fermented, *are* bad," he conceded, staring at her in fascination. "But I have a feeling I'll lose this argument regardless. Let me just ask you if you trust me."

"Sure," she said.

"Good, then when I tell you sauerkraut is good, you'll trust me, right?"

She hesitated, and he glared at her. She raised both hands in mock surrender. "I'll try it. But I don't know why you'd want to eat something bad."

"It's not bad. It's like silage."

"Silage." She beamed. "That's bad hay given to cows." And then she frowned. "So ..."

"Stop," Mack warned. "Don't even say it." Her lips twitched. He pointed a finger at her. "No, no, no, no, no, you don't get to say it."

"Which part? I am confused now, so I don't know how I should feel about you feeding me bad cabbage or implying I'm a cow."

He stared at her, threw up his hands, then picked her up in his arms, swung her around in the kitchen, and, when he put her down, he gave her a smacking long kiss.

"Don't ever change," he whispered. And, with that, he was gone.

Chapter 13

Wednesday Morning …

THE NEXT MORNING, Doreen woke with a bright smile on her face. Considering she was dealing with two cases—one of which she wasn't allowed to have anything to do with, but could hardly not, and one that had zero information about a couple missing for twenty-five years—it was an odd state to be in. She still hadn't spent more than a moment or two looking up this Stanley Gupta guy either. Still, what she had seen was a grieving father wanting to help someone else. And he'd passed away a few years back.

On the other hand, Mack had been in such a good mood when he left yesterday, and his goodbye kiss was responsible for her smile this morning, even though she was a little confused about the reason behind his kiss. Still, she certainly didn't object to it and knew it was much nicer to focus on good things than sad ones. On that note, it reminded her that she still had one major problem.

She picked up her phone and quickly texted Nick. **Did you hear back?** She got a thumbs-down. **How long do we wait?**

You in a rush now?

Maybe.

She got a thumbs-up for that.

Doreen sighed. Not anything she could do about it. She rolled over to see Mugs, lying here, snoring away. She checked him out, and, sure enough, she noted just a bit more *chubs* than she was used to seeing on him. "Up and at it," she told Mugs. "Let's go outside and get some gardening done."

He snuffled and looked at her and then rolled over and ignored her. She got up and dressed quickly, and Mugs was still lying on the bed, snoring. Goliath was right beside him. Both of them turned when she called their names and looked at her.

"Hey, slugs, come on. Let's go."

Goliath bounced up and walked toward her, before throwing himself onto the floor at her feet.

She sighed. "Wow, what is going on with you guys?"

She walked over to Mugs, scratched his belly, and repeated, "Come on, buddy. Let's go."

He just looked at her, slowly got up, and then she added, "Let's go play with sticks."

He snorted at her. But she got him down the stairs and outside. She was getting a little worried about him now. Still, when she opened the door, he raced outside and immediately brought her a stick. She laughed. "You're acting more and more like a typical dog than I would have expected, but it's all good."

Then she noted Thaddeus was missing. She walked up to the patio and called out to him, "Thaddeus, come on. Come on outside and join us."

When she heard no answer, she called again. Still nothing. She sighed, tossed a stick again for Mugs, and raced upstairs to her bedroom, finding the bird huddled on his perch, sound asleep. She walked over and gently stroked his back. He opened an eye and squawked at her. "We're outside. Don't you want to come?" She held out her arm, and he climbed up until he sat against her neck. "Wow," she muttered. "Seems as if everybody needs a holiday."

But then, as she thought about it, they'd had had weeks and weeks and weeks—if not months—of excitement. Obviously everybody had hit the wall, and maybe even Doreen had too; she just didn't want to admit it. And she had other cases to worry about. She took Thaddeus outside and parked him on the patio before picking up the stick that Mugs had brought back and flung it for him again. She played with him for a good fifteen minutes, until he collapsed beside her.

As she headed inside, she made coffee, still wondering how come he had gained weight on her.

She stopped when she heard him woofing. And Thaddeus was cackling, "Wait your turn. Wait your turn." She froze and peered into the open pantry, where Thaddeus was busy pulling dog treats out of the bag and dropping them to the floor. Mugs was scarfing them up in great big bites.

"Whoa, whoa, whoa, whoa," she said.

Thaddeus gave a squawk and bounced back.

"You can't do that, Thaddeus."

He gave her a gimlet eye.

"No, no, no, no, no," she told him. "Mugs can't have that many."

But that certainly explained where the extra weight had come from. She sighed. "Nope, that won't happen, Mugs." She looked down at him and shook her head.

He gave her the most woebegone look. "No, no, no, you know better," she muttered.

Almost as if he understood Doreen, Mugs snorted. Then Thaddeus repeated the sound himself.

"No, that's enough of that," she declared. "Man, the attitude you guys have." She turned to face Thaddaeus. "Where did you learn to do that?"

"Where did you learn to do that?" he repeated. "Where'd you learn to do that?"

"Stop, stop, stop," she said, glaring at him, her fists on her hips.

And didn't he fold his wings back right then, as if imitating her.

She raised her hands. Immediately his wings went up. "You're mocking me, aren't you?"

"Nope, not mocking you, not mocking you," he muttered.

She laughed, beside herself. "Fine, you're not mocking me. You're just having fun at my expense. You and Mack are in cahoots on this, aren't you? But never mind. Mugs can't have that many treats. It's not good for him."

Thaddeus looked at her and then defiantly reached into the bag, pulled out one more, and dropped it onto the floor. Mugs raced to grab it before Doreen could.

She snatched the bag of treats and said, "That means we can't keep the treats here in the pantry anymore." She turned around, looking for a better place for them. Yet it must be a place that Thaddeus couldn't open. Even as she studied the kitchen, looking for the ideal spot, Thaddeus walked onto her foot and said, "Thaddeus wants up. Thaddeus wants up."

She stared down on him. "You say the darndest things."

And she quickly reached down and picked him up and put him on her shoulder. And then she continued to look for a better hiding place for the treats.

As she opened one cupboard and murmured, "I wonder how this one would do."

Thaddeus laughed again. "*He-he-he-he.*"

Doreen shook her head. "No point in trying to hide anything from you if you're standing right here watching me," she muttered.

"*He-he-he-he.*"

She glared at him. "Just for that, you can go sit on your roost. Meanwhile, I'll find a new hiding place for these." She walked into the living room and put him on his roost, much to his disgust, and then quickly walked back into the kitchen and hid them in a cupboard over the fridge. "You won't get them there."

She turned and glared at Mugs. He gave her another woebegone look and went outside. "Yep, we'll go play some more. You have to wear off all those extra calories," she muttered.

She paused to grab her phone and texted Mack, saying that she had the answer to how Mugs had gained weight. Then she took another moment and explained, trying to make it as brief as possible.

When her phone rang a few minutes later, he asked, "Are you serious?"

She laughed. "Yes, I just caught Thaddeus giving him a whole pile of treats." And she explained to him how he was asking Mugs to *wait your turn.*

"Does that mean Goliath was eating the others?"

"Oh, I never even thought about Goliath, that sneaky little boy." She raced to the pantry to check out the other treats. "His treats are almost gone too," she cried out.

"That answers that. Goliath is just better at hiding a few extra pounds, what with all that fur."

"Not that much better," she noted grimly. "Now I know why he usually doesn't eat all that much now. They all have treats on the side."

"Mugs has obviously become way too accustomed to getting those."

"I've hidden them," she shared, deliberately not telling him about the problem she had trying to hide things from Thaddeus.

"Good luck with that." Mack laughed. "That bird appears to find everything."

"I know," she agreed. "I hadn't thought of that as a challenging aspect of having him as part of the family."

"But it doesn't really matter though, does it?"

"Only that we want to make sure Mugs doesn't get too many of these treats," she muttered.

"I almost sympathize with the poor guy," Mack replied. "I happen to like my treats myself, especially brownies."

"Right," she said, "and, speaking of brownies, I want to see about baking something again. So brownies?"

"You could always try baking some," he suggested. "Gives you something else to think about."

"Yeah, that doesn't sound terribly fun though," she told him. "Now, I used to love getting a brownie with my tea, but, when you have to make them yourself, … it does take away some of the fun."

"For a lot of people it's more fun to do the cooking. It's up to you really, however you want to look at it." And he added in a hurried tone, "I have to go. See you later." And, with that, he was gone again.

She frowned at her phone because, of course, it was one of those life lessons on work versus hobby versus enjoying your time. And was it worth it trying to make brownies on her own again for that sense of accomplishment? She pondered that while taking her coffee outside, where she stood, throwing the stick a few more times, until she figured Mugs may have worn off the extra treats. And then she contemplated the same problem for herself. If she made brownies, then she would probably feel like she had to do extra physical work to wear off the brownies.

Then she thought about it. "Whoa, whoa. No, no, no. I am no longer under Mathew's thumb. I don't have to do an extra-heavy workout because I had potatoes for dinner," she muttered.

She laughed at that. She almost never had potatoes, and, the one time she had, Mathew had been quite perturbed that she would gain a lot of weight very quickly. She'd learned after that to not eat anything even like potatoes around him. Otherwise she would end up with the same comments.

There was a lot about Mathew to *not* like, yet she'd also learned a lot, and she was a very different person now. Still she wouldn't want to necessarily put it to the test. Her husband hadn't been the easiest person to get along with, and apparently neither was she.

Frowning at that, she walked over to her laptop to see how hard it would be to make brownies.

She'd managed to make a few simpler things to take to his place when Mack got hurt, and they'd had a lovely birthday coffee cake, but now she had a hankering for brownies. And Mack just told her they were a favorite of his too.

So she grabbed a recipe that looked promising. She quickly put everything together, mixed it all up, and put it into the oven. The best part of all this was, she would have one with her afternoon tea. She hovered every few minutes to check on it. She took out the pan very carefully and put it on the top of the stove. Then sent a picture to Mack. **I did it.**

He sent her a big happy face emoji and wrote **I'll be over in five.**

But the text that followed had an LOL laughter emoji, so she knew he wasn't coming. At least she didn't think so. She stared at the pan, wondering if she should hide some. And then decided, no, he really hadn't meant it. With a sense of satisfaction, she went outside to do some gardening. A couple hours later she came back in, looking for a cup of tea, hopefully a brownie too, when she heard a truck pull up in the driveway. She walked to the front, and, sure enough, there was Mack. But the look on his face wasn't happy. She frowned. "Here I thought you were coming for a treat."

He smiled. "I won't say no to a brownie, but it's not why I came, no."

"Why did you come then?"

He hesitated and then said, "We have another body."

Chapter 14

A T HIS WORDS, Doreen turned and walked into the kitchen, Mack hot on her heels.

"Any chance of coffee?" he asked, vexed and frustrated.

She sensed that urgency to get somewhere from his tone, yet with no place to go. She was all too familiar with that urge and that addiction. "Absolutely," she replied calmly.

He spied the pan of brownies. "Wow."

She smiled at him. "I know, right? I'm getting there."

"You're doing better than *getting there*," he clarified, turning to her. "Take it easy on yourself. All of this is a big change. No need to overwhelm yourself. And remember to celebrate the victories. Brownies are victories."

She smiled, as she put on the coffee. "Back to that cheer-leader part, *huh?*" she replied in a teasing voice.

He shrugged. "Sometimes I think we forget to remember the good things in life. We're just so busy trying to accomplish stuff that … it doesn't always work out."

She pondered that, as she filled the carafe with water and put on the pot. "Maybe that's part of it," she murmured. "A lot of it is just … so much of it's new for me that it's still an accomplishment, but I also know that it's not an accomplishment for anybody else. So it feels weird to make a big deal out of it."

He shook his head. "Make a big deal out of it," he argued, "make a really big deal. If there's nothing else beyond what all these cases are showing us, ... there is a need to spend more time making a big deal about the things that are important to you."

She laughed, picked up a knife and cut the brownies. "Since when are brownies important?"

He snagged one off the pan and replied, "Honestly? Since you started making them, they're very important," he noted. "They should be a food group."

"Pretty sure you mentioned something similar about pizza."

He looked at her. "Is pizza not a food group?" he asked in astonishment.

She rolled her eyes at his joking and realized just how much he was trying to lighten the air. "So who died?" she asked because, let's face it, even though rattled, she still wanted the truth.

He stared at her for a long moment. "We're not sure. We're waiting on an ID."

"But," she pointed out, "you came here for a reason."

He smiled at her. "Brownies and coffee?"

"No, you think this second death is connected to me in some way, to the cold case and even your current case."

He shook his head. "I'm not sure it's connected at all," he clarified. "I guess I'm wondering about the man we heard at the wisteria."

She frowned. "You think the dead guy is him?"

He frowned, as he stared at the brownie in his hand. "I think ..." He took a deep breath, before adding, "It's a possibility."

She let out her breath slowly. "Wow, that would suck, wouldn't it?"

"It would suck for anybody," he noted. "Nobody wants to be found dead, but people need to wait for a positive ID. It could be him. I don't have a good-enough description, and I didn't get a look at him when we were in the park."

She studied Mack, as she thought back. "He wore a hoodie. I just remember a big cowlick." When Mack frowned, she explained, "Above his right eye, a lock of hair, with a mind of its own, was going in the opposite direction of the rest of his hair."

He pondered that. "Have you met anybody else in this case?"

"Only over the phone, except Roscoe," she replied. "Why?" And then she knew it because that just clicked. "You're thinking it's the boyfriend, aren't you?"

Mack winced. "Thinking is one thing, but I'm waiting on an ID first, before we go there."

"Right, of course you are. If it is the boyfriend, ... if it is, indeed, Oscar, it shouldn't be all that hard to match up. I gave you his name already."

"I know, and we haven't been able to reach him."

"Did you call his girlfriend?"

"I did. I haven't been able to reach her either."

Doreen stared at Mack, pulled out her phone, and quickly dialed Gina's number.

The girlfriend answered, her voice harried, as she asked, "Who is this, and what's going on? I'm really busy at the moment."

"Sorry, this is Doreen. I talked to you about Edwin's death."

After a moment of shocked silence, Gina muttered, "Oh, I remember you. ... Can this wait until another time? I'm really in a rush."

"Possibly," Doreen replied. "What's going on?"

"I can't find Oscar," she wailed. "I don't want to call the cops because I know it'll really upset him, but I haven't been able to find him."

"When did you see him last?" she asked, putting her cell on Speakerphone.

"This morning. We had quite a row, and then he took off in the middle of that argument, just in a huff, and he drove off crazy. I am worried. He drives rash, and he was really upset."

"Was the row about Edwin?"

"Yes, of course it was," she snapped bitterly. "Every row we've ever had has been about him."

"I'm sorry," Doreen murmured. Then she hesitated and looked over at Mack. "Another reason I'm calling was to ask a couple questions. Did Oscar show up at work or do you have any idea where he might have gone? Where have you tried?"

"I've tried everywhere," she wailed. "He didn't show up at work, and I have no idea what happened to him. I've even called the hospitals, and there's nothing."

Doreen looked over at Mack and raised an eyebrow. He nodded, and, on his cue, Doreen added, "Look. One of my friends is a police officer, and he was trying to get a hold of Oscar earlier today."

"Why?" she asked in astonishment, and then she hesitated. "Has he done something wrong?"

"I'm not sure that he's done something wrong, but I'll let you speak to my friend." And, with that, she handed the phone over to Mack. Doreen listened while he identified himself to Gina and then told her what he'd found. Doreen heard Gina gasping on the other end. Mack added, "Now we don't know for sure that it's Oscar. We're looking to ID him."

"Oh my God, oh my God," Gina cried out into the phone.

"It doesn't mean it's him," Mack repeated cautiously.

"I need to see him," Gina stated. "I'll identify him. ... Is it terrible? To go down there?"

At that, he shrugged, then replied, "For some people, yeah. It can be bad, and they need somebody with them." He asked Gina, "Do you have somebody to come with you?"

"No," she wailed, tears in her voice. "I don't."

At that, Doreen snatched her phone from Mack's hand. "Do you want me to come? I can meet you down there."

Gina asked, "Would you? I just ... I don't ... If it's not him, it's, ... it's fine." She continued. "Outside of seeing a dead body, which I've never seen before," she muttered, grasping for coherence. "But if it is him ..."

"Why don't I meet you there? We both will." She turned and looked at Mack. "When can we arrange this?"

But he was already on his phone.

"My friend is calling to arrange a time right now," Doreen explained to Gina.

"It needs to be now," Gina demanded. "I've been beside myself all day. It's almost as if I knew," she murmured.

"Again," Doreen noted, "let's not jump the gun. It may not be him."

"No, it's probably him," Gina muttered. "He would do something like that."

"Like what?" Doreen asked, frowning.

"Go off half-cocked and get himself into trouble."

"And you don't know anyone he would have talked to today, nothing? Edwin's dead. Edwin's dead, he certainly couldn't have killed Oscar."

"I know. I know." And then Gina started to bawl.

At that, Doreen winced. "Look. Let me call you right back, as soon as I have a time and place."

And Gina ended the call, without even saying anything else.

Doreen waited for Mack to get off the phone.

He looked at her, holding her phone in her hand, and asked, "Is she gone?"

Doreen nodded. "She was heading into a deep crying jag, so I had to let her go. I was waiting for you to get back with a time frame."

He said, "We can go now."

She called Gina again. When the woman answered, her voice still teary, Doreen told her, "We can go now. Do you want me to come pick you up? I don't think you should be driving."

Gina gasped. "Why are you being so nice?"

Doreen shrugged. "It's who I am. Let me come pick you up, and I'll take you down there." Gina was grateful for the assistance, and Doreen confirmed the time she would pick up Gina—just enough time to get to her place. As Doreen disconnected, she looked at Mack. "So much for coffee."

He winced. "Do you have a travel mug?"

She nodded. "That's a good idea." She quickly packed up two travel mugs, one for him and one for her, and watched as he snagged another brownie.

He shrugged. "It could be a long day."

Realizing it could more than that—it could be a very

emotional day—she wondered if she should grab one too but decided against it.

As she headed out the door, Mack added, "I'll meet you there in a few minutes."

She nodded. "Hopefully I can get her in the vehicle and get her down there."

He shrugged. "It may not be Oscar. That's my only concern."

"We'll know soon enough," Doreen murmured. "If it isn't? Well, that's good. If it is? … Well, there's your next stage of this investigation."

He grimaced. "An investigation that's turning pretty ugly. We already had a dead body, topped off with two mysterious disappearances from twenty-five years ago, and now this."

And, with a wave, he hopped into his truck and drove out, and she followed.

She left the animals at home this time. Although she really wanted them with her, it could have been too overwhelming for her to have them for a morgue identification or to interact with the already stressed Gina. How did she react to animals? Although Mugs might have made a good therapy dog, Mugs also didn't know Gina.

Doreen quickly followed the directions to the address to find a woman standing outside, nervously jiggling her weight from foot to foot as she waited. When she saw Doreen pull up, Gina looked at her and frowned.

Doreen opened the window and greeted her. "Hi, I'm Doreen."

Gina raced around and jumped into the passenger side. "Thank you for picking me up. I don't think I could have driven."

"No, I'm sure you couldn't have, and, at this point, that's not an issue," Doreen stated, looking at her in understanding. "Let's get you down there and figure this out."

Gina hardly said two words the whole way down, and, when the two women arrived at the morgue, Mack stood outside, waiting for them.

"This is Mack. You spoke to him earlier," Doreen murmured.

Gina looked at her and nodded. "I guess the police really need to know, don't they?" She stood outside the car nervously, as Doreen locked up. Then, with Doreen at Gina's side, they headed toward the morgue.

Doreen nodded to Mack. "This is Gina."

He looked at her, smiled, introduced himself, and added, "I'm sorry to ask you to do this."

Gina shook her head. "It's okay. I've been beside myself all day, wondering what could possibly have happened. But, inside, … I knew."

"Let's not get ahead of ourselves, not until we see, not until we are sure," Mack stated, as he led the way.

When the process was to the point of seeing the dead man's face, Gina turned to Doreen. "What if it's not him?"

"Then we'll keep looking for Oscar," Doreen replied. "Let's hope it's not him."

The woman nodded and then turned to the body again. As the sheet was pulled back to reveal his face, Gina slapped a hand over her mouth and gasped.

"So does that mean yes or no?" Doreen asked.

Gina, tears welling in her eyes, nodded. "That's him." And she collapsed onto the floor, crying.

Doreen sat down beside her, wrapped her arms around Gina and just held her. Doreen looked up at Mack and nodded. "You're right. This was the guy I saw at the park."

He asked Doreen, "Are you two okay?"

She nodded and said, "We'll be here for a few minutes, and then I'll take her home."

Things were taking a turn, for all of them. Doreen was sure something else had been shaken loose again, and it would get uglier before it was sorted for good.

Chapter 15

DOREEN CALLED A couple of Gina's girlfriends to come keep Gina company for the afternoon. She was in bad shape, when Doreen dropped Gina off at her home. Doreen promised to call Gina later in the day to ensure she was doing okay. Gina had gotten out of the car and stiffly made her way up to her apartment. Doreen had wondered about staying, but Gina didn't want anybody here right now; she just wanted to be alone.

Doreen understood that. It was tough enough right now to deal with the confirmation of Oscar's death just moments ago.

When Doreen got home, she snatched a brownie, needing the sugar hit, and went outside with the animals. She went to the patio beyond the deck and just sat, realizing once again how absolutely lucky she was to have this peace and quiet to come home to. If that had been her down in the morgue, identifying somebody she knew and cared for, there would be very little solace to be found in that place. Even though the news was still so fresh, even being at your own home, with familiar surroundings, would make a difference too.

At least Doreen was willing to try and believe that. She sat here, pushing back the memory of the heartbroken woman's reaction to seeing her dead loved one. Goliath jumped up onto the table and whacked a piece of brownie off the table. Mugs jumped for it at the same time that Thaddeus did. And what had been a somber moment turned into absolute chaos, as everybody dove for the piece of brownie to try and get it first.

Thankfully Doreen snatched it up before either of them could eat it and could get sick. She was both shocked and laughing by the time she snagged Thaddeus and put him on the table. Thaddeus had beat Goliath to the brownie bit— just short of getting the piece of chocolate. Goliath lost to him by a narrow margin, and he was now lying in the grass, staring at Doreen with disdain.

"Did you do that on purpose?" she scolded him but still with a smile on her face. She almost wanted to reward him for easing up the heaviness of the day. He just flicked his tail at her. She walked into the kitchen, pulled out the animals' treats and walked back out and gave Goliath one.

Mugs gave her his woebegone expression once more, staring up at her, and she sighed and relented. "Fine, you can have one." And she headed back inside to where she'd hidden the treats and pulled out one for him. She didn't dare give him too many, and she had to keep the location still hidden. Now much happier and lighter at heart, she walked down to the river, picked up several sticks and played with Mugs for a good ten minutes. Feeling better, she turned and pondered what to do next.

The question rattling around in her brain really was how would they find out what happened to that family? Going for an hours-long drive wouldn't be a whole lot of help, not without a specific destination in mind, but then she thought about Google Maps. Pondering that, she walked back inside, wondering if any local groups dealt with some of this stuff. And who would know?

As she considered that, she thought about the search and rescue guys she'd connected with over the little boy who had drowned in the lake in a truck so many years ago. She went back through her contacts, trying to find a name and a number. *Nathan*, a former scuba diver, knew of more people in the search and rescue field, and she had a number for him.

When she called him, he recognized her immediately.

"Hey," he greeted her in a bright, cheerful voice. "How're you doing? Solved any more mysteries?"

She chuckled. "Oh, I don't know about solved, but I'm working on one right now."

"Oh good. What do you need?"

And thankfully he was the person who just flat-out asked what she needed. "I'm wondering, and it's probably not very likely, but can you find somebody who went missing on land many, many years ago?"

Nathan replied, "Maybe you need to explain that a little further."

"I am working on another cold case, where two people went missing twenty-five years ago in a vehicle, and they were driving up from the coast. Could we review any aerial map of the land involved in that road trip? Both from back then and also a current view?"

"I never heard about that couple," he noted thoughtful-ly. "Obviously there's money involved in trying to get the manpower to physically search, especially so late in the game."

"So many locals drove the highway over and over again

back in the day," she shared. "Some people dedicated every weekend for weeks, driving up and down, looking for a vehicle that could have gone off the road—or any signs of it."

"Hundreds of miles are between those two cities," Nathan pointed out, "and I mean *hundreds* of miles. The chances of somebody happening upon that specific car off the road are not great."

"I was thinking about that too. So, what would have changed in the last twenty-five years? Not only the landscape but the technology, if nothing else. Mack mentioned a lot of the geography would have changed because of the forest fires."

At that, Nathan agreed. "Now of course there could be twenty-five years' worth of additional growth. However, Mack's quite right. That's exactly what has happened. With the forest fires, an awful lot of now-open ground has been brought to life again. Not everyone knows that the forest fires can sometimes rebuild a forest, depending on the trees. If they have an extensive root system, any dormant buds underground are protected. Nutrients stored in the root system allow for quick sprouting after a fire. Or, if pine trees are involved, some pine cones only release their seeds in a fire, rejuvenating the forest."

"Oh, wow," Doreen murmured.

Nathan continued. "We do have some aerial tools, and I know a whole group of internet sleuths who enjoy searching online for this kind of a thing. We use their services every once in a while for search and rescue work, and a couple of our guys even belong to the group."

"Really? What a great idea."

"Sure, they can get very involved when somebody goes

missing. Granted, they prefer to search for the recently missing, as it improves the chances of finding someone. Regardless, it puts a lot of eyes on a problem."

"And in this case," Doreen said, "I don't know what vehicle they were driving. It may have been buried or stuck for twenty-five years and then potentially caught in a fire. ... So what would that even look like?"

Nathan stated succinctly, "*Brown*. My guess is, it would blend right in. But that doesn't mean that some of the metal didn't survive, so any reflection could be caught. I can put you in touch with these guys, if you want."

"Yeah, I would love that. Thank you."

"No guarantee that they'll help you," he noted cautiously.

"No, no, I know, but if people are bored ..."

"Exactly, which is why you do this too, isn't it?" he asked in a joking manner.

"Bored, and now I can't leave these people alone and lost forever," she murmured.

"Oh, I know," Nathan agreed. "Why do you think I do the work I do? Most of our team are volunteers, and we all have other jobs, and then we come home at night to find out that somebody has gone missing on an ATV or someone has fallen someplace, and we're all out there helping."

"And that's because you're very good people," she declared. "The world needs more like you."

He chuckled at that. "Just trying to get some good karma stored up."

"Hey, you never know," she shared. "I've gotten into trouble more than a few times. And you can bet some of my friends would like me to stop this *hobby*."

"Oh, I can imagine," Nathan replied. "I did hear a few

of the tales, but anytime you want to go for coffee and just visit and talk, I'm always up for it."

"Thanks," she said in pleased surprise.

"Hang on a sec, while I go grab some numbers for you," he muttered. "Most of them will be emails though."

"That's fine. As long as I have a way to contact people, I don't have a problem reaching out."

"I think it's because you *do* reach out," Nathan stated, "that makes you good at what you do. A lot of people struggle with that aspect."

"I never really understood that," she admitted. "If you need to know something, isn't it best to just ask?"

He burst out laughing. "Absolutely, and because you do reach out and ask, ... you often put people on the spot, I imagine, and they don't quite know what to say."

"Maybe, but sometimes they just blurt out the truth, and that makes it much easier for me."

"I agree," he murmured. "I definitely agree with that. Hang on." When he came back on the phone, he said, "I have three emails here. What's your email, and I'll send them to you."

She quickly gave him her email address, and, when she got off the phone, promising to meet him for a cup of coffee down the road, she opened up her email and waited for his to come in. When it did, she quickly drafted an email and then let it sit for a minute, while she pondered what she needed to say. She gave the details—as much as she had them—and really needed more details on the car. A quick phone call to Roscoe confirmed it was a light-blue Toyota Corolla.

"Almost silvery," he added. "It was a weird color. But it was secondhand when they bought it, and I don't imagine that time would have been very kind to it."

"I don't know," she said.

"Why's that?" he asked. "Are you getting somewhere?" He sounded positively thrilled.

"I don't know that I'm getting anywhere," she clarified, "It won't help to just go in blind to some of these details."

"No, no, you're right," Roscoe confirmed. "I should have given you that from the first."

When she hung up, she quickly finished off the draft email and gave the three online search guys the route that the earlier searchers had assumed had been taken and the last checkpoint of the vehicle. She sent it off with a personal reference added. *Hey, if you have any questions about who I am, feel free to contact Nathan, who I understand you already know.*

She got an email back almost immediately. This guy must have been sitting at his computer, reading his emails.

Hey, fun. I'll take a gander and contact some of my buddies. No promises.

And that's all there was. But still, *No promises* was all she could give to anybody too. And then she called Nathan back and asked, "Hey, if I wanted to waste some time searching online, where would I go?"

He quickly gave her instructions to get the best aerial view of the area and added, "Really it's just a matter of poring over slides and being on Google Earth."

"Right," she muttered. "That can take a lot of time."

"Which is also why you try to get as many people on this as you can. Those guys who do it, it is their hobby. They can spend hours, but they also know what they're looking for."

"I contacted them, all three of them, and one got back to me right away, saying that it looked like a fun search but no promises. Yet he would contact a few of his friends."

"That was probably Donnie, wasn't it?"

She checked her email. "Yeah, that's exactly who it was."

"Good. He's one of the better ones. He doesn't talk to people often, so that he even answered you meant something in your request appealed."

"I tried to give him all the information he would need to get started," she shared, "but what do I know."

Nathan laughed. "Don't knock yourself down. You're starting to be one of those local people who does know. None of us really know who and what you'll pop up with next."

"I appreciate the assistance, thank you."

"No problem." And they rang off.

At least with the idea that maybe, just maybe, something would come out of this, and, if nothing else, she had gotten a start on something, she made notes on everyone she had contacted, when and why. When the phone rang a bit later, she answered absentmindedly.

"I signed. There you go. You happy?" Mathew snapped into the phone.

She straightened. "Did you?" she asked. "Because it seemed obvious to me that you were not signing all of it on purpose." He just grumbled something that she didn't understand. "Did you say something?" she asked. "I can't really hear."

"If you would take all those dreams of riches out of your ears," he spat, "you would hear just fine." And, with that, growled loud and clear then smack, the phone went dead.

She stared at hers in consternation. It was odd to hear him be that angry and yet not be within striking distance. It was great. It was absolutely lovely; at the same time, it was odd. It seemed to be a lifetime ago for her, a lifetime that she had no idea could even have been possible. Yet here she was, so far away from that whole scenario that it was almost something that brought tears of joy to her eyes. She quickly phoned Nick, but, when she couldn't get through, she left him a message about Mathew's phone call.

When he called her back about twenty minutes later, he asked, "Did you answer another call from him?"

She winced. "Of course you would pick up on that," she cried out. "How about, *Hi, Doreen? How are you, Doreen? How's my brother, Doreen?*"

He burst out laughing. "Yes, of course I picked up on that. I thought we decided you wouldn't take his calls, wouldn't talk to him anymore."

"I know, and I was really caught up in what I was doing," she explained, "so I forgot to check the number."

"At least he gave you a message that's helpful. I still haven't got the paperwork though."

"Of course. Just because he *said* that he followed through doesn't mean he did it, I suppose."

"Let's hope he did," Nick stated calmly. "We're getting down to the wire now. That hearing is still set to be heard."

"He didn't sound very good, and for him to hang up on me is very out of character," she noted. "I hope we haven't completely destroyed his life."

Nick paused on the other end, as if contemplating her words. "You're way too nice, you know that?"

She stared down at the phone. "I don't know about that," she replied cautiously. "But, as you are well aware, all kinds of problems are in other people's lives. ... So, do they really have to go out of their way to ruin someone else's life?"

"You tell me, given what you've been learning about

humanity for these past several months," Nick replied. "I deal with people like this all the time, and it's not very nice sometimes."

"No, you're right," she agreed. "I'll be a nice person as it sounds like the world needs more nice people. I'm happy to be one of them."

He chuckled. "You sure you don't have a sister around?"

"Nope, no sisters at all. Why?" At that, he really burst out laughing. She sighed. "Another one of those jokes, *huh?*"

"Nope, not a joke at all," Nick corrected, "but my brother is very lucky to have found you."

"You can always come out to Kelowna and find somebody yourself."

"Or I could find somebody down here," he noted, with a chuckle. "Up there isn't any guarantee of finding anybody, especially since I certainly didn't find anybody all those years ago."

"*Aah.*" Doreen sensed something in his tone. "And maybe whoever you walked away from back then is free now."

Silence came on the other end. "Did I say I walked away from anybody?"

"Didn't have to," she said. "I got it in your tone."

"Wow," Nick said, "you're dangerous."

"No, I'm not dangerous to anybody," she stated. "However, life only gives you so many options and so many chances and choices. So, maybe you should try picking up one of those."

"Yeah, maybe," he conceded, yet with no intent on doing that, as if it would be the last thing he ever did.

"Or not," she added, "as apparently that's bad news there."

"When somebody walks away from you, it's pretty hard

to walk back from that."

"It depends whether you want to walk back or not," she declared cheerfully. "Depends on the value of what you lost and what it is worth to you."

"What do you do when the trust is gone?" Nick asked.

"Ah, trust is a big one," she agreed. "I should know."

"You lost trust early on?"

"Yep, and then I was just in a holding pattern, for a very long time. I'm really grateful I'm not back in that anymore. I was thinking about that this morning and how many things have changed in my life and how grateful I am that they have."

"Good," Nick replied. "Keep up the cheerfulness. It'll get you through the rest of this lovely divorce."

She winced at that, but he was already gone. How much more could there be? When it came to Robin's estate, Doreen had thought there had been almost nothing left to do but sell her assets, yet Nick made it sound like they still had a process.

Maybe that's because he still hadn't gotten the paperwork on Robin or from Mathew. Doreen didn't know but was hoping, hoping, and hoping that maybe, just maybe, her divorce would be over soon.

When she was sitting outside later that afternoon, staring at her laptop, fighting with the sunlight, trying to tilt the angle so that she could see some of the ground photos that she was looking at, Mack arrived. She looked up. "Hey. What's this? Back for more brownies?"

He smiled. "Wouldn't be so bad to have brownies either, but I did pick up burritos."

She looked at the bag and frowned. "What's a burrito?" He slowly lowered the bag and stared at her. She shrugged.

"Sounds Mexican."

"It is Mexican. Please tell me that you've had burritos."

She wrinkled up her nose. "See now? You're heading into that territory that makes me feel like I should know something, but I really don't." And she wagged her finger at him. "You shouldn't do that."

He sighed. "Who knew you wouldn't know what a burrito is."

"Maybe, when I see it, I'll recognize it," she offered.

He nodded. "*Maybe.*"

But he sounded so doubtful that she burst out laughing. "Okay, okay," she said dismissively. "I hope you're happy because I've been sitting at home, doing nothing."

"That really surprises me," he said.

"You won't let me in on your case—although you're certainly happy to come here and get my help when needed," she muttered. "You could let me do more than that."

"What would you like to do?" he asked, with a note of amusement. "We've got cops all over this. Now that we have two bodies, you can bet we have things that need to be done. *Cop* things."

"I'm sure you've traced the boyfriend's path and all that good stuff," she replied.

"We have." But his tone was quiet, almost pensive.

"And?"

He looked over at her and smiled. "And what?"

She sighed. "Fine, you don't want to tell me. That's okay."

"Good," he said. "I *do* want to tell you, but I can't tell you."

She nodded. "Yeah, I get that. I don't like it, but okay." He looked at her. She shrugged. "It is what it is. Besides, I just want to make sure the girlfriend didn't do it."

"What?"

She looked at him. "What's the surprise for? If you think about it, Gina had the most motive."

"What motive did she have?" he asked, staring at her.

"Gina and Oscar had a big fight over Edwin, among other big fights over Edwin, and now both guys are dead. So maybe Gina's fight got a little bit out of control."

"She did fight with him. Maybe something is there, but what about Oscar's body?"

"You didn't tell me where they found the body, how he died, so I can't answer that."

"Right." Mack stared off into space. "I don't think she killed him."

"Good," Doreen noted, "because I would really hate to think that I went down to the morgue to help her put on a display."

"Unless ..." He pondered that.

"Yeah, I know," Doreen agreed, "*unless.*"

"No, no, we're not going there," Mack muttered. "Besides I'm taking the evening off, and the rest of the team had time off yesterday, so now they're back on it."

"Good. I gather that means burritos are next." She eyed the bag in his hand. "Are they meant to be eaten hot?"

He gave a headshake and focused on her. "Wow, yes, they are meant to be eaten hot. Come on. Let's grab plates. I'll show you what to do with these."

Eating them was a no-brainer, except, when holding them in your hand, trying not to get both hands completely covered with the contents in the wrap. Doreen found she certainly couldn't stop once she started because otherwise everything went everywhere. By the time she had eaten half of hers, Mack had already scarfed his down.

He sat, staring at her. "Even that you eat very elegantly."

Her eyebrows shot up. "How is *this* being elegant?" she muttered. "I feel like I'm losing three-quarters of it."

"That's because you are," he said cheerfully. And he reached over and tweaked the tin foil that wrapped the bottom of it. "That might help."

She sighed but kept on plowing through it.

"What do you think of it?" he asked curiously.

She nodded. "It's good, and, no, I've never had one before."

He shook his head. "Wow, your education is so basic in food." She glared at him. He grinned and added, "That's okay."

"But you still didn't tell me where you found the body."

"The first one we found in the City Park area, which was Edwin," Mack stated, "and the other one, Oscar, we just found in Mission Creek Park."

She straightened up and stared down at her little creek. "What?"

"Up at the Eco Center," Mack clarified. "It's closed right now for forensics to work on."

"Of course," she muttered. "Why didn't I ask that earlier?"

"Because, once you locked on to who it was, you were more concerned about getting Gina's information."

"Right." Doreen stared at Mack. "Mission Creek though, *huh?*" And again she turned to look at her little creek.

"Don't tell me," Mack began. "You want to go for a walk up there later," he guessed, with a sigh.

"Absolutely," she declared. "It does help to get the location fixed in my head."

"But this isn't for you to sort out," Mack reminded her.

"No, it isn't. … However, when I picked her up and took her to the morgue, Gina doesn't live very far from where Oscar was found. Of course they lived together in that apartment, not far from where that new center is going up."

"Which is right across from where the body was found," Mack confirmed. "And I'm sure you noticed, when we were all in the morgue to ID the body, that Gina never asked where Oscar's body was found."

Doreen stared at Mack, her mouth slowly opening. "Neither did Gina ask anything about what happened, how Oscar died, what time, nothing. Now we could just go out on a limb and assume she was so shocked that it didn't make any difference at the time," Doreen suggested.

"We could," Mack noted cheerfully. "And, of course, we still have some questions to sort out."

She nodded passively, not really liking anything about this. "And yet you were just saying that you don't think she killed him."

"I don't," he agreed, "but that doesn't mean she didn't have something to do with it."

"I really don't like hearing that."

"I know," he said. "I shouldn't tell you about it, but, dang, you're a little too easy to talk to." He glared at her.

She beamed. "I also got a phone call from Mathew today."

He stopped and stared. "When is that ever a good line to open with?"

She burst out laughing. "When he hangs up on me."

"So you answered it?" He stared at her, dumbfounded.

She glared at him. "Great, that's the one thing your

brother glommed onto as well."

"Yeah, because we can't understand why this intelligent woman in front of us keeps doing things like that."

She smiled. "I forgot."

"Right. How is that even possible?" he asked, staring at her in disbelief.

She sighed. "I was really hooked on what I was doing. So, when the phone rang, I just automatically answered it. I didn't even pick it up. I just hit Talk."

"Right, and what did he want?" Mack asked.

"He told me that he signed the paperwork and that I should be happy."

And she had said it so cheerfully that he looked at her, her happiness reflecting off him, and asked, "And are you happy?"

"Sure I am, if it's over," she declared. "I would love for this to be over."

He nodded. "And does my brother have the paperwork?"

"Nope, not yet." She frowned. "Not at the time that I contacted him. But then I don't know if Mathew's lawyer had to do something with it first." Mack didn't say anything, just stared at her. She smiled at him and asked, "Now that we've eaten, you want to go for a walk?"

"You want to walk to the Eco Center?" he asked in a dry tone.

She winced. "Surely it can't hurt. Besides, I've been a help so far."

He nodded grimly at that. "Fine, but we're not going into the crime scene area."

"No, of course not," she agreed.

He stared at her. "How is it you can make something so simple so complex?"

"It's a gift," she declared, and then she burst out laughing. When she came back from the washroom, picking up the leashes, Mugs was half on Mack's lap and half off. "He's become such a suck-up," she said.

"He's a good boy."

She smiled. "That he is. And I told you about Thaddeus feeding treats to everyone, so I had to hide the treats." As it was funny enough, she retold him the story, adding in the details she'd missed the first time.

He burst out laughing to the point that he was almost rolling off the chair, with Mugs falling off his lap and giving Mack a disgruntled look.

"Oh my," Mack said, wiping tears from his eyes a few minutes later. "I really needed that. I couldn't have imagined."

"Yeah, well, they had quite the team thing going between them," she muttered. "Now I have safely moved the treats to another cupboard."

"Yeah, and how safe is that, once Thaddeus knows where they are? Can he open cupboards yet?"

She pondered that and then shook her head. "I don't think so. I'd gotten in the habit of leaving the pantry door wide open, so opening a door wasn't really an issue there, but now it's above the fridge."

And then she stopped and turned toward Thaddeus, glaring at him.

He tilted his head. "Above the fridge. Above the fridge."

She sighed. "The good thing is, he might mimic, but he doesn't know how to open cupboards yet."

At that, Mack chuckled. "I wouldn't count on it. He's pretty smart."

"He's *too* smart," she muttered. "Besides, Mugs was just

getting a little too complacent about treats."

"It's all good," Mack stated. "Animals will be animals."

"And people will be people," she added in a firm voice, "as we keep finding out."

He nodded and smiled. "And you keep growing and changing in ways that surprise me."

"I don't know about that," she said. "I don't think there should be any surprise—except that, well, I guess I'm constantly surprised too."

He laughed. "And sometimes you say the darndest things, as if you don't even know what's going on in your own head."

"And lots of times I don't," she admitted.

"So what was keeping you so busy?" he asked, as they walked down to the river, "that you didn't realize you needed to check who was phoning you?" he asked, glancing over at her.

She smiled. "Remember Nathan, the scuba diver with ties to local search and rescue?"

He nodded. "I know Nathan pretty well. Why?"

"I contacted him and asked him about trying to find a vehicle that may have gone missing twenty-five years ago in the area."

He stared at her in astonishment. "Search and rescue really doesn't have the time or the budget money for something like that," he replied slowly.

"I know. I know, and I wasn't asking him to physically go out and do something like that," she explained. "I was wondering if there was another way. Did you know that there is a group of internet sleuths, people Nathan knew that I could get in touch with?"

At that, Mack stopped and turned and looked at her.

She shrugged. "It was just an idea."

"It's a really good idea," he confirmed, still staring at her.

"Knew you would get there soon." She shrugged, pleased with herself. "Anyway, I contacted all three of the names Nathan gave me, and I did hear back from one, and he told me that it looked like an interesting project and that he might get a few people on it."

"That would be huge," Mack replied. "I never even considered something like that."

"Why not?" she asked, looking at him. "Or is it a foolish idea?"

"No, not at all," he said, "but you do need people who have time, no axe to grind, and the ability to sit there and hunt that down. It is quite a skill."

"I'm sure it is," she agreed. "I don't have that same skill myself, but I just thought maybe, if some people out there were bored …"

"And there's always people out there who are bored," Mack said, with a smile. "So, if you found somebody who was part of one of those big groups, you never know what might come up." He wrapped an arm around her shoulders, tucked her up close, and muttered, "Wow, I didn't realize just how brilliant you are."

She looked up at him and smirked. "How could you *not* realize?" she cried out in mock horror.

He chuckled. "Hey, you know, when you got this much figured out, you're doing really well."

"That doesn't mean we'll get any answers, though."

"No, sure doesn't," he noted, "but you're doing what you can do, and you've contacted people who are doing what they can do. That's all any of us can do in this life." He shrugged. "And we hope that it's enough, and sometimes it is, and sometimes it isn't. ... Coming to peace with that? That's huge."

She smiled. "We'll see. I don't know whether I can contact them down the road or they just contact me," she noted, "but the bottom line is, I, at least, got something started."

Chapter 16

A T THE ECO Center, Doreen and Mack and the animals stopped to enjoy a brief rest. It had been a beautiful walk up here, a bit long, but a nice day and surely was good for Mugs too. At least she thought so, as she looked down at him. He was still full of energy and raring to go. "What do you expect to see here?" she murmured.

"I'm not expecting to see anything," Mack replied, looking at her. "What are *you* expecting to see?"

She frowned. "You won't like it."

"No, I probably won't," he muttered, with a pained smile. "Doesn't mean I won't listen though."

She sighed. "I just want to make sure that the people who are here aren't any of the people who had anything to do with that murder."

"I do have police officers keeping an eye on the crowd," Mack noted. "However, most of them have gone by now. This was all happening earlier today."

She nodded. "We do know that crowds like to come back and forth."

"And even people connected to the crime. Don't forget. Oscar had a mother and sisters."

"Ouch," Doreen whispered. "That's sad, isn't it?"

"It is. It's also life."

They walked up and around to the crime scene tape. One of the cops lifted a hand in acknowledgment to Mack.

He raised a hand back and then told Doreen, "Stay here." And Mack walked over and spoke with the officer for a few minutes. When Mack returned to stand beside Doreen, he didn't appear to be concerned.

"So no problems?" Doreen asked Mack.

He shook his head. "No, no problems."

"Good," she muttered.

She wandered around the crime scene tape, looking at the space and surrounding park. Yet it was just a park. It was just the same park that she had walked many times before. Nothing stood out. "I wonder why you would choose a public place like this?" she asked.

"Usually because you want the body found fast," Mack shared. "If you didn't want it discovered soon, you would take it out anywhere up and down on the highway, wouldn't you?"

"Wouldn't that be a thing, someone disappearing down the highway?" She gave Mack a knowing look. As she wandered around, she studied the area the crime tape had cordoned off. "When do you let the public in?" Doreen asked Mack.

"Not until everything's processed. As much as I want answers fast, it is up to the forensic team, and we follow their lead."

"I would have thought it would have been completed already."

"Yeah, so did I." Mack frowned. "Stay here again." And he walked over and spoke to two men, wearing full protective suits, covered from head to toe. When he rejoined Doreen, he nodded. "They're done now. They were called off to another space as well."

"Another space?"

"Yes," Mack confirmed. "No, not another crime scene just another space in this park that they also considered to be ... interesting."

At that, she turned and stared at him, as if considering the new information. "You mean, a place where they may have entered and left by?"

He looked at her and then shrugged. "Can't say yet. We're waiting on forensics."

"Right," she muttered. "You guys wait a lot, don't you?"

"Yep," Mack agreed, "we're at the *collection of evidence* stage. We need to know how Oscar was killed."

"And whether his death was connected to Edwin's death," she added, with a nod.

He looked at her and smiled. "Exactly. So no speculation until we know."

"Too late," she argued cheerfully. She called Mugs toward her, but he suddenly veered off and went under the crime scene tape.

The leash snapped from her hand, and she called out, "Mugs, come back here. Mugs."

Mack looked at her and asked, "Did you do that on purpose?"

She glared at him and snapped, "No."

Mack was already heading under the crime scene tape and over to a spot in the ground where Mugs sniffed all the way around. She wondered just what scent Mugs was catching. If that's where the body had lain, that would explain it. By the time Mack caught up to Mugs, the dog had picked something up off the grass and brought it to her. With relief, she saw it was a stick.

"Really, you had to have *that* stick?" she cried out. Then looked over at Mack. "I really didn't do it on purpose."

"I know."

"Can he have the stick?"

He looked at it and said, "They're done here anyway, so yes."

"Okay, good." With that, she petted Mugs and noted, "Maybe we should walk back home." When Mack hesitated, she asked him, "Do you need to stay?"

He pondered that for just a quick minute, then one of the other men called him.

She added, "You do need to stay. Go on. I'll walk home." He glared at her, but she smiled at him. "It's fine. You go do you. This is just part of the job."

"It is part of the job, but I don't want to leave you alone."

"Nothing to worry about," she said, with a shrug. "The animals are with me. It's all good. We'll just walk back the same way we came."

He nodded. "Are you sure you're okay?"

"I am, not a problem," she replied. "*Go.*"

And she watched as he hesitantly took off in the direction where he needed to go. She called Mugs and Goliath to head down the opposite direction because Mugs was still very much interested in following Mack, but that wasn't to be

Finally, with the animals corralled, she walked toward home, with Mugs dragging his stick along. When he dropped it, he barked at her. She stopped to pick it up and went to throw it, when she looked at it carefully. "*Uh-oh,*" she muttered, staring at it. She fished her phone from her pocket and called Mack.

"Wow, you got far, didn't you?" he remarked, with a humorous note.

"The stick," she began, "the one that Mugs got? Dried wisteria blossoms are jammed into the bark." There was a moment of silence, and then Mack swore into the phone. She smirked. "Yeah, so I gather you want me to walk back with it."

"I'll meet you halfway," he offered. "I'm coming with an evidence bag."

"Good luck with that," she said. "You'll need something bigger and better than that to get the stick away from Mugs."

"Maybe you should just grab it and don't let him have it any longer," Mack noted in alarm. "Valuable evidence is on it."

She laughed. "I have it in my hand. We're on our way back toward you."

"Okay, I'll see you in a few minutes."

With the animals in tow, she quickly fast-walked back to Mack. Mugs was quite excited and not too sure just what was going on, but he didn't seem to mind. Goliath, on the other hand, was not impressed; he wanted to go home and was letting her know it by plopping on the ground, now being dragged by his leash.

Doreen groaned. "Come on, Goliath. I need to give this to Mack. Then we can go home." But Goliath just glared at her.

Finally she looked up to see Mack racing toward them. She raised her hands when she saw him. "Mugs is quite excited to see you as always," she said, "but Goliath here did not want to come back."

"Hey, I understand," Mack replied.

She held out the stick that she hadn't let go of. "I've only gripped it here, but I'm sure you guys can take my finger-prints off any other number of samples I've given you to let them know that it was mine and not somebody else's."

And with her other hand holding Mugs's leash, she pointed out the dried purple wisteria flowers tucked into the bark. "Did you know that a late-blooming special variety of wisteria was trialed a few years back, right here in Kelowna?"

Mack frowned. "Can't say that I did. Wow, you do keep in the know about your gardening, don't you?"

"Just look at this. That special variety has thrived."

Mack nodded, then his face turned grim. "It's hard to see, evidence-wise. I think when Mugs was dragging it around, the bark came a little bit loose here."

"Unfortunately there's also a lot of Mugs's slobber and bite marks."

"That's all right," Mack said. "I'll take this. If forensics confirms these are your special wisteria blossoms, well, you know what that means."

"Yeah, sure do," she claimed. "It means it's connected to the other death, which we already knew."

He nodded. "But now we have forensic evidence that connects the two dead bodies, and that makes all the difference in the world." And, with that, he looked at her, down at the animals, and frowned. "Why don't I get somebody to drive you home."

She chuckled. "No, we're good. I can't let Goliath get away with this either."

He pointed out, "But it's darker now."

She smiled. "And we've done this trip many, many times."

He hesitated, clearly not impressed with the idea of her leaving once again on her own.

She smiled and gave him a wave. "Go. You still have to come back to my house and get your truck."

He shook his head, cursing under his breath again.

She laughed. "That's all right. Go. I'll talk to you when you get there."

And, with that, she turned and resolutely headed back again toward home, and this time the animals were more than willing to pick up the pace and to race beside her, especially Goliath.

She asked him as they walked, "Why are you so anxious to get home?"

Goliath kept up a lope the whole time, pulling on the leash, then running faster to the point that she realized maybe something was wrong. On the other hand, it was Goliath. Could it be just that it was naptime, and he was racing toward his bed?

As soon as she made it home, Goliath raced up the backyard and, instead of going to the kitchen door, he raced around to the front of the house. Mugs, by now, was on the same path of whatever was bothering Goliath. Following their instincts, Doreen headed around to the front and stopped.

"Look. Nothing is here, guys, but Mack's truck," she muttered. And she looked over to see a vehicle parked in front of Richard's house. Shaking her head, she addressed her animals again. "Nobody is here. Nothing is wrong," she cried out.

Mugs barked at her ferociously, and then, all of a sudden, he dropped down. She frowned at him and then turned to Goliath, who was sitting on the front steps, staring over at

Richard's.

"Okay, so was that just a false alarm?" she asked in an exasperated voice, still huffing from the race home.

She texted Mack to say that they were back home already.

He replied, **That was fast.**

She responded, **Blame Goliath. He wouldn't slow down.**

He phoned her immediately. "Is anything wrong at the house?"

"Instead of going to the back door at the kitchen, they insisted on coming straight through to the front yard, yet nothing suspicious is here."

"Have you been inside yet?"

"No, not yet. I'm just unlocking right now."

She unlocked, opened the door, disarmed the alarm, and called the animals inside. "They don't seem to care."

"And you're comfortable in the house?"

"Yes," she replied, as she wandered through. "They're completely relaxed too."

"Nobody's outside?"

"It looks like Richard's brother, Roscoe, is visiting," she added, "but I've got no reason to be suspicious of him."

"No, of course not," Mack noted. "Besides, he has a perfectly legitimate reason for being there. They are brothers."

"Right." She sighed. "Still, I don't know why the animals are acting like something's wrong. It's worrisome."

"We have to respect their actions because they've held you in good stead all this time," Mack stated. "So just stay safe, will you? I'll be there as soon as I can." And, with that, he hung up.

Doreen walked into the kitchen and muttered, "Now,

it's time for a cup of tea, unless you guys object to that too."

She put on the kettle. While the water boiled, she fed the animals their dinner. Now waiting for Mack, she sipped her tea and returned to her online searching through the canyons between here and Vancouver. Some 242 miles. It was a daunting task. She could probably spend the next twenty years doing this and still not get anywhere. The thought of losing somebody in that vast space was also pretty shocking.

It must be so hard for all those people who spent years, decades, waiting for answers. Of course she'd seen it more than a few times in other cold cases, particularly in the little boy's case, where he was eventually found in the lake. That was the case where she'd first met Nathan. He lived along the lake and was a scuba diver and was instrumental in locating that long-lost little boy.

Regardless, when there were no answers, everybody did the best they could, and then the search for these missing folks had to stop—but, of course, it never really stopped. Everybody remained on the lookout.

She wasn't even sure where the internet hunters would end up looking, and she had no way to know if the missing couple had made it almost to Kelowna or driven off the road during a fight just before reaching here. or disappeared somewhere else entirely. Still, she dug into Google Earth, easily spending hours trying to locate geographical landmarks and any steep drop-offs near the main highway from here all the way to Vancouver. She actually enjoyed this. She could see how people could get hooked on searching Google Earth for whatever they needed.

With her next break, and a second cup of tea, she sat outside on the deck, enjoying the peace and quiet and just the calmness of the moment. When she heard a vehicle out front, Mugs started barking like crazy. "Is that Mack?" she asked. "One of the cops just dropped him off?"

From across the fence Richard snarled, "Can you shut that dog up?"

"Not easily," she replied in a cheerful voice. With that, she went inside, and, sure enough, Mack had arrived. She smiled when he got out of the vehicle. He turned toward her, and she watched the expression of relief revealed on his face. "See? I told you that I was safe." She looked over at her neighbor's house, and Roscoe's truck was gone. "Richard, of course, is in a fine stew though."

"Why is that?" Mack asked.

"Mugs was barking like crazy. It was disturbing him."

Mack's eyebrows shot up, as he crouched in front of Mugs and gave him a good cuddle. "It doesn't matter if he was or not. I would hope Mugs barks when there's a reason to bark, instead of being silent when there was a need."

She understood because Mugs had saved her bacon plenty of times.

"And nothing else from the ex?" he asked, without looking up from Mugs.

"Nope, I haven't asked Nick though if he got the paperwork."

"I'm sure he'll let you know when he does."

"Right. Seems foolish that Mathew would take all this time and effort to get out of it though."

"Maybe, maybe not," Mack muttered.

She walked back into the kitchen. "I'm just having tea. Did you want a cup?" He hesitated. "Or you have to run?"

"I need to run," he confirmed. "It is ten o'clock, and I haven't slept very much in the last few nights. I just wanted to make sure that everything here was okay."

She smiled. "Not to mention you got dropped off because your truck was here."

He laughed. "There is that too."

She smiled. "Go get some sleep. I'll see you tomorrow or the next day." He nodded, then hesitated. She laughed, "What? Do you want some brownies to go?"

"I would like something sweet to go," he muttered, with a teasing look, "but it might make it harder to sleep tonight."

She immediately flushed. "Definitely a hug would be nice," she ventured.

He gave her a wry look. "The hugs are very nice, especially if they go along with something else."

She sighed. "You're getting difficult, aren't you?"

He burst out laughing. "I hope not. I've had a lot of patience, up until now."

"Yep, you sure have." She walked to him, gave him a hug, and said, "So that's what you get. A hug for your patience."

He chuckled. "I'll take it." He wrapped her up in a big hug and just held her.

She snuggled in close, wrapping her arms around his large frame. "It does feel nice to be held."

"Exactly," he agreed, "and sometimes that's all we need. To know that we're not alone."

She thought of all the times in the last year when she'd felt very much alone and realized just how absolutely correct he was. "I don't even think we necessarily understand when we're alone that that's what we need," she murmured. "Sometimes the loneliness just creeps up, and it hits you like a two-by-four."

He smiled, tilted up her chin, gave her a hard kiss, and

muttered, "Now go to sleep."

"I'll sleep," she replied, batting her eyes at him. "Hopefully you will too."

"I will. Happy thoughts. Let's get that stupid paperwork from your ex signed, so we can move on." And, with that, he was gone.

Doreen realized that she and Mack were heading toward a juncture in her life where she had to make a decision. The trouble was, she already felt like the decision had been made. She was just waiting for the details to get ironed out. Smiling, she headed to bed and a good night's sleep.

Chapter 17

Thursday Morning ...

DOREEN WOKE UP the next morning, yawning and stretching. Mugs was flat on his back beside her, looking all for the world as if he'd died during the night. Yet his chest systematically rising and falling reassured her.

She smiled, reached over, gave him a big hug, and whispered, "You big galoot, I don't want anything to happen to you."

He gave a snuffle and yawned and went back to sleep. She got up and Thaddeus looked at her and went, "*He-he-he-he.*"

She glared at him. "You don't have to laugh at me as soon as I get up in the morning."

"*He-he-he-he-he.*"

"Fine, okay. Do you want to come have a shower with me?"

He tilted his head to the side.

She asked him, "You want a bath?"

He flapped his wings. "Bath. Bath."

She wondered if he knew what she was talking about. Still, she headed in and turned on the shower. As she turned to take off her pajamas, she realized he'd booked it. "So much for that idea," she noted, laughing.

She'd read somewhere that birds liked to have baths, so she wasn't sure whether she should give him a bowl of tap water to flounce around in and if she should let the shower run, just to see how he reacted to that. Something else she would have to look into. As she pulled back the curtain and stepped inside, she froze because, strutting back and forth under the shower, was Thaddeus, preening, ruffling his feathers, and generally having a gay old time.

She laughed. "Well, you did understand what I meant."

He continuously surprised her with his intelligence and his easy comprehension. As she watched, he looked to be having an absolute ball.

"So is there room in there for me too, buddy?"

He looked up at her and cawed several times, then replied, "Thaddeus is here. Thaddeus is here."

"I get it," she said. "The question is whether you share or not." Deciding it was worth taking a chance, she stepped into the shower and stood under the water too. He didn't appear to be bothered at the disrupted flow, instead walking back and forth as if thoroughly enjoying himself.

She smiled and proceeded to have her shower too, hoping that it wouldn't bother him, careful to keep any soap from getting in his face. Then, when she was ready to step out, she said, "Okay, shower's over. I'm turning off the water."

He stared at her as she shut off the water. Immediately he made a weird cawing sound.

"No, that's it for now," she repeated. She reached down, picked him up, and muttered, "Now let's dry you off."

And she flapped him up and down a little bit, so he

opened his wings. Catching on, he fluttered his wings several times, trying to shake off as much of the water as he could. She put him on the counter, as she grabbed a towel and dried off herself. Then leaving him where he was, she went into the bedroom and got dressed. When he hadn't come out yet, she headed back into the bathroom to check on him. Silly bird was giving the stink eye to his buddy in the mirror.

Chuckling, she headed downstairs with a still damp Thaddeus on her shoulder. When he made a sad-sounding caw, she put him up on the living room roost and moved it so it was in the morning sun. Then she took a paper towel and gently blotted him off.

He snuggled into her hand and whispered, "Thaddeus loves Doreen."

This bird could break her heart without even trying. She knew he didn't really understand, yet she wanted to believe that he understood. And she whispered right back, "Doreen loves Thaddeus."

A weird sound came from his throat; she wasn't sure what it was, but it was almost … She looked down to see Goliath at her heels, his engine loud and strong, and then Doreen looked back at Thaddeus. "Are you purring?" she asked.

That wasn't a thing for birds, was it? But it sure sounded like it. He *was* imitating the cat, who was obviously very happy to see her. Yet, at the same time, it was the most bizarre and yet lovely sound to hear. She cuddled Thaddeus close for a moment and then stepped back, gave Goliath several good scrubs and hugs, picked him up, swung him around, and cuddled him for a little bit.

"Everybody's quite needy today," she murmured. "What's going on?"

But, of course, she got no answer out of any of them. Then she realized Goliath's food bowl was empty. She snorted. "Really? It's all about food, isn't it? You're waiting for me to feed you."

And, with that, she put him down in front of his bowl, picked up the bowl, and opened up a can of wet food for him. When she dished it out and placed it in front of him, his engine kicked into even higher gear, and he sat down and ate. She smiled at that. And then she proceeded to give Thaddeus his food, and finally Mugs got his.

And, with that, she asked, "Okay, you guys, now how about me? I could use something too."

She put on the coffee, rousted up her normal toast, put on several pieces, grabbed her trusty peanut butter and her quince jelly—reminding her that she still wanted to visit with Esther to confirm she was doing okay. Maybe they would do that after breakfast.

As she walked out to the backyard with her coffee and toast, she sat down at the patio table. Her animals now milling all around her, she muttered, "It's a beautiful day, you know."

Then came a weird echo, like when you put a phone too close to a radio, that grating feedback, which surprised her. She stared over at Richard's place. When she heard that same noise a second time, she called out, "Hey, have you got a radio on?" But she got no answer.

Struggling, she grabbed one of her deck chairs, headed over to the fence, hopped up, and took a look into Richard's backyard. She couldn't see much of note back there. As she hopped back down again, Mugs was now barking.

"It's okay, Mugs. It's okay, buddy." But again came that weird electronic sound. Frowning, she called over once more,

"Richard, you in there?" Still no answer.

He may have gone out, or he could be just ignoring her, seeing as how he always seemed to think that she was a pain. Maybe she was, and she would give him credit for that. It's not like he'd seen her at her most stay-out-of-everybody's-way mode.

But then, what the heck? Life was crazy enough these days that she didn't need to be bothered about worrying what the neighbors thought either. As she headed back to her patio table, that squeal repeated. She cried out, covering her ears, with even Mugs snapping and barking. Finally, when it stopped, she pounded on the fence.

Richard came out, roaring at her, "What's the matter?"

She yelled back, "I don't know what you got going on over there, but it's killing my ears."

She heard Richard slam a chair against the fence, and he popped his head over. "What are you talking about? I haven't got anything going on."

Just then came that same weird electronic sound. He looked at her in shock and disappeared over the fence.

"Maybe you didn't set that up," she called back, "but somebody sure did."

He soon appeared over the fence again and held up a small device. "I don't know what this is," he admitted, "or where it came from."

She stared at it. "Isn't that a listening device or something?"

He shrugged. "I have no idea. It's not my thing."

She groaned. "Hopefully, now that you unplugged it, maybe it won't work because that was killing my ears."

"Yeah, mine too." He glared at it. "I don't know anything about it."

"Somebody must have put it in your backyard," she muttered.

He glared at her. "Probably because of you."

She snorted. "What did I do?"

"I don't know, but somebody probably crept into my backyard, wanting to sneak up on you or something."

She stared at him. "So they came to your backyard? Listening for me?"

"Yours has the barking dog," he pointed out.

"Ha. You could be right there."

He nodded. "It does happen."

"It's quite possible someone wanted to listen in on me in my backyard. I just don't know why anybody would care."

"Maybe because you're always interfering in everybody's life," Richard complained.

"Sure," she replied, "go ahead. Blame me. I'm just trying to help people find closure, but that's all right. Make me feel like I'm a terrible person."

He handed her the contraption.

He certainly didn't apologize or back off in any way, and she realized he probably never would. She raised her hands. "Thank you for disconnecting it. My ears are a whole lot better."

He nodded stiffly and disappeared.

She went over to the patio to find her coffee was cold. Glaring down at her cup, she headed inside to refill it with hot coffee and took the first sip, smiling because at least now it was hot enough to drink and not so cold that it would go to waste. Feeling better, she sat outside again, but her mind was now preoccupied with the idea of somebody having gone into Richard's backyard to put in a listening device.

Of course her mind went to his brother, Roscoe. But

there was no reason for that, outside of the fact that he'd just recently been at Richard's house. But then why wouldn't he be there? She couldn't remember seeing Roscoe there before, but that didn't mean much because she didn't spy on Richard. He spied on her as much as anything.

She sat here for a long moment and then called out, "Richard, are you there?"

"Yeah, I'm here," he grumped. "Now what?"

But he wasn't quite so cranky now, as if realizing that something was going on that needed to be dealt with. "I guess your brother wouldn't have left that, *huh?*"

Immediately he popped his head over and glared at her. "Whatever you're messed up in, don't you involve my brother in it."

"Not trying to," she said. "I just know your brother was here visiting you."

"Yeah, he was, but he wasn't in the backyard."

"You're sure about that?"

He nodded. "Yeah, he wasn't here very long. So, no, it wasn't him."

"Okay, good. I didn't want to have to put him on my suspect list."

Richard stared at her in shock. "Why would you have a suspect list?"

"Why would somebody put a listening device like that in your backyard?" She pondered the horrific noise. "You were probably what, adjusting your ham radio? That would have set off that horrid squeal."

He looked at her and slowly nodded. "Yeah, that's exactly what I was doing."

"So then the frequency messed up that audio device." Then she stopped, pursed her lips. "When was the last time you adjusted your ham radio?"

He shrugged. "I haven't had much time for them lately, so it's been a while."

"Dang, I was hoping you would say yesterday because then the audio *thingamajiggy* would have been placed yesterday."

He shook his head. "I was last on the ham radio a few days ago, but you weren't home at the time."

"Right, so I wouldn't have noticed this feedback noise."

"Nope, you sure wouldn't have."

"Fine," she muttered. "I still don't know what to think, but I'll probably contact the police."

He stared at her in horror. "Oh no you don't. You're not involving me in any of that stuff."

"You have to tell me where it was," she cried out. "I need to know exactly where you found it."

"I'll send you a picture." And almost immediately her phone beeped.

She looked down to see that the device had been placed just literally on the other side of the fence.

She stared at the photo and asked Richard, "How many people would have access to your backyard?"

"Nobody," he cried out. "Nobody, nobody, nobody. I don't like people back here."

"You might not *like* people back there, but somebody was there."

"There wasn't anybody," he snapped.

"Okay, so then why did *you* put that listening device on your fence? Are you trying to listen in to my conversations?"

His head popped out over the fence, and he glared at her.

She shrugged. "If nobody else was in your backyard,

then, well, it means *you* did this."

He slowly let out his breath, and she could see the wheels working.

"No," he declared, "I didn't do this. However, somebody could have hopped the fence. Maybe come in from the river, who knows?"

"But they had to have known if you were away."

"I'm never away. I live here. Remember that part?"

She smiled. "How could I forget," she muttered. "How else would somebody know that you weren't here? You're often outside, so, if they knew that you were here in your backyard, they wouldn't jump over the fence then. And, if it looked like you were not home, they still couldn't have taken a chance because you might have just been inside, making tea or coffee."

He nodded. "I know," he agreed.

For the first time she caught the note of worry in Richard's tone.

He looked back toward the river. "It still wouldn't have taken very long to drop that thing here. For that matter," he added, "they could have grabbed that ladder."

He pointed to the one behind her. "Put it up, jumped over to my side from your yard, and then come back over onto your place again."

She looked at it and nodded slowly. "That's one way to look at it, but then wouldn't he need the ladder to get back out of your yard and over the fence again?" she noted. "I don't know why they would have done it that way. They could have installed it on my side then."

"With me at home all the time, entering my backyard is riskier. However, because you're gone a lot, maybe they figured entering your yard was easier," he suggested. "If they saw you walking down the river, they would have assumed that you'd gone to your grandmother's, giving them time to do this."

"Maybe," she muttered. "Now I have to think about this."

He gave her a fat smirk. "Just keep me out of it. I didn't have anything to do with it."

She smiled and nodded. "Good enough," she said cheerfully. "I'll try to keep you out of it."

Richard grimaced. "There is no such thing as *try*. It's either *do* or *don't*. Everything in between doesn't work for me." And, with that gem of wisdom, he jumped back down off his chair.

She sighed, as she looked at the fence. "It would be nice if you were friendlier."

"Yeah, well, look what happens when I'm friendlier," he pointed out. "People use my place to get back at you. It would be nice if *you* were friendlier, so you don't have so many enemies."

He had a point. She hadn't really thought that she had all these enemies, but the more cases she got involved in, the fewer people she could count as friendly. That was a little distressing too. Still, Richard quickly disappeared on the other side, and she heard his door slam, as he went back into his house.

"I really am not trying to be difficult," she shared with Mugs. He sat beside her, staring at her, yet completely relaxed. "And how come you didn't bark when somebody was in his backyard?"

But then why would he? It wasn't *his* backyard. It was Richard's backyard, which is why it made a whole lot more sense that somebody had done it from Richard's backyard. It was bothersome to consider such a thing, but, knowing that Mugs probably wouldn't have welcomed anybody in their backyard, it did make a strange sense.

She pondered that for a moment and knew that she would have to tell Mack, but he wouldn't be very happy. When Mack wasn't very happy, generally he was pretty upset at Doreen. She shouldn't have to take the blame for this one, but somehow she knew that it would be directed at her.

She sighed. "You know, he'll be madder if I *don't* tell him," she muttered.

Almost as if he knew that she was talking about him, her phone rang. She stared down at the number and answered it. "Are you psychic?"

"Nope, but I am feeling much better, after a good night's sleep."

At the sound of his teasing tone, she sighed. "Good thing you're not here right now."

"Why is that?" he asked.

"Because I'm fifty shades of red."

He quipped, "Isn't that *Fifty Shades of Grey*?"

Considering it was a very popular erotica book, she felt her cheeks heating up yet again. "I won't answer that."

He burst out laughing. "You already did. That's fine. I won't tease you."

"Too late," she muttered. "Besides, it's not a teasing morning."

"What happened?" he asked, his tone turning sharp, as he realized something was wrong. She explained about what Richard had found. "Seriously?" Mack cried out.

"Yeah, I just don't know why."

There was silence on the other end, while he thought about it. "I'll come by and pick up the listening device. I'll be right there."

She smiled, as he hung up. "Look at that, guys. Mack is visiting again too. Although a mad Mack, *huh*?"

She chuckled. She really liked having him close like this. Still, it was taking way too much of his time, but she didn't think the captain would have a problem with it. She was starting to build a few enemies around town, and they were just enough to be a little unnerving every once in a while.

She sighed, as her animals now slept. Thaddeus was asleep atop the patio table. "I can see you're all really bothered about the listening device. At least Mack had the right response."

With a sniff of disdain in their direction, she headed back inside, knowing that Mack would need coffee. As she was just getting another pot dripping, she heard a vehicle pulling up in the driveway. She raced to the living room window, sure it was Mack, only stopped in shock.

Her ex-husband, Mathew, was pounding on the door. "Doreen, open this door."

"If I don't?" she asked, crying out through the locked door. "What are you doing here? You told me that you signed all the paperwork. Why are you here now?"

"Because I don't want to give you that much money," he roared. "Since when did you become such a greedy idiot, you witch."

She wasn't sure that *greedy* and *idiot* went together, but he was obviously quickly losing his temper again. *Witch* was a nice touch. Right up his alley. "So you flew all the way up here just to tell me how angry you are?"

"Actually I drove," he snapped.

"Oh, did you see any vehicles off the road, … like down in a ravine or anything like that?" She opened the door and looked at him curiously. "I'm looking for a vehicle that went off the road a couple decades ago."

He stared at her. "Oddly enough I saw something that seemed suspicious, but I was too angry to even think about it."

She stared at him. "Location?"

"What do you mean, *location*?" he asked. "What's this got to do with you?"

"Stop. Where was that vehicle?"

He stopped to consider her question. "It was just on the other side of West Kelowna, where one of the big fires was, over there."

"Okay. What made you look there?"

"I don't know. I just saw something." He glared at her. "And if you want something from me, I want something from you."

She rolled her eyes at that. "I shouldn't even be talking to you."

He gave her a fat smile. "Nope, you shouldn't be, but you opened the door." He looked down, and there was Mugs, staring up at her. "Wow, he does not look good. What did you do to him?"

She glared at Mathew. "I didn't do anything."

"Yeah, you can tell," he quipped. "He hasn't been in for a good grooming or anything. He looks on the wild side." And then Mathew stared at her. "But then so do you. Boy, you sure let yourself go, didn't you?"

As far as personality went, Mathew never would have won awards, but right now he was definitely not making any gains with her. "Did you just come up here to insult me?" she asked her voice low, giving him a hard glare.

"Maybe," he replied cheerfully. "It improves my mood

to think that you're not getting away with everything."

"I'm just trying to get divorced. If you hadn't tried to cheat me out of a proper divorce settlement and got poor Robin involved in your lies and deception …"

He laughed. "Poor Robin was only too willing to screw you out of everything. I'll tell you there is nothing worse than women, particularly women who have been crossed."

"You ended up crossing her too. I don't think she was very happy about it."

"Nope, she sure wasn't." He shook his head. "And I'm here because I heard how much money you're getting from her estate," he spat in disgust. "So I don't want to give you anything."

"Of course you don't. I could go after the big fancy house. Oh, but I think you have what? Six of them? So I should be taking three of them."

He glared at her. In the distance she heard a very reassuring rumbling. She studied Mathew curiously. "Now you'll get in trouble."

"Why am I in trouble?" He scoffed at her. "Nobody even knows I'm here. It's one of the reasons I drove."

"Right, well, that won't work out for you so well, or it won't in a few minutes."

"What are you talking about? Let me in. We need to talk."

As Mathew pushed her out of the way, Mack came around the corner of the cul-de-sac and pulled up just to see it happen again. Now Mathew pushed Doreen harder a second time, and she fell backward.

"Stop it," she cried out. "I don't want you in my house."

"Too bad," he cried out. "You can't stop me."

Immediately another man added, "She can't, but I can."

And Mack picked up Mathew and pinned him against the exterior wall.

Mathew glared at him and looked at her. "Where did he come from?" he roared. "You didn't even have time to call him."

"No, he came because I had a police matter completely unrelated to you." She glared at him, as she brushed off her clothing.

Mugs was milling around in confusion. "I know, buddy. You don't quite know what to do when it's him, do you?" She reached down and added, "Unfortunately he's no longer a friend."

Mugs turned to Mathew and started growling.

Mack looked down at him and nodded. "Good boy, good boy. Not a friend." And Mack slowly released Mathew to address him. "Since I witnessed you assaulting her, believe me when I say her lawyer's about to find out, and I'm taking you down for questioning."

"Oh no you're not," Mathew argued. "I didn't assault her. She just wouldn't let me in."

Mack glared at him. "You know that there's a reason why we have things like *assault* and *forcible entry* charges? Doreen didn't have to let you in. It's her house."

Mathew glared at him, straightened his suit, and replied, "You might be some country-bumpkin copper, but it doesn't change the fact that she is still my wife."

"But being your wife," she added, her head poking around Mack, "doesn't mean I'm your punching bag. I was for too long," she muttered, snarling at him. "I'm not anymore. You don't get to hit me or to push me around now." And she kicked him in the shin, hard.

He bounced up and down, swearing and yelling, "Ow,

ow, ow, ow."

She glared at him. "Mack can take you down to the station and book you, for all I care."

"That won't happen. I've already got my lawyer here."

Mack frowned at him. "So, hang on a minute. You *knew* you would break the law, so you brought your lawyer ahead of time? Wow, that's *premeditated* assault. You know that, right?"

"I came to sign the stupid papers she wanted me to sign, and then I got emotionally overwrought." And he gave Mack this sweet smile.

Doreen snorted. "You didn't bring me any papers. You didn't show me any papers, and you just tried to force yourself into my house." She glared at him. "That is against the law. Even I know that."

"*Even you,*" Mathew repeated her words, with a shake of his head. "You don't know anything. You just keep talking like you do. You're an airhead."

She fisted her hands on her hips and replied, "I'm really getting tired of listening to you bad-mouth me all the time. I'm a nice person. I'm a good person, and I don't need you in my life. I need you to get out of here and to stay out of here. And, if you have the paperwork, great. We'll get it *to my lawyer* and make sure it's completely signed this time," she declared. "If you don't have the paperwork, Mathew, I'll see you in court." She looked over to Mack. "Can you take him out of here?"

Mack gave her a fat smile. "Oh, with great pleasure." And he grabbed Mathew by his collar and walked him to the driveway.

Doreen noted Arnold and Chester were now here in a black-and-white.

Mack looked over at them and said, "Take him in for assault. *Premeditated* assault."

"My lawyer will have me out in five minutes."

"Yeah, we'll see about that," Mack said, with a hard smile. "You come back to Doreen's again, and believe me, the law won't look at you kindly."

Mathew turned to Doreen and pointed a finger. "I'm warning you."

"Yeah, I know you're warning me again," she quipped. "You said you came to sign papers, so just sign the stupid thing, so I never have to see your ugly face. I shouldn't have had to see you this time."

"Yeah, but you couldn't resist. You opened the door."

She looked at him and shrugged. "Hardly. I thought it was Mack."

Mathew frowned at her and then at Mack standing there, and a sour look came over Mathew's face. "Don't tell me that you're sleeping with him." He shuddered. "Good Lord, how the mighty have fallen."

At that, Chester grabbed him, pinned his hands behind his back, and handcuffed him. "That'll be enough of that. Doreen is highly thought of in this town. We don't need people like you, coming from the big city, looking to hurt her," he muttered. And then he pushed him down the driveway toward the black-and-white.

She stared at Chester and Arnold, then called out, "Hey, guys, thanks so much."

Chester gave her a beaming smile and lifted a hand. With Mathew loaded up, they took off with him. She stayed on the front step and then turned to look at Mack. "I did open the door," she admitted, her shoulders sagging. "I shouldn't have, should I?"

He slowly shook his head. "No, you shouldn't have, …
and I shouldn't have to tell you."

She nodded. "No, you're right." She pinched the bridge
of her nose and added, "It seemed natural to do it."

"And then when he started to knock you around, how
did that feel?"

She looked at him, and—for the first time in a long
time—she admitted, "It felt natural."

"*Aah*, sweetheart." He pulled her into his arms and just
held her. That moment of sweetness would have lasted,
except Richard opened his front door and started yelling at
her.

"See, see? You just bring all the riffraff into town."

She turned to him, gave him a hard look, and replied,
"And you're the one with the listening device pointing to my
backyard," she snapped. "You're hardly the one to talk."

When a look of absolute horror crossed his face, Richard
raced inside and slammed his door shut.

Chapter 18

D OREEN SAT INSIDE the kitchen and watched as Mack put on a pot of tea. "You're almost as good at that as Nan is," she commented.

He looked over at her. "It helps to have something to do."

"Instead of wrapping your hands around Mathew's neck and choking him?" she teased, with a chuckle.

He grinned. "As long as you're laughing about that, then, yes, I do have to admit every once in a while that my limits get tested."

"Of course, when I opened the door to my ex," she muttered. "It was a stupid thing to do."

"You've come a long way," Mack said. "Stop knocking yourself."

She shrugged.

He looked around the kitchen and asked, "Where'd the brownies go?"

She got up, walked over to a cupboard, and pulled out the plate.

"You keep a plate of brownies in the cupboard?"

"What else am I supposed to do with these animals

around who steal food?"

He looked at her, and his lips twitched.

She glared. "This is not a good day for you to laugh at me."

"No, it sure isn't," he agreed, "which is surprising because we've had a lot of days where it *was* a good day to do that."

She continued to glare at him. "So what else am I supposed to do with the brownies?"

"Most people would put them into an airtight container or a sealed baggie."

"Why?" she asked, looking down at them. "Then you just have to open it and throw the bag away or wash your container. They're just on a plate. Why can't they stay like that?"

"Because they'll dry out."

"They will?" She looked at him in horror, picked up a brownie, and bit into it. It was definitely not the same texture as it was before. She stared down at the brownies. "I didn't know," she muttered.

"Remember when we have leftovers? I put them in containers in the fridge."

"Yeah, but that's because they can't stay in the pots or on a dirty plate," she replied, looking up at him.

He didn't know what to say, obviously. He gave her a long look. "All food has to be put away. You can't leave it out on the counters. Think contamination, bacteria, et cetera."

"I always put fresh food in the fridge, but I thought brownies could go into the cupboard, especially since dogs can't have chocolate," she explained. As she looked at the plate, her shoulders sagged. Glancing at Mack, she caught his lips twitching. She glared. "Remember that part about it's not a good day to be teasing me?"

He nodded. "Remember that part about sometimes it's a little hard not to?" And he burst out laughing.

She picked up a brownie and threw it at him, but he caught it midair and promptly bit down on it. "See? I still have teeth, so it's all good. Besides you ate most of them anyway."

"Not most of them. I was saving a few for tomorrow," she said.

"And if you put these in a baggie right now," he suggested, "chances are, they'll soften up overnight."

She looked up at him. "Really?"

"Absolutely. Not everything in life is irreparable."

She shook her head but got up and found a baggie. She turned and looked at him.

He nodded, as he snagged a second brownie off the plate. "That'll do."

She stared at the plate and asked, "Will there be any left to put away?"

"That's one way to save your baggie," he noted, with a fat grin, as he snagged a third one.

She rolled her eyes and grabbed two for herself, while he checked the pot of tea.

"Looks like it's brewed, but I'm not the expert."

She smiled. "It'll be fine. I'm sure all kinds of people in this world could tell me exactly how to make it, but chances are, they'll be very different instructions as we go from person to person."

"It's like everything else." Mack chuckled. "They all have their own idea of the best way to do something." He poured tea, even getting himself a cup.

Surprised, she asked, "Did you really want to drink that?"

"I'll try. You know it was suggested that maybe I'm drinking too much coffee." She stared at him in horror. He smiled. "No, I'm not cutting back or down. I just was looking for another drink that I might enjoy in the evenings."

"I don't know that tea's any better. If you think about it, tea still has caffeine."

"I know." He gave a shrug. "Still, I'll try it today." And, with that, he poured two cups. She added milk to hers and stirred. He looked at the milk, shrugged, and said, "I'll try it this way first."

"You do that." Doreen smiled. "And, if you want milk or sugar, they're both here." And she patted the sugar bowl. His face twisted, and she nodded. "Yeah, I know. Sugar bowls, right?" He chuckled. "Just think of all the things that we look at differently now. ... I only keep it around for company."

"And *company* being what it is, that's generally me."

"Or Nan," she added. "Anybody else who comes tends *not* to be what I would necessarily call *company*."

"What would you call it?"

She shrugged. "It's not as if they're friends because I don't have any friends, and generally anybody who comes calling is looking for something. And not always in a nice way."

"Right," Mack agreed. "What about Bernard?"

"Bernard's an interesting character." She smiled. "However, he lives in the world that I left behind."

"He could put you back into that world again, if you wanted."

She gave a mock shudder. "No thanks. I was a caged bird already. I plan on singing freely for a long time now."

"Good," Mack replied.

She looked over at him. "He's a nice guy, but not for me."

He smiled at her. "Also good that you know that."

"Not that he doesn't, you mean?" she asked, with a chuckle.

"Oh, I'm pretty sure that, if you were interested, he'd be interested, but he's smart enough to know that that's not where you're at right now."

"Did you warn him off?" she asked, with a sideways look.

"Nope, I didn't have to," he declared.

And such a sense of complacency filled his tone of voice that she burst out laughing. "I'm glad to hear that," she stated. "Then we don't have any issues."

"No, no issues. As long as everybody keeps to where they belong, we're all good. I was a little worried about Bernard there for a while, but he seems to have calmed down."

"It's not as if I've contacted him, at least not often," she admitted. "If I thought he had anything he could do to help find that couple who went missing so long ago, I would contact him in a heartbeat."

"Sure, but then you'd be contacting him for assistance, not for personal reasons. Shall we?" he asked, and he picked up the two cups of tea and headed outside. He sat down at the patio table and looked around at the deck and the patio. "We did good on these projects."

"You did very good," she agreed, "and I do feel guilty sometimes that I couldn't do more to help you guys."

"Nope, not needed," Mack declared. "We're all fine."

"Sure, fine is fine, but it doesn't change the fact that sometimes you need to say *thank you.*"

He looked at her. "And sometimes there's no need to say anything because we already know."

"See? That's the thing, I'm not really sure that I know what that means anymore."

"You're learning, so don't keep worrying about something that's not worth worrying about."

She chuckled. "Still, I think brownies for the office would be appreciated."

He raised his eyebrows at her. "I'm not against you getting into this whole brownies thing. Just remember that a lot of people are at the office."

"So one dozen won't cut it, *huh?*"

"No." He chuckled. "Not only won't a dozen cut it, but they would disappear with the first person."

She latched her gaze on his, considering his words. "So nobody at the station has manners."

"Not when it comes to brownies. Now if you wanted to bake up maybe ..." He considered it and estimated, "Four dozen? That's not hard to do."

"No." She frowned. "I guess I just have to do multiple brownie pans, right?" she asked, turning to look at him.

"Exactly, most brownie recipes you can multiply easily enough."

"That's the thing. I don't have any experience in that."

"Google is your friend at all times, especially when it comes to something like that."

She frowned at him, while nodding her head. "You're right. That would be an easy answer."

"But don't do something like that unless you really feel up to it." He stretched out his legs and sat back, and said,

"Now, tell me what's going on with this listening device." She quickly went through what had happened. He asked her, "And yet, why would that weird sound have come up all of a sudden?"

"Ah, I forgot about that." And she explained about Richard's ham radio.

Mack nodded thoughtfully. "That might do it."

"I don't know what was doing it, but something was interfering and making this godawful noise," she added, with a shudder.

"That's good because at least then you found it."

She got up, walked back into the kitchen, picked up what Richard had given her, and put it on the patio table in front of Mack. "This is it. I don't know anything about them."

Mack picked it up, studied it, and nodded. "It's a pretty simple device. You can get these in any electronics store around here. Or on the internet."

"How is it that things like this could even be sold?" she asked.

"Anyone can purchase way-more-sophisticated ones quite easily too," he muttered. "Still, this gives us something." He eyed her. "Do you have any suspicions who placed it?"

"Of course my mind went to his brother, but I have absolutely no reason to even suspect him of anything."

"Of course not," Mack said. "Plus Roscoe did spend a lot of time looking for his friends."

"Right, and there's no suspicion of foul play against his friends, so it seems ludicrous to pin something like this on Roscoe. Now, if it *was* him, that's a game changer."

"Not only ludicrous, not exactly effective," Mack noted,

with a smile.

"It all just seems a little too ridiculous. Why were they trying to listen in on Richard or on me?"

Mack shrugged. "And that's another question we don't have an answer for. For all you know, Richard's planning on selling, and somebody hoped they'd learn something about the property or his plans."

She frowned at Mack, not buying that suggestion.

He raised his hands. "I don't know why people would do something like that." And then he smiled. "But you have this, and now, of course, it's covered in fingerprints."

She winced and nodded. "Yeah, and obviously I can't really do anything about Richard's prints all over it."

Mack agreed. "We can get his for comparison, but chances are it was wiped clean. Plus, depending on how long it's been out here, it's had plenty of weathering."

"Right, so, in other words, we can't get anything off of it."

"I wouldn't think so, but I will take it into forensics and find out." He picked up his tea, took a sip absentmindedly, and stared out toward the river. "His fence is closed up all the way back there, isn't it?"

"Yeah, but it's not exactly hard to jump over. He hops up on a chair to talk to me all the time, and, every once in a while, I do the same with him."

"So anybody tall could probably kick themselves up and over easily enough. And Richard doesn't leave home often, does he?"

She shook her head. "No, but still somebody got in his backyard without any trouble and without Richard noticing it."

"Absolutely," Mack acknowledged. "If somebody wants

to get somewhere, we know perfectly well how easy that is."

"Which is another part of my problem. We don't know why somebody did this, but were they after something Richard would say, or me? That's what I would like to know."

"We'll have to assume that it's both at this point in time," Mack replied, "considering that he also talks to you."

"Not very often," she pointed out, "and rarely in a nice tone. Although lately, we have talked more pleasantly."

He smiled at her. "Like when you guys are flinging insults back and forth at each other from the front steps?" he asked.

She sighed. "I keep trying to be a nice person, but then I do things like that," she muttered contritely. "You know he is no better either, right?"

"Oh, I wouldn't worry about it." Mack laughed. "I'm pretty sure he's done way more mudslinging than you have."

"Maybe," she conceded, "but it's still not right."

He looked at her with the gentlest of smiles. "Never doubt that you're a good person. Whether other people agree isn't the point. You have to do what you need to do for yourself."

"Like my ex?" She threw up her hands. "I just want him to sign the papers, and I want him to go back to Vancouver and stay there. Instead he shows up on my doorstep."

"Do you have any idea why he came up? Surely a phone call would have sufficed."

"No, it makes no sense. He mentioned that he drove here, which presumably is why you didn't know that he was here." She turned to face Mack. "Or are you not following Mathew anymore?"

"I haven't gotten any alerts, and I didn't check today to

see if he was coming. So, now that I know he's driving, there's no point. I can keep doing it on the odd occasion, but it won't necessarily help, not if he thinks nothing about the five-hour drive. He also could have flown into one of the other airports, rented a vehicle, and come down here," he explained.

"I didn't think any of it was worth his time to be honest," she stated bluntly. "He makes no bones of the fact that I'm just a pain in his life right now. He was also furious about Robin's will."

"Yet you're a pain that he's not willing to quite sign off on."

"He thinks I'm getting enough from Robin so I shouldn't get anything from him."

"It doesn't work that way. Regardless, we'll park him for the moment, and let's deal with the listening device. Unless …" Mack studied the device and asked, "Would Mathew have used something like this?"

She looked at him and smiled. "Absolutely he would have, but it wouldn't have been a cheap one. That I am sure of."

"No, of course not. He would have used the best and only the best."

"And then he would have complained when it didn't work the way he wanted it to because there's no technology out there to do what he wants it to do."

"What technology would he want?" Mack asked curiously.

"Knowing him, anything from trying to read minds so he can guess what his opponent will do ahead of time to who knows?" She added, "Maybe putting suggestions in other people's heads."

"Now that's technology I really don't want to deal with anytime soon," Mack declared, staring at her. "Your ex is definitely not someone who should have access to that technology."

"No, but people like him drive the technology demand and build it for control."

Mack laughed. "That and governments."

She wrinkled up her nose. "Yeah, I'm not going down that road. That's just a nightmare waiting to happen." She watched him as he finished his tea. "I was waiting for you to make a face over the tea."

"It wasn't bad," he replied. "I didn't want to add milk or sugar just yet. I was trying to give it a decent test by drinking it plain. It was okay. I can't say it's anything I would necessarily jump for joy at having, not quite the way you and Nan do."

"I think it's an acquired taste," she noted honestly.

"I haven't acquired it then." He got up and grabbed the device and said, "I'll take this into the office in the morning."

"Good. I'm glad you didn't say you'd take that to the office tonight. You need to go home and get some rest." She stopped and looked at him. "Did you ever think that whoever did this was hoping to get information on you and the case?"

He looked down at the device and shrugged. "I guess that's possible. It doesn't make a whole lot of sense though."

"None of this does," she muttered. "Whenever we're looking for common sense out of these guys, you know it's not there. It's all about survival."

He studied the device and nodded. "I won't say yes or no either way. The fact is, people do know that you're involved in a lot of these cases, so maybe …"

As he walked toward the front door, she asked, "What about your case? Have you had any progress?"

He shook his head. "Not yet, we're still working on it. It's taking time to gather the information."

She didn't want to say anything because obviously it did take time, and sometimes it took way more time than anybody had patience for, yet she had to be patient. She walked with him to her front door, and then he headed out to his truck.

As he drove away, she looked over at Richard's house and saw the curtains twitch. She should probably apologize, but maybe now he could relax too, knowing that Mack hadn't even gone over to talk to him. She pondered that and quickly sent him a text. **Any reason you didn't talk to Richard?**

He phoned her back and said, with a laugh, "I was waiting for him to calm down. Figured he would be too panic-stricken right now to have a decent conversation. Don't worry. I'll talk to him and get his prints soon." And, at that, he hung up.

Chapter 19

Friday Morning ...

THE NEXT MORNING, Doreen woke up with a lot of energy and a sense of accomplishment. Although for what, she had no idea. But, as she looked around the house, carrying her first cup of coffee, she realized that she wanted to get something done. So she started in on the housework, never realizing that it was simple and easy to do, but still there sure was a lot of it.

She knew a lot of people would probably shoot her for saying housework was easy. Yet it wasn't that hard to do. It was just something you *had* to do, and, so far, it was a novelty to her. Maybe at one point in time she would get to hating it as much as a lot of people did, but right now it was kinda fun. She quickly vacuumed, mopped floors, and cleaned up bathrooms, then gave the kitchen a quick wipe down. Just as she was finishing, Nan called her.

"What are you doing?" she asked in that voice that belied she was up to something.

"I just finished the housework," Doreen said.

"Oh, good. Did you hear any more news about our idea?"

"I did talk to Mack about it," she replied, "but we need more than just supposition."

At that, Nan sighed. "You guys are such party poopers."

The phrase made Doreen chuckle. "According to Mack, it's got to be all about facts. So far, there have been no facts supporting your idea."

"We know that the facts don't always fit the circumstances either," she muttered.

"It needs to, Nan." Doreen stared at her phone. "You know that as well as I do."

"Posh. That just sounds like an excuse."

"No, and yes, I know I sound more and more like Mack every day."

"It is amazing that you do," Nan said. "You're picking up a lot from him."

"Whether it's a good thing or not, I don't know," she muttered.

Nan added in a brighter voice, "Are you coming down for tea?"

"Maybe," Doreen replied. "It's a good time for me to take a break, if you're up for company."

"I'm always up for your company," Nan said. "Hurry up. I'll go put on the teapot." And Nan disconnected.

At that, Doreen laughed, grabbed the animals, and asked, "You guys ready to go see Nan?"

There was general excitement, as she opened the back door. Everybody was happy to head down to Nan's, as far as Doreen could tell. But then they always were. It was an adventure to them. As she wandered down the creek, she stopped at Richard's fence, checking to see if anybody could easily scale it. She certainly couldn't, but she could imagine that lots of people could. That just made her leery. Just because some people could didn't mean that they should, and that was a lesson that she knew a lot of people didn't care to learn either.

As she walked down to Nan's, she checked the other houses along the path. Nothing appeared suspicious. As she came around the corner, Nan sat outside on her patio at the bistro table, waiting for her. Doreen smiled as the animals pulled on their leashes to race over, so she quickly unhooked them and let them go.

Mugs ran toward Nan. Goliath, being Goliath, raced toward the flower boxes and then sprawled just out of arm's reach, so Nan couldn't quite greet him.

As Doreen walked up, Nan looked over at the cat and noted, "He's really got an attitude, doesn't he?"

Doreen chuckled. "I think all cats do, but definitely this one's over the top."

Nan got up and greeted Goliath. As she bent over, Thaddeus hopped off Doreen's shoulder and jumped onto Nan's back. Giving a startled exclamation, Nan straightened up quickly, and Thaddeus flew up, his wings fluttering in her face.

"Easy, easy, easy," Doreen told him. "No scaring Nan."

Nan chuckled. "Hardly an issue. He just startled me." She reached up and cuddled Thaddeus. "He's just happy to see me."

"Yet we see you almost every day," Doreen noted in a wry tone.

"*Almost* isn't quite good enough, not according to these guys." Nan pointed at the tea and the table. "Now sit down, and I'll pour."

"I gather it's your teatime."

"Absolutely. We've been lawn bowling all morning. So

I'm ready for my tea. Oh, hang on a minute." She hopped up and disappeared into the kitchen.

Doreen waited for the inevitable basket of goodies. At least she hoped it would be a basket of goodies because, after her morning of housecleaning, she was on the hungry side. She needed to go shopping for groceries again.

That was one of those jobs that just never seemed to go away. You couldn't do it once and have it be done, as it just came back around again. She wondered how people managed to sort out all this stuff all the time. If she had a full-time job and got home at a specific time and still had all these other things that she had to do, she didn't think she'd have time to even eat—or the inclination, for that matter.

As Nan came bustling out, she did have a basket.

Doreen perked up. "Is this food?"

"It is," Nan declared. "You did say you were doing a lot of housework."

"I was, and I am hungry," she admitted.

"Good. These are a few things that Richie had from yesterday, and then I grabbed a couple muffins this morning to have for tea. So it's a good thing you came. Otherwise it would be too much."

At that, knowing that Nan was doing this on purpose, Doreen said, "I just don't want you to get in trouble."

"I won't get in trouble," she replied. "I think sometimes the cooks make extra to be sure that whoever needs it has all that they want."

"As long as you guys aren't starving," Doreen added.

"That would never go down well."

"Maybe not, but it can happen," Doreen said. "Let's hope it doesn't happen anytime for you."

"Not me," she muttered. "I like my groceries too much.

I make sure I get fed. Don't you worry."

Doreen chuckled at that. "I'm glad to hear it." She lifted the tea towel covering the basket of goodies and smiled. "Wow, quite a selection here."

"Richie does like to bring over anything that's extra in case you come along. So whatever's here that we don't eat, you're taking home with you."

"What?" Doreen asked, staring at her grandmother.

"Yeah, that's the way we work it. And then Richie doesn't feel bad if he has extra because it won't go to waste."

"So I've become a dumping ground?" Doreen asked, with a wry tone.

"Oh dear, I hope not," Nan replied. "That would be pretty bad. Why don't we just enjoy these and not worry about it."

As it was, there wasn't very much of Richie's spare treats here anyway. By the time Doreen had had three treats, she held up a hand and sighed. "I'm good. I'm done. That was lovely though."

"I do tell them in the kitchen how much you enjoy everybody's cooking," Nan shared, "so it's not as if they don't know you come and go all the time here."

Doreen winced at that. "Sure I come, but I really didn't want them to think that I came for food all the time."

Nan chuckled. "Whyever not?" she asked. "It's what you do."

"No, I come to see you," Doreen stated firmly.

Nan stopped, looked up at her, and her eyes got misty. "And believe me. I appreciate it." As she poured another cup of tea, she asked, "So what's new?"

Doreen rolled her eyes at her. "Not a whole lot." Then she thought about the listening device. "Except for one thing." And when she told her about what Richard had found on his side of the fence, Nan stared at her in astonishment.

"Well," she cried out, "the nerve of some people."

"That's what I was thinking," Doreen muttered. "It's hardly anything I wanted to think of Richard doing, and, for him to have done it, he wouldn't have been mad to find it there."

"No, of course not," Nan agreed, staring at her. "That wouldn't make any sense."

"No, I don't think Richard did it, but I wouldn't put it past all kinds of people. His brother, Roscoe, was there earlier, but I don't want to automatically suspect his brother either."

"I haven't had much to do with him," Nan noted.

"Me neither," Doreen said. "He must visit Richard every once in a while. I think he gets quite lonely, so it's not something we want to stop. However, if there's any chance that Roscoe did this, ... then that would be bad news."

"You would hope not," Nan said.

Doreen nodded. "Enough is going on in our world that we don't need things like that happening. Right in our backyard too."

Nan nodded, but she was thoughtful. After a few minutes she just shook her head. "It's silly I know, but I just can't see Richard doing something like that."

"I don't think it was Richard at all," Doreen replied. "But what I don't know is who would have had access to his backyard, and, in theory, ... it could have been anybody. They could have hopped the fence and, you know, come into his yard, without him even knowing it. I don't have any way to know how often he's in his backyard because I can't see."

Nan nodded. "There was a gate at one time along the back fence to his property, but I think it's overgrown in weeds. That guy was always lurking in his backyard when I lived there."

Doreen frowned. "I don't think I've ever seen a gate there." But Nan was right; it was overgrown back there.

"Still, once again, somebody's using somebody else's space and trying to make nefarious use of that space."

Doreen chuckled. "Maybe." With a side glance, she watched as Thaddaeus snuck up closer to Nan's plate. "Are you done eating, Nan?" she asked.

Nan looked at her. "Sure, why? Are you still hungry?" Nan frowned.

"No, but Thaddeus is trying to tackle your plate."

And a few crumbs were left on it, but Nan, being Nan, shoved it closer to Thaddeus and said, "In that case, he's welcome to it."

Doreen watched as Thaddeus proceeded to clean up all the little bits and pieces on Nan's plate. "I don't even know how healthy any of this stuff is for him."

"It's probably not at all," Nan noted. "It's one of those tricky things about pets. You do the best you can, but you still never really know how much of these treats are allowed to be given to them."

"More than *not allowed* but hurting them."

But Thaddeus had already scarfed up everything on Nan's plate and then turned to look at Doreen.

She pressed a finger gently against his beak and whispered, "Don't say it."

He cocked his head to the side and said, "Thaddeus loves Nan."

"Right, Thaddeus loves Nan, but Thaddeus doesn't love Doreen."

And he started to cackle again, with that same weird laughter.

Nan shook her head. "I don't know where he gets some of these things from."

"He's come up with a few new ones lately too," Doreen muttered. "He definitely keeps me on my toes."

"That's a good thing." Nan smiled. "And, if he keeps you smiling, he keeps you happy. I can't find any fault with that."

By the time Doreen was ready to return home again, several other people had popped in to see if Doreen had gotten anywhere on the case.

She looked over at Nan. "Apparently you are Grand Central Station. Are you okay with that?"

"I don't mind," she replied. "It lends a certain credence to my position here."

Doreen rolled her eyes at that. "Doesn't mean it's a good thing," she muttered. But she stood up when it was time to go, smiled at the collection of people, and announced, "I do need to take the animals home again."

There was a mutual crying out of goodbyes, and she quickly packed up everybody and headed to the river again. She wasn't exactly sure what was going on down at the home or whether Nan was betting on the results or not. As Doreen considered that, she frowned and phoned her grandmother. "Please tell me that you're not placing bets on this case."

"Of course not," Nan stated, but way too much innocence filled her tone.

"*Nan*," Doreen muttered.

"Don't you worry, child," Nan replied. "I promise I'm

not doing anything bad."

"No, but you're probably not doing anything good either," Doreen retorted.

"If I have to do everything good and nothing bad, I won't have any fun at all," she declared crossly. "You just go home and have fun."

"What will you do?" Doreen asked, with a note of humor.

"Oh dear, don't you worry about me. I've got all kinds of plans this afternoon." And she laughed. "I probably have way more fun than you do." And, with that, she hung up the phone, leaving Doreen staring down at it, nonplussed.

Chances were, Nan *did* have way more fun than Doreen. Doreen was spending way too much time on cases instead of getting out and doing things. At that, she wondered if maybe Mack was up for either paddleboarding or a hike this weekend, something to get them all out and away from the cases that were starting to dominate everything.

And, with that, she sent Mack a text. **Hey, do you want to do something this weekend?**

He came back almost immediately. **Sure. What's on your mind?**

She wrote back. **Paddleboarding, a hike, a drive. Take your pick.**

He phoned her then. "Is this connected to the case?"

"No, I was trying to get away from the cases."

"In that case, absolutely, unless you want to take a drive down the highway and see if you can find anything about this vehicle."

"Yeah, there's what, 250 miles to cover? I don't think I'll find anything myself."

"Okay, good enough. Maybe we'll just go out for a drive

and hike around."

"Now that sounds good," she said.

"What brought this on?" he asked curiously.

"Nan just told me that she has more fun than I do." Doreen laughed. "I realized she was right. She does have way more fun. I just need to get out more."

"This is a good start. By the way, Mathew left Kelowna early this morning."

"He was released already?" she cried out.

"Yep, his lawyer managed it."

"*Great,*" she muttered. "How do you know he's left for sure?"

"He was escorted to the city limits."

"That's nothing. He could have come back again."

"He was also instructed to check in once he's home. Apparently he did just check in. So I am pretty confident in the news."

"Great, well, that's something at least. If he's out of my life for a day or so, that would help."

"Remember. No opening the door to him or strangers."

"Which means just don't open the door then," she replied, with a note of humor.

"Unless it's me or my brother."

"Okay, good enough."

"Anything else happening over at Richard's?"

"Not that I know of. I'm just coming up to my backyard now."

As she reached the side of Richard's fence, she heard a heavy *bang*, and somebody jumped over the fence, took one startled look at her, and booked it.

She immediately dropped the leash and said, "Go, Mugs, go." She cried out to Mack, "Somebody just jumped over

Richard's fence, and now he's racing down the river. Mugs is after him."

"Good Lord, call him back. You can't catch him. I don't want you getting into any confrontations."

But she was already running down the creek, and she screamed into the phone, "Too late."

And hung up.

Chapter 20

DOREEN RACED BEHIND Mugs, calling him back. The guy was ahead of them, but, as she watched, Mugs was gaining. She wasn't even sure what Mugs would do with the stranger, if Mugs caught him. Still, Doreen picked up the pace as fast as she could. Meanwhile, Thaddeus's claws gripped her neck, and he was screaming in her ear, "Giddy-up, giddyup, giddyup."

"Could you just stop that?" she cried out.

"Giddyup, giddyup, giddyup."

She groaned, remembered thinking having a talking parrot was cool. Then there was Goliath, who was even worse. She turned to look for the big Maine coon cat and got caught up on a rock and ended up sprawled on the ground. She bounded to her feet, Mugs still racing ahead.

She screamed at him, "Mugs, Mugs, get back here. Come back here, Mugs!" She kept running behind him, but now she was limping and sore.

She was still looking for Goliath, but she saw no sign of him. When she finally caught up with Mugs, he was milling around in the creek, sniffing the rocks. Either the guy had found a quick hiding space or the guy had jumped the creek, but Mugs hadn't seen him. The creek was an odd thing too. It was much deeper here; it was also freezing cold. Her phone was screaming at her as well, and she knew it would be Mack. She sighed as she answered it. She stood, watching Mugs. "Looks like Mugs lost him," she said into the phone, her whole body screaming in pain.

Mack may have picked up on that, sensing something was wrong. "What happened?"

"What happened is I fell," she muttered. "Between Thaddeus gripping my neck and a missing Goliath, it hasn't been a great chase."

"You aren't supposed to chase after intruders," Mack muttered. "Do I need to come?"

"No," she said. "It's fine. Mugs is calming down."

"Any idea where this guy went?"

"No, that's a mystery." She glared down at her knee. "And I scraped my knee."

"Go home," he said in a soothing tone. "I'll come over, and you can give me the details."

"No details. Somebody just jumped Richard's fence—right in front of me—took one look at me, and booked it, but I don't think Richard even knew."

"Would you recognize this guy?"

"I possibly would. Of course all I can think about is how somebody was over there, maybe putting new listening devices there again."

Silence came for a moment. "Right," Mack agreed. "Why don't you go put on some coffee, and I'll be there in a few minutes." And, with that, he hung up.

She smiled at the critters. "At least Mack's coming. That's about the only good thing to come out of this."

They started to walk away, but she heard a noise. When

she turned to look back, she saw a guy pulling out of the river from the deep part. He took one look at her, and he raced away again. She decided not to track him down because he was just that much farther ahead again. Plus now he was on the other side of the river, and this was the deep end.

She sighed, as she looked down at Mugs. "That's why you lost him, buddy. He stayed under the water." As she slowly made her way home, her knee started to stiffen up. And there at her place, right on her creekside bench, waiting for them, was Goliath. Doreen glared at the cat. "What happened to you?" she muttered. "I thought this was supposed to be a family thing."

But obviously Goliath had made the decision that it was a family thing, *providing* it didn't involve water.

Doreen petted him, and he hopped up on his back legs, so that she could pick him up. She immediately did and cuddled him. "You were the smartest one of us all," she muttered, as she slowly carried him up to the house.

As she got closer, he jumped down, and she unlocked the door, disarmed the alarm, and then stepped inside. As soon as she did so, she had a thought and stepped back out on the deck. "Richard, are you there?"

Only silence came, but then what did she expect? If there'd been an intruder back there, chances were good that Richard wouldn't be around to witness that. It just said a whole lot about the craziness that was their life right now.

She wanted to go knock on Richard's door but figured, since Mack was coming, she'd leave that up to him. Because, for sure, now Mack would have to talk to Richard. Even though Mack was supposed to do it earlier, maybe he would have held this off. Yet she didn't think so. Whoever was there had been very much interested in Richard's backyard, and the only thing that came to mind for her was the fact that they had removed the other listening device.

With that thought uppermost she turned her attention to the coffeepot, then sat and waited for Mack.

Chapter 21

WHEN MACK WALKED in the front door, Doreen noted, "That took you way longer than I expected."

"Yeah, it sure did." He dropped his huge frame onto the kitchen chair with enough force that she was afraid it would break. He caught the look on her face and shook his head. "Honest, I haven't broken a kitchen chair in my lifetime."

She nodded and then added, "*Yet.*"

He glared at her and asked, "Are you telling me that I'm fat?"

She snickered. "Nope. It would take a bigger person than me to say that."

He burst out laughing. "My mom used to give me heck all the time for the way I used to throw myself into the chairs, but it seemed to be just the way my mind was working right now," he said, shaking his head. "This case is just too stupid."

"Am I a case now?" she asked, eyeing him with interest.

He rolled his eyes. "I don't know what this is. I'll have to go talk to Richard."

"I called over the fence earlier, but he didn't answer."

"It would make sense that he's not home, or at least not

in his backyard, considering that somebody was just there. I will go see if anything else has been disturbed, or maybe his house has even been broken into."

She pondered that and then admitted, "I didn't even think of that. All I thought about was the listening device."

"Yet not everything is about you," he noted gently.

"Good," she declared promptly. "I would be totally happy to not have this be about me."

He nodded. "I'm with you there."

"Did you tell anybody at work?"

"I did, so we're all waiting to see what comes back from forensics on this. Nobody's happy at the idea of planting listening devices next door."

"It's stupid. Nobody should care about what I'm doing. Maybe it really is just about Richard. That was Nan's suggestion."

"That's something we'll have to get to the bottom of," Mack confirmed. "Either way, we can't have it continuing, and we had somebody in Richard's backyard, which just adds a whole new element to it."

"It's not a good element," she muttered. "Nobody wants to think of people breaking into our backyards, but to think that he might have left something?"

When they finished their first shared coffee, Mack stood. "I'll go see if Richard's home." And, with that, he went out the front door.

She got another cup of coffee and moved out to the deck table, her animals following her. "It's a little bit crazy these days, but we're supposed to stay out of trouble." She wasn't sure how one was supposed to do that when it seemed like there was no end of headaches, but, hey, she was happy to have Mack deal with Richard right now. And Richard would deal with Mack in a completely different way because it was Mack. With her, Richard would probably just shout and scream through the fence.

When the silence was suddenly split with Richard literally shouting and screaming at Mack, she realized it really didn't make a difference who was talking to Richard. That's who he was as a person. She snickered as she listened. And then Richard's face popped over the edge of the fence, and he glared at her.

"Hey, I had nothing to do with it." She showed her palms. "We tried to catch the guy who was in your yard."

Richard looked at her suspiciously. "Maybe it wasn't my yard. Maybe it was your yard."

"Sure, like I'll mistake my yard for yours, especially when yours is fenced and mine isn't," she replied, with an eye roll. "He hopped *over* your fence. So I don't know whether you got broken into or they planted more listening devices."

He stared at her and then quickly disappeared again.

She figured that was an answer he didn't like either. When she heard low voices, she realized Richard had calmed down enough to talk to Mack, so eventually Mack would get back to her. She walked into her kitchen, trying to figure out what she could have for lunch, knowing that Mack probably hadn't eaten either. There were sandwiches to be made, but that wouldn't make him happy.

Then she shrugged. She hadn't been grocery shopping, hadn't had a chance to do anything between the housework this morning, then going down to Nan's. And thinking about that, she realized she still had the leftovers from Nan, and it hadn't been very long since Doreen had eaten, so really she wasn't even hungry. She was just … She stopped and gave her head a shake.

"You're just still dealing with the shock of it all," she muttered. "Now stop it. Bring out the treats, let Mack have some, and you can wait to eat until dinner. You certainly don't need to eat again now."

And, with that, she sat outside on the deck and prepared to wait.

Chapter 22

AN HOUR LATER Mack finally showed up again. Doreen stared at him. "Really? And here I thought you would be gone for like five minutes."

He shrugged. "Sorry about that."

But he didn't sound sorry. She glared at him.

He smiled. "You shouldn't frown so much. It'll put wrinkles on your face."

At that, she rolled her eyes. "Will you still love me if I have wrinkles?"

His response was instantaneous. "Of course."

She sighed. "I'm glad to hear that because Mathew would have given me a completely different answer."

"And we aren't discussing him," Mack noted calmly.

She nodded. "No, we'll discuss this." She pointed to Richard's house.

"It looks like somebody was trying to get into his back door. I had forensics come and check for fingerprints."

"Oh." She studied him. "So maybe it has nothing to do with me."

"I don't know about that yet. We did find another listening device outside though."

She stared at him in shock. "What?"

He nodded. "Somebody is determined to hear either what you say or what Richard says outside."

She stared, dumbfounded, as Mack held up yet a second device in his hand. "Wow. ... I don't even know what to say."

"It's just been that kind of a day." His gaze landed on the plate of treats, and his face lit up. Then he stopped and asked, "You got these from Nan's, didn't you?"

"I did. Apparently Richie takes a little extra these days, so that he doesn't starve and then pawns the extras off on Nan for me." She sighed. "Everybody is afraid I'll starve."

"Everybody is caring," Mack corrected. "I am sure they want to ensure that you're doing okay."

"Yes, that's one way to look at it." She smirked. "Sometimes it just doesn't feel like that."

"That's because you're looking at it from you trying to be independent versus them trying to help you out."

She chuckled. "That's fine. I'll take food, whatever way they want to give it to me."

"Exactly." Mack pointed at the device. "Now ... this one appears to be exactly the same as the one that was here before. Only a bit newer."

She pondered that. "What do you think's going on?" she asked.

He shook his head. "I can't tell if it's targeted at you or Richard—although, if Richard, maybe that's why they were trying to get inside his house, to place another device there."

"Did you ask Richard if he's in any trouble or if he has any idea why someone would do that?"

"Richard told me that he has no idea why." Mack's lips twitched. "He did suggest that it was all because of you, though."

She chuckled. "I'm not at all surprised. He doesn't want anything to mess up his nice, peaceful little world."

"I think that went out the window when you moved in."

"So true." She nudged the plate of treats toward him, and he immediately picked one. "It is a good system. I do quite like getting treats myself," he admitted, with such boyish charm that she was laughing.

"You and me both," she agreed. "I mean, ... it's almost expected, and I have to watch that because I don't want to go down there and then not get something one day and be really disappointed."

"And it is hard because very quickly, after you've gotten something on a regular basis, you do come to expect it. It's a case now of remembering to be grateful for everything that you do get," he pointed out. "I'm definitely grateful when you get treats like this." And he took a big bite into a muffin.

She smiled. "You don't even get half of what I get." He stopped and stared. She shrugged. "What can I say? Sometimes there's quite a pile of treats. And they do send me home with them. So it's not that I'm *not* eating. It's just I don't need to eat as much because I get a lot from them."

"I won't argue with it, if it keeps you interested in food. Besides, you always share." And he gave her a big fat smile, as he took another bite. Then he surveyed what was still on the plate.

She laughed at him. "Go ahead. I've already had three or four." He stared at her in mock outrage and picked up two more. She added, "You're just like a little kid."

"Hey, it goes along with the brownies," he explained. "Remember that the way to a man's heart is through his stomach."

"Yeah, I didn't quite understand that before," she said. "Now I'm getting it."

"Yeah, you just have to keep trying."

"What if I don't want to try?" she asked, teasing.

He gave her a mock look of horror. "Don't ever say that. As far as I'm concerned, it's a done deal anyway. But you? You still need to keep trying."

She burst out laughing. And then, as soon as the laughter died away, she looked at him and turned serious. "So now what will we do?"

His voice was calm, his tone steady, as he told her, "We'll wait and see if this guy comes back. I'll keep some unmarked vehicles in the area, maybe even a guy somewhere along the creek."

Chapter 23

L ATER, CLOSE TO sunset, Doreen sat outside with her notes, and she got an email from the Google Earth group she had contacted about searching. She clicked on it eagerly. Not much was in it.

Hey, Doreen. Just an update. Nothing found yet. It would help if we had a confirmation of any other sightings.

She pondered that. She had already told them where the couple were last seen. Remembering Mathew's comment, she sent a quick note on his observation and got a thumbs-up in response.

As she sat there, she phoned Roscoe.

"Hey," he greeted her, his voice curious. "Does this mean you're getting somewhere?"

"I don't know about getting somewhere," she clarified, "but I would like to think so."

"If you're calling me and you haven't announced it to the world," he replied, "then you haven't found them. I really would like to find them."

"Me too. I guess I was just wondering if there was any way to know whether they went missing closer to Kelowna or farther away."

"How would I know that?" he asked in exasperation. "I only have the last known contact."

"Nobody saw them in West Kelowna? Nobody saw them in Merritt or anywhere around there, right?"

"Nope, not that I know of. We did stop in and talk to local people at the time. And nobody had seen them, but it was a small car that got good gas mileage. Therefore, Zeus would not have needed to stop anywhere in between."

She pondered that. "Did you have anybody else who searched with you?"

"I told you there were lots of us."

"I get that," she said. "I guess I'm just looking at anybody else I could talk to, anybody else who might know something."

"A couple guys are still around. I talked to them, told them how you're on the case. Most of them just thought it was a bit of a joke at this point. I agree that I think the chances are very slim. I just keep hoping that you do find something."

"That's the plan," she noted, "but I can't guarantee that we'll find anything very quickly."

"There are no guarantees," Roscoe muttered. "That's the one thing you learn with searches like this. When you lose a good friend, it just haunts you."

"Was he just coming up for a visit or was it business? Was there anything else going on?"

"I'm not sure what you mean by that. He wanted to talk to a couple buddies here about some business investments, maybe moving to Kelowna. I know he wasn't too thrilled about the idea of living and working in a small town like Kelowna, but he was really big on the idea of making money, so he may have had something in mind." Roscoe laughed.

"We were just kids back then, but we had such dreams. And then it just ends up becoming nothing, no answers, no nothing. It's still a shock. You don't know quite how to deal with it, and I think for years I just coasted. I didn't even know what to think. I kept going, putting one foot in front of the other because, well, what else can you do? Yet I really do need answers about Zeus," Roscoe repeated, his voice becoming hoarse.

"I'm doing what I can," she told him. "Do you come over to Richard's very often?"

"No," he replied. "I mean, every once in a while I do. I was over there just the other day. We were talking about you," he stated. "I was a little concerned that you were pretty fly-by-night about all this. Richard, on the other hand, was more concerned about you bringing more trouble and Japanese tourists to his corner of the world." Roscoe snickered. "I have to admit that, as much as I hope you do succeed, I sure wouldn't want to live next to you. That is a given."

"Right," she declared, with more feeling than she intended. "I know he doesn't always get along or appreciate that I'm here."

"Nope, he sure doesn't. We did talk about a bunch of the problems that he's had, but again there's only so much anybody can do. In your case, you're trying to help somebody, so I told him to have a bit of patience."

"You just went over alone?"

"Yeah, sure did. No reason to go over there with anybody. Richard doesn't know too many of my friends, and I don't know too many of his friends. Of course the one that he did know was someone who Richard didn't like at all and wouldn't have in his house." Roscoe's voice hardened. "So I guess that pretty well stopped me from bringing *any* friends over."

"Who was that?" she asked curiously.

"Jesse," he replied. "Jesse's a good bud, and he was there for me at the time I was searching for my friend Zeus."

"Did he know Zeus?"

"Jesse was one of the guys Zeus had talked to and wanted to see about going into business with. However, when Zeus didn't show up, well, ... Jesse did suggest at the time that maybe Zeus was just flaky and had taken off because he didn't want to do a business deal. However, I told Jesse that Zeus wasn't like that at all. He wasn't. He would want to come up and meet the guys in person before going into business with them, but that's just good sense on anybody's part. Everyone does their due diligence, before getting into bed together, so to speak."

She nodded. "Jesse was here the weekend that Zeus went missing?"

"Yep, sure was. Not everybody understood what I was going through, but Jesse did. He understood, and he was there for me. When you have somebody who stands by you when the trouble comes," Roscoe pointed out, "it's a friend you keep."

"It's also a friend who, even now, after all this time, can relate," she murmured. "What business were you guys getting into?"

Roscoe hesitated, and then he laughed. "It's stupid now," he admitted, "but we figured, since we're far enough away from the law, being in a small town like this, that we could probably grow some marijuana and sell it in Vancouver. Jesse would move it from point A to point B. Zeus wouldn't have to move here. Zeus could be the sales point on the other end in Vancouver, and he could make some money on the side. We would keep it pretty small to stay under the radar, but we all needed some bucks back then."

She winced at that. "But it was illegal way back then, right?"

"Sure," he agreed. "We were young and stupid. Just another reason why my brother didn't want anything to do with Jesse, as he was part of that scenario."

"So Richard knew what you were up to?" She added, "I can't imagine that that was his scene."

"Oh, it wasn't. He's way too Goody-Two-Shoes for that." And then he burst out laughing. "Richard is the moral one in the family."

She nodded. "He's always seemed that way to me."

"Yeah, sure is, but that was just an idea we had. Jesse's quite a gardener, and he figured he could grow a few plants," Roscoe said casually, but something was in his tone.

"You mean, a few *more* plants," she clarified, with a knowing smile. "He was probably already growing them quite nicely in his backyard, wasn't he?"

"Now, that he was," Roscoe admitted, with a laugh. "Not anymore though."

"No need to tell me that. It's legal everywhere now. I think you can grow four plants on your own, can't you?"

"Yeah, sure can," he confirmed. "I'm surprised you know about it."

"I read the news," she explained. "It's not really my scene, but, as you know, there's enough criminal activity around there to stay on top of the legislation."

"Of course you would keep track of that," he noted. "Anyway, back then, we planned to do a twenty-to-forty plant operation and figured that, if we grew it up here, and trucked it down to Vancouver, nobody ever stops you on the highway, so it would all be all good."

"Right, and do you think, looking back, that this partnership would have done well?"

"Nope, sure don't think so now," Roscoe shared. "At the time I was all for it. I thought we would make some money. Don't get me wrong. We wouldn't, you know, make enough money to go off and do anything with our lives, but it would have paid the bills and given us a step up. Then Zeus and Rosalina went missing. After that, I didn't have the heart for it either. It was almost as if we were being punished for all that nonsense."

"Ah." Doreen nodded. "I imagine that would have been pretty painful."

"It was. I felt terribly guilty for my involvement in bringing Zeus up here. I wanted him, me, and Jesse to work out the details."

"They hadn't met before?"

"No. ... Come to think of it, Zeus called me the night before. We talked on the phone all the time, but this time he really wanted to talk to Jesse."

"*Hmm*. Any reason why?"

"Nope, no clue. As far as I knew, he and Jesse hadn't had anything to do with each other, except for our phone calls back and forth. As we made plans back then, we had to do things pretty cryptically anyway," he noted. "So Zeus was coming up, just so we could lock things down. However, Zeus did sound a little bit upset, maybe somewhat angry on the phone."

"Could that have just been something his wife did to piss him off?"

"Yeah, you're not kidding. Rosalina did that on a regular

basis, which used to make Zeus really angry too."

Doreen winced at that. "Was he the kind to hit her?"

"Yeah, he was. He knocked her around a little bit, never very bad. Just enough to tune her up. You know?"

"Yeah, I do know," she stated, her voice sad. "I feel sorry for her."

"Yeah, me too. Believe me. We tried to get Zeus to stop it, and he used to get mad at us and told us to go get our own punching bags and that she was his."

"Wow, nice guy," she muttered in a caustic tone.

"He had some things to learn, but he wasn't all bad, and anytime I saw him get really angry, I would calm him down and tell him that he couldn't keep doing that. He would be good for a while, all remorseful, saying, he was getting his temper under control. But, you know, then he would go do it again."

Doreen didn't want to deal with how she thought about that.

"It doesn't change the search, does it?" Roscoe asked in alarm.

"No, no, because, if nothing else, Rosalina needs to be found too."

As he spoke, relief filled his voice. "I never even thought how people would react to that, but I guess most people don't think highly of anybody who beats up people."

"No, especially beating up women, his own wife," she declared in a harsh tone. "I'm particularly against that."

"Yeah? How do you feel about women beating up on men?" he asked in a disgruntled tone. "Do you ever worry about that?"

"Absolutely," she stated. "I hate to see anyone hurt someone else, but particularly when it's for a vulnerable member of society." She had to give herself a headshake. "Anyway, it doesn't affect the search. We still need to know what happened to them."

"Good. ... I'm really sorry. I probably shouldn't have told you."

"Obviously, to you, it's not a big deal."

"It's not a big deal," he argued, "because I did see him trying to work on it. I figured he was trying hard to become a better person, and, if we gave him enough support, he would."

"Of course he never had a chance to get better."

"And that makes me angry too."

"Good point," she noted, reminding herself that she shouldn't judge anybody either. "What about this Jesse person? Any chance I can talk to him?"

"Sure. I don't care. I've got his number. I'll give him a heads-up though."

"Okay, good, thanks." She quickly wrote down the number and asked, "Where does he live?"

"Not too far from where you are. His house is next to the Rec Center."

"Ah, right, that's not that far away."

"I've got the address here too somewhere. Just a sec." He came back a few minutes later and said, "Here it is." And he gave it to her.

She stared down at it, but she didn't recognize it. "Okay, I'll get in touch with him."

"I don't know why you would want to," Roscoe replied, "but, hey, if it puts your mind at rest over something, then fine. Just please do what you can to find these guys. I know Zeus may not have been an angel in your eyes, but he was working on it."

"And, in that case, it's too bad he didn't get a chance to

work on it a little longer," she said and quickly hung up.

It was something that she had to watch because her own personal judgment was at work here, and that wasn't good either. At the same time, she didn't want anything to put off the search for this couple, given a young boy had grown up without a family. Almost as if realizing that she had been talking and thinking about the mother, Bessie called.

"Any news?" she barked into the phone.

"No, not yet, but it's continuing to build as a case."

"That doesn't sound good."

"Maybe not, but I don't know if you heard a second body was found."

"Yes, Oscar. I did hear." She hesitated, "Do you think, … do you know that it was him? That Oscar killed my grandson? My Edwin?"

"The second body has been confirmed as Oscar. We don't necessarily know that Oscar killed Edwin," she replied calmly. "I also don't know that any of that's related to the original couple going missing."

"I'm not expecting you to find any answers on that, after so many years," Bessie muttered, her voice heavy. "Yet I really want answers on Edwin. Preferably before I die."

"We're doing our best. We're getting closer."

"Are you?" Bessie asked.

Such hope filled her voice that Doreen wasn't sure how to backtrack from it. She clarified, "Absolutely we're getting closer. I just don't have any final answers."

"Keep in touch," Bessie snapped. "I'm not getting any younger." And, with that, she hung up.

Doreen winced, knowing that she shouldn't have mentioned anything about getting closer in that case, but how did you not give people hope? Without hope, nothing was left. At least *with* hope, any number of answers were possible.

Chapter 24

DOREEN MADE HERSELF dinner and then sat outside down at the river with a cup of herbal tea. She pondered whether she should phone this Jesse guy. However, to *not* call was to leave a rock unturned. And that went against every fiber of her being. Finally she dialed the number, and, when he answered, she explained who she was.

"Oh, hey," Jesse replied. "Yeah, Roscoe told me that you might call." But his tone was definitely not friendly or happy.

"I know it's dragging up memories you would just as soon not revisit," she apologized.

He snorted. "I doubt it. Most people say things like that, but they don't really mean it. You would still call back, even if I tell you to go away. People continue to ask questions, even if we don't want to hear ourselves reliving the answers."

This guy was seriously unimpressed. She winced. "That's because I'm still trying to find these friends of Roscoe's."

"I never understood all the fuss. That guy was a loose cannon."

"Roscoe?"

"No, Zeus," he replied. "Every time I talked to him, I

got weird vibes from him. But Roscoe was gung-ho about Zeus. Not me. I just didn't trust Zeus."

"Interesting. I didn't hear any of that from Roscoe."

"Of course not. Why would you?" he asked. "What reason would Roscoe have to tell you that I didn't like Zeus."

"According to Roscoe, you wanted to go into business together with Zeus and Roscoe. So, why would you do that with somebody you don't like or trust? It's a fair question but for someone prickly already ..."

"That's why I wanted to meet Zeus. As far as Roscoe believed, Zeus was the one who wanted us to meet him, but I'm the one who requested the meeting. Just to make sure Zeus was okay."

"Zeus phoned Roscoe the night before, and he sounded a little bit wild and wanted to have a private talk."

"Private talk?" Jesse repeated.

"Yeah, that was my understanding."

"I don't know about any private talk," Jesse said. "I know Zeus wanted to talk, but I don't think it was intended to be without me."

"*Hmm.* I'll have to ask Roscoe about it."

"I don't think any of it matters now, does it? It's not as if Zeus ever showed up."

"Do you think that was on purpose?"

"At the time I certainly did. I figured he got scared, maybe nervous. I don't know. As I've said before, Zeus was flaky. For all I know, he was planning deals with multiple people."

"But Roscoe did tell me about your marijuana production plans."

He snorted at that. "Yeah, when we were young and stupid. That's nothing compared to the ideas this Zeus guy had."

"In what way?"

"Oh, I don't remember specifics. He was always coming up with fanciful ways to make money, and yet nobody really had any idea whether he was serious or not."

"Interesting. Do you remember what ideas?"

"Not really. I mean, he was working in a bank, and he would say things like, *What if we ripped off the bank? What if I went in one day, and I just opened up the safe deposit boxes and took everything?* We'd be like, *Dude, don't even talk about that. That's not funny.* Then Zeus would laugh, as if it were the funniest thing in the world."

"Oh, he was an interesting character then."

"Exactly," Jesse confirmed. "I wouldn't have been at all surprised if he hadn't stolen from the bank on the day they disappeared. He would have done it, if he thought he could get away with it."

She stared at the phone. "Then it gave him an excuse to disappear?"

"Exactly," Jesse said. "I did mention it to Roscoe, but he got pretty upset."

"Yeah, because that would have meant that his friend had taken off without him."

"More than that, his friend hadn't shared. Believe me. That's what this Zeus guy was like. Everything was about him. He used to beat that poor wife of his, just for saying the wrong thing. Smack her across the face at the table with Roscoe right there."

"Yet according to Roscoe, Zeus was attempting to work on improving his bad behavior."

"He would say he was. Roscoe would say Zeus was improving, but yet, hearing Roscoe speak about Zeus all the time, Zeus never did."

She hesitated for a moment, not sure what to ask. "Where were you supposed to meet him?"

"Originally we would meet him in Merritt. Why make the whole trip up there, when he could meet us partway? Then he decided he wanted to come for the weekend."

She stared at the phone. "That's the first I heard about the Merritt option."

"Because we ended up deciding to meet up here anyway. So it was no big deal."

"Interesting, and why Merritt?"

"It was a midway point—obviously still more driving on his part."

"Right, but then he wouldn't come up to see Roscoe?"

"Roscoe was the one pushing for Zeus to come spend time together, but Roscoe would go to Merritt with me regardless."

"When was the plan changed?"

"The day before, I think. Then Zeus decided that he would come up."

"Who made the change of plans?"

Jesse's voice got testy. "Why all the questions? God, you're being nosy. Zeus did, I think, but I can't remember. It didn't matter because we didn't meet them."

"No, I just wonder if they made it as far as Merritt."

"Why would they have?" he asked curiously.

She couldn't detect anything in his voice. "I don't know. I just wish I could pinpoint somewhere along that four-plus-hour drive, where it ended."

"You think we don't wish the same thing? We drove forever. We had a lot of coffee in Merritt, as we thought about places where they could have driven off."

"Did you focus on the Chilliwack to Merritt or the Merritt to Kelowna section?"

"I don't think we focused on anything. We just checked all of it. The passes were the biggest part. You know that you can go off the road and go down into a ravine in so many places along there. The trouble is, lots of skid marks still exist where other vehicles drove off the road. So it's not as if we were the only ones dealing with potential accident sites. ... Honestly I'm still not sure that Zeus didn't just disappear. And maybe I didn't give Roscoe the best effort that I had within me and just went along for the ride because, at the time, I was just like, you know, *The guy's booked it.* He probably stole some money from the bank, and that was it. But then nobody ever mentioned anything about him stealing anything, so maybe not."

"Interesting," she said.

"Now if you don't mind," Jesse declared, his voice turning harsh, "enough questions. If you find them, great. If you don't, well, that's just life. I don't know what happened to Zeus. I just know that I'm rather grateful I didn't end up going into business with him. I was pretty sure I wouldn't like the guy anyway, and it just saved me a lot of trouble trying to convince Roscoe that Zeus was bad news." And, with that, Jesse hung up on her.

She stared down at the phone, and an odd feeling rose in the back of her mind. She quickly emailed the Google Earth guys. And gave them a more specific area to search for. It was a long shot, and, outside of their time spent searching, it wasn't really wasting anything, but maybe it would have some results. At least she hoped so. By the time she headed to bed, she couldn't put the idea out of her mind.

Chapter 25

Saturday Morning …

WHEN DOREEN WOKE up the next morning, she was still restless after not having slept well.

She got up, headed downstairs and wondered, her mind once again going back over the same scenario. She picked up the phone, even though it was early, and phoned Roscoe.

"What now?" he asked curiously. "Surely there can't be anything new."

"No. I did talk to Jesse yesterday."

"Yeah, he told me how you pissed him off."

"Yeah, sorry about that," she muttered. "Asking questions tends to upset people."

"Whatever," Roscoe replied. "I presume you have more questions for me too."

"I just wondered how you guys planned to meet in Merritt?"

"Yeah, that was the first plan. Then his mother-in-law wanted them to take off for the weekend. So, I convinced him to come up here for a full visit. Zeus was stressed and upset, you know, worried about whether they should go into business or not." Roscoe continued. "So we wanted a chance to convince Zeus, and that meant a person-to-person meeting. I wanted him to come up long enough that we could have an impact."

"Right. When was the plan changed?"

"Oh, I don't know. The day before I think, when the mother-in-law said it was okay to keep the kid while they visited here. Zeus contacted me, telling me how they had the weekend off, and maybe he would come up. It's fuzzy. That was a long time ago."

"Who made all the arrangements?"

"I did normally, but Zeus and Jesse had been talking too. I know that they had some conversations back and forth. Zeus was having some phone problems. We didn't have cell phones back then. Zeus and Rosalina were supposed to stop at Merritt and phone us. I was working that day, so Zeus was supposed to phone Jesse and let us know that he had arrived in Merritt, but he never made it."

"So then you do have a better idea of where they went missing."

"Not really, because he wasn't good at phoning anyway," Roscoe shared. "If I'd known, if he always could be counted on to make his phone calls, then yes—but because he didn't, … I didn't want the whole search to be completely suspended or focused on one particular area. Not when I knew that the guy was bad for things like that. In theory, Zeus and Rosalina could have gone missing anywhere. When we didn't find them initially, we expanded the search area. But, of course, with him not making the phone call, then we didn't even look in that area. We just ended up focusing all the way down to Chilliwack because that made the most sense."

And it did make sense in a way, but it also made her a

little bit suspicious. "Okay. It helps, just not a whole lot."

"I told you," he said. "We searched for days and days and days, but we found nothing."

"Right, anyway that's what I was asking about." Just as he went to hang up, she added, "By the way, Jesse told me that he really believed that Zeus just took off, at least at the time."

"Yeah, he did. Jesse wasn't too sure about going into business with Zeus anyway, and I was trying to pull the deal together. They needed to be comfortable with each other because both of them were suspicious. Now I can look back and see that it was probably a good thing we didn't do a business deal together, but, at the time, it seemed like the end of the world that they went missing and that we couldn't pull this deal together."

"Of course," she agreed. "At the same time Jesse also wondered if Zeus had stolen a bunch of money from the bank and had just booked it."

Roscoe snorted at that. "That is giving Zeus more credit than I think he had in his brain. Zeus wasn't the most intelligent of the bunch. He wasn't all that great at putting plans together, and he certainly had a lot of get-rich-quick schemes, but he had no intention of going to jail."

"Which is why Jesse thinks Zeus just booked it, and nobody ever heard from them again."

"Rosalina wouldn't have left her son. Rosalina loved Edwin too much for that. No way," Roscoe declared.

"Would Zeus have done something to Rosalina in order to book it?"

An ugly silence came on the other end, and Roscoe slowly let out his breath. "Wow, you don't pull your punches, do you?"

"No. When people go missing like this, all kinds of ugly scenarios come to light."

More silence came, much longer than she was comfortable with, but Roscoe finally replied, "I can't say no—because of the way he treated her. I wanted him to be a better person and to not beat her around like that, but he hit her too much. Even if he'd hit her on the road and had knocked her out or had killed her, I ... I don't know what he would have done. It's possible he would have ditched her on the side of the road and then taken off, but I just don't know," he muttered. "And now that you've put that thought in my brain, I'll do nothing but think about it."

"I'm sorry. I'm certainly not trying to set off a chain reaction here, but obviously we have to consider all avenues."

"That wasn't an avenue anybody brought up before," he snapped. "It's ugly."

"Yes, it's ugly, but you've got a guy who beats up his wife. She's got a new baby. She may not be in great shape. She could be feeling particularly vulnerable. She maybe didn't want to make this trip in the first place. You don't know all the circumstances that they were going through, and it's quite possible that maybe she had to go for a pee break or something, and it set off Zeus."

"She always had to do that, and he was complaining about it before they ever left," Roscoe noted, his voice heavy. "God, I hope you're wrong."

"I hope I am too," she said. "It still would mean that Zeus managed to disappear, and nobody ever found out anything about him—which doesn't sound like Zeus was really somebody who could do that very well."

"No, no," Roscoe said, his voice gaining in strength. "That was something I always could count on. He didn't have that brainpower." He stopped. "However, if he had friends to help, Zeus might have tried that."

"Meaning, friends who weren't you?"

"That's another aspect I don't want to even think about either," he replied bitterly. "I defended him heavily against people who were much less than accepting about it all. But everybody's excuse or suggestion so far was something that I couldn't come to terms with. I didn't think Zeus would have done any of those things—until now."

"Until I brought up him killing his wife?"

"Yeah, because that ... unfortunately I could see happening." He cursed. "I wish you hadn't called." And, without anything further to add, he hung up on her.

She should be used to people hanging up on her, and, sure enough, she had done plenty of hanging up on others herself. Still, at this point in time, she knew that this upset feeling was more because Roscoe didn't want to face something that she had brought up versus an actual insult to her.

She sat here, wondering what she should do for her next step and if she should even bring this up with Mack. When her phone rang again, it was the mother.

"I just talked to Roscoe," Bessie began.

"Oh? I did too," Doreen confirmed.

"Yeah, he's wondering right now just how bad the abuse was. I told him how bad it was. And it was bad."

"I'm sorry," Doreen said. "I made a suggestion to him about a possible scenario that needed to be considered. I didn't say it definitely happened, just that it was possible."

"He told me." Bessie's voice was heavy. "You've no idea how many times I tried to get Rosalina to leave Zeus."

"I'm sorry," Doreen whispered. "It's got to be hard, and I'm not trying to bring up all that pain. But, with your grandson saying that he'd had an idea what happened, … it just made me realize that there could be so many other circumstances surrounding what could have gone on."

"And you're right," Bessie agreed. "It never occurred to me that that would be one of them. Zeus really wasn't the guy to pull off something like that though."

"What did Roscoe want to know?"

"Just whether Zeus had any other friends down here who could have helped him with any of his get-rich schemes, whether there was any hint that the bank was missing any money, anything along that line. I didn't have any answers for him. He's pretty upset right now though, so whatever you did, you shook him up pretty good. I may be upset, but I'm not against that. We need to shake some things up."

"I am going to be upset if this theory doesn't do any good," Doreen admitted. "I'm not here to throw suspicion or to make people accuse each other of wrongdoings. I'm trying to get to the bottom of the mystery. And, by getting to the bottom of it, I have to ask the hard questions."

"And, for that reason alone, I'm glad that you did," Bessie stated. "Maybe something will rise up from this." And, with that, she said, "I'll talk to you later." And hung up.

Doreen stared down at the phone, wondering at the morning that had started so crazy. And it was crazy. Still, she also had several different hypotheses coming to the surface. She wondered if any of Mack's other law enforcement buddies had been involved in the search and rescue and may have had any further ideas.

When Mack called a couple hours later, he asked, "Are you okay?"

"Yeah, I'm okay," she said. "I've been trying to line up all the ideas that are coming through right now about the missing vehicle from twenty-five years ago."

"How many ideas could there possibly be?" Mack asked. "The vehicle likely went off the road at a critical juncture."

"Maybe," she hedged. "No way to know, is there?"

"Nope, not until we find their bodies. Even then, after all this time, answers will be a little slim on the ground."

She sighed. "I upset Richard's brother with some questions, leading to one of my suggestions."

"Oh? What's the theory that you put forth?" She gave it to him, and he muttered, "*Ooh*, that's an interesting one. You should take that a step further. If they had a fight in the vehicle, that could have been enough to cause the accident."

"Right? I was thinking of that too, but I didn't want to bring it up, not after I upset Roscoe with that first theory."

"No, and, as you told the mother, asking the hard questions is what we do, and people don't always like it."

"No, they sure don't. I guess I'm also wondering if anybody did go meet them because that's another option."

"You're talking about them being murdered?"

"Yeah, I am," she said. "I just don't know who could have done something like that."

"Got it," Mack replied. "I just wanted to tell you that we ID'd the store where the listening devices were sold, but we don't have an ID of the buyer. He paid cash for them, of course. No inside store cameras to get a visual."

"And, of course, all you got was something like, five-ten, brown hair, slim build."

He chuckled. "Which is the same description you gave us of Richard's intruder."

"Exactly. What I do know is that he wasn't old, Zeus's age now, like mid-fifties or thereabouts. Yet I could be wrong. A lot of people carry themselves in a younger manner, and some young people carry themselves in an older manner."

"And, when you're in a panic, like running, you also have no idea how people will react when they're under stress. Old people can run pretty-darn fast when they need to."

She nodded. "I wanted to take a walk up to the Rec Center and go past this Jesse guy's house just because."

"Just because why?"

"Because he got angry at me," she noted.

"Okay, so because you got some guy pissed off with all your questions, you now feel you should go into his personal space and see how that goes?"

"I don't like the way you said that," she murmured. "You know that seeing the area helps me to put things into perspective, especially when I get a view of where they live, how they live, things like that."

"Right," Mack muttered. "Please don't get involved in any more confrontations. And, if this Jesse guy doesn't want to talk, he doesn't want to talk."

"Got it," she said.

Chapter 26

DOREEN MADE TOAST, finished off her coffee, and gathered the animals.

"We can walk this time," she declared, hooking up both Goliath's and Mugs's leashes. It was a beautiful day and a little cool, so she grabbed a sweater and headed out in the direction of Jesse's address. It was pretty close to her and to the Recreation Center. Also some beautiful fields were up there, so she and Mugs could go grab some sticks and play. At that, she remembered the stick kept as evidence, and she texted Mack, asking if he had the forensic results.

He sent back a text. **Yes, nothing found.**

"Of course not," she muttered.

As she headed toward the Rec Center, she pondered the circumstances of the two most recent murders. When her phone rang, she answered it.

"Hey, this is Edwin's cousin, Sylvee. I spoke to you earlier."

"Oh hey," Doreen replied. "Yes, I remember. What's up?"

"Look. I found his email address, but I don't have a password to get in."

"Right, the police probably want that too."

"I also wondered if you had any ideas. You seem to have all these tricks."

"Did you send me something?"

"I did. There's a journal of his that I was trying to figure out what it meant. It wasn't necessarily in code or anything." She laughed. "Yet it's not very clear. I didn't understand it. There were some notes about a Roscoe and some other people."

"You already mailed it?" Doreen asked, her voice sharp.

"Yep, you should get it today or tomorrow."

"Perfect," Doreen said, with a smile.

"Why? Does that name mean anything to you?"

"Yeah, it does. It really does."

"Oh good. I'll email you Edwin's username for his Gmail account, and you can see if you can get into it yourself. Honestly this whole thing is pretty upsetting. I would like to not have a whole lot to do with it."

"That's fine. Are you okay if I give the journal to the police?"

"Absolutely," Sylvee replied. "That's probably the ones I should be calling in the first place but, well ..."

"It's fine," Doreen noted. "As long as you've given it to me, and I can send it to the police, I will. I do know somebody there who will help."

"Oh good," Sylvee muttered. "I really hope you get to the bottom of this."

When the phone call was over, Doreen was almost at Jesse's address. She stopped outside, studying the exterior. It was a really nice house. Quite a nice house, as in surprisingly good for him. And yet she had no reason to be suspicious or judgmental, considering what his financial situation had been back then. Just because he'd been a broke criminal back then didn't mean he hadn't turned his life around. Still, heading down that pathway was hard to turn around. She quickly phoned Roscoe again. "Hey, did you ever have anything to do with Zeus's son?"

"No, I didn't. He was a toddler back then, under his grandma's care. And Bessie sure wouldn't have liked me, not as Zeus's friend and all. However, Edwin did call me a couple times over the later years, and it was always to ask about his parents' deaths, and I didn't know what to tell him. So I would talk to him, but it's not as if we really kept in touch."

"Right, so did you know anything about him looking into his parents' deaths?"

"No, sure don't, but I'm not surprised," he replied. "When you think about it, there's always that thought in the back of everybody's head as to what really happened to them."

"Okay, and what about Jesse? You think Edwin talked to him?"

"It's possible he called him too, but I don't know. I wouldn't get in touch with him right now. He's still cranky."

"Yeah, ya think?" she quipped and laughed. "I'll leave him alone." As she studied the house in front of her, sure enough, Jesse stepped out, looked at her, and asked, "Can I help you?"

She looked over at him, smiled, and replied, "Hey, I'm Doreen."

He crossed his arms, leaned against his door, and asked, "What are you doing here?"

"Oh, I just got off the phone with Edwin's cousin. Did Edwin ever talk to you?"

"Yeah, a couple times over the years. Why?" he asked, glaring at her.

"Apparently he was getting pretty excited because he thought he had solved his parents' disappearance."

At that, he stared at her. "I don't know what you're talking about. Now you're starting to harass me."

"I didn't say anything harassing," she argued in astonishment. "I just asked if you had talked to Edwin."

"You seem to be accusing me of something I didn't do." He glared at her. "You keep your mouth shut." And he turned and headed back inside.

Doreen added, "Even if it does look that way, it still doesn't mean you had anything to do with their deaths."

He turned to look back at her and nodded. "Good, because I didn't."

"Did you see them there? You know that I'll go to Merritt, and I'll talk to the locals."

"Doesn't matter whether you do or not."

"Good," she said. "In that case, you won't mind if I ask them about you and show pictures of you from twenty-five years ago."

He stood there, his hands on his hips. "You're nothing but an interfering old bat. Do you think we didn't ask time and time again?" he muttered.

"I'm not old, and I'm not a bat," she stated calmly. As she turned toward home, she called back, "Seems you're trash-talking because you are running scared."

He just went inside and slammed the front door.

Chapter 27

BY THE TIME Doreen got home, she knew that Mack would be angry with her again. She should be used to it, but still it was not the easiest thing to deal with. She sighed as she walked up to the back door, just to hear her front doorbell ring. With Mugs barking like crazy, she raced forward to see a delivery truck, and the uniformed guy held out a parcel for her. She had to sign for it. As she took it inside, she realized this was the package she'd been expecting from Sylvee.

"Edwin, let's see what you left behind."

She put on the teakettle and opened the parcel on the kitchen table. There were just a few notes, with the name *Roscoe* and just beside it was scribbled *Jess*, who she figured was *Jesse*.

As she sat there, she noted Edwin had jotted down disjointed bits and pieces. It had probably made sense to him at the time but not to anybody else. Yet, as she studied it, she could see an interesting pattern. And, of course, there was a mention of Merritt. What stood out was a name followed by a phone number. She immediately dialed the number.

When a man with an old cranky voice answered, she

said, "I'm looking for Horace."

"Yes, speaking to him," he grumped.

"Ah, my name is Doreen, and I'm looking into the death of a young man you spoke to."

Silence came from on the other end.

"His name was Edwin, and he was looking into a vehicle that disappeared between Chilliwack and Kelowna many years ago."

"Twenty-five years ago," he claimed, with a snort. "Yeah, I remember. I talked to him. He was pretty pushy too, same as you."

She winced. She'd just got started. "Edwin was recently murdered," she said. "So we're all trying to backtrack through his life to figure out what could possibly have gone wrong and what he was doing that maybe pissed somebody off."

"If he was looking into that disappearance so many years ago, that would have done it. Maybe you should take note."

"Can you tell me what questions he asked you and what information you gave him?"

"He asked me about whether his parents ever showed up at the coffee shop, and they did," he stated, "but so did somebody else. The three of them were sitting there for a good half hour, waiting for somebody else to join them. They said that they had stopped in Chilliwack and had called to arrange this meeting because they decided they would take a few days to themselves and not come to Kelowna. Therefore, they wanted to meet in Merritt."

"Oh, interesting." Plus not what Jesse or Roscoe had divulged.

"Yeah."

"So did Roscoe meet them?"

"I don't know who met up with the couple," he snapped.

"Did you know who they expected to meet?"

"No, I don't."

"Did you know what vehicle the guy they met with drove there?"

"Yeah, a truck. An old Ford truck, big old thing," Horace muttered. "Kind of a pale green-blue, but it was a big tank of a thing."

"Right, and you didn't hear anybody say any names?"

"I just heard the name Roscoe."

"But were they talking about a Roscoe or were they talking *to* a Roscoe?"

The old man hesitated. "It's been a long time ago. I don't know."

"Okay, that's fine. Anything else that Edwin asked?"

"Yeah, he wanted to know if I could recognize someone in some pictures, but my eyes aren't very good now," he shared, "so I don't see too well."

"Did you own the restaurant where those three people met some twenty-five years ago?"

"I did, long ago. Had it for a lot of years but not sure I owned it then. I got pretty sick back then. Ended up in the hospital. Not sure I was ever questioned about that missing couple before. Although I was more concerned with how quickly my health was sliding at the time. Plus I'd just lost my sister. I was trying to sell the restaurant around that time too, I think, so might have told everyone to just eff off," he grumped. "Anyway that's all I had to say." He stopped, then quickly added, "That young man's dead?"

"Yes, and he had just been killed after others heard him telling people that he figured he knew what happened to his parents."

"Never good to do that," Horace said. "Good way to get yourself killed."

Chapter 28

LONG AFTER THEY ended the call, Doreen had to wonder about that. She looked down at Edwin's notes and brought up Gmail, looking at the sign-in page to his account. Doreen considered what Edwin would use as a password. What would he possibly make into an email password? She tried all kinds of variations of his name, and then she tried his parents' names. And, sure enough, there popped up his emails. She shook her head at that.

"We're such creatures of habit, and we're so sentimental," she murmured.

She wrote down the password and changed it—in case anybody else was trying to get into it. Then she sorted through his emails. And, sure enough, there was one. One that made her heart freeze. As she sat, staring at it, she picked up the phone and called Mack. "Mack, you need to come over here right now."

"Doreen, I have a job to do," he replied, with exaggerated patience.

"Yeah, well, maybe, but I know who killed Edwin. I know who killed him, and I know what happened to the vehicle twenty-five years ago. You really need to come now."

And, with that, she quickly forwarded him emails, copying herself so that she had them for safekeeping.

When hands grabbed the back of her neck, she let out a squawk. And realized that she was inside, but Mugs was lying in the backyard, sprawled out in the garden. Goliath was on the patio table, and Thaddeus was sleeping in a rosebush.

"Not a word," said the man behind her. "I don't want you alerting your animals, or I'll have to kill them too."

She nodded ever-so-slightly, knowing the kitchen door was still ajar. He forced her upright, and she turned ever-so-slowly, already knowing who it was. "Hello, Jesse."

The hand squeezed even tighter against her throat.

"How did you figure it out?" he asked.

She sighed. "Not sure I've figured out all of it yet. Still, what I do know is that you met Edwin's parents in Merritt, and either things blew up or you planned it ahead of time. I don't know, but you ended up either running them off the road or killing them, dumping their bodies and their vehicle off the road, somewhere close to Merritt. Then you came home and pretended to join in the search. And somehow enough money found its way into your hands to help you along in life."

"I don't know about that," he grumbled, shoving her back into the chair and glaring at her.

She looked at the small black revolver in his hand and asked, "Is this the one you used to kill Edwin, by any chance?"

He nodded. "Because, just like you, he was nosy."

"You killed his parents," she declared, her voice hard, while staring at him. "Then you used Roscoe here to access his brother's yard, so that you could listen in on my conversations to see if I was getting anywhere."

"You weren't getting anywhere, so it was safe, but then you found the listening device. So I realized things were getting a little bit too dicey."

"At which point, you had to kill Oscar."

"Sure, because he also started to ask questions," Jesse noted. "I just figured you wouldn't find anything out, but look at you," he spat. "You think you've got it all figured out, don't you?"

"Not all of it," she admitted, "but I think I probably got the bulk of it figured out."

"That you did. Unfortunately." He glared at the small kitchen. "I wanted Zeus to completely walk away from the business deal. I didn't like the guy right from the beginning, and, when I got there, he was in a pissy mood, so full of himself. So, when I followed him out to his car afterward, I told him that he didn't need to continue to Kelowna. That I wouldn't go into business with him. That I didn't like him. That he was a two-bit con artist. And then his wife piped up and said something snarky. So Zeus turned and belted her one. I just saw red. I turned around, and I picked up a rock, and I pounded his head with it." Jesse groaned, pushing his hat off his head. "But she was out, unconscious, and so was he. I just thought, you know, what a perfect way to end this. So I got us all in their vehicle, and I drove it up the road, parked it on the edge, with the brake off. Then I got out and just pushed it over an embankment, and it just soared into the ravine. Nobody will ever find that thing."

"Then what? You just walked back to your vehicle?"

"Yeah, but I was carrying something that I'd found in his vehicle. Remember when I told you that Zeus probably stole a bunch of money from the bank and had to escape? I don't know where he stole the money from, but I found ten grand in one of his bags." Jesse laughed hysterically. "Believe me. I put that to good use. I built up my marijuana business, and I ran drugs back and forth myself for quite a few years. I didn't have to share the profits that way."

He continued. "Never selling enough marijuana to raise suspicions, just enough to keep myself in change and to build up a nest egg slowly. Then I could do okay. Finally I bought a legitimate business and have been doing great ever since. But no way I would ever have that truth be known."

"Yeah, because just imagine how Roscoe would feel when he found out his best friend killed his other best friend and betrayed him." She glared at Jesse. "Some friend you were. I suppose you didn't let Roscoe into the marijuana business either, did you?"

"No, not after Zeus failed to show up. … Roscoe spent weeks and weeks and weeks looking for Zeus. But I found a perfect spot just outside of the town limits. Couldn't be seen from the highway. They're still there too. But Roscoe's searching all day every day was pathetic. I knew I couldn't trust him at that point. Bloody bleeding heart. With the 10K seed money, I didn't need anyone else. I would just save the profits, and I wouldn't split any of that. And Roscoe would have needed an explanation of where the start-up money came from. And that, well, I couldn't give him."

"But how did Zeus come up with that money?"

Jesse nodded. "Yeah, if he was coming into our business deal, he was supposed to bring ten Gs. I had heard the bank where he worked had been robbed at the time and a suspect killed. So, at first, I thought Zeus was the dead robber. However, the dead guy's name was released soon afterward. And those stupid cops thought he was acting solo. Then I thought, well, Zeus would need help with this robbery, so surely his partner knew enough not to trust Zeus to handle all that money. Therefore, the dead robber must have had the money on him—or at least half of it. Either way, I just knew Zeus didn't have it. Still, it nagged at me, so I looked for it when I was putting them into the car. Color me surprised when I found out that he did have the cash. I admit I was shocked."

She looked at him and asked, "Now what? You really expect to just shoot me in my own kitchen and get away with it?"

He hesitated. "I didn't think that far. This is out of control now."

"You can't just expect to kill me and get away with it. A lot of people here know what I'm doing. I've already emailed all kinds of people about the info that Edwin had collected."

"That punk kid, he's the one who blew this up. He kept bugging me and poking and prodding and said he'd found somebody in Merritt to talk to. I couldn't even figure out who it would have been, and back then I wouldn't have had a name. I wouldn't have had any way to track them down. They didn't see me hit Zeus," he said. "They just saw me there in the café, meeting him and Rosalina. That meeting nobody had known about but me. Zeus had phoned me from Chilliwack, and I arranged to meet him there alone, knowing Roscoe was expecting them to show up in Kelowna hours later. I needed to see what Zeus was like as a person. I went in. I had coffee, and then I basically walked out to talk to him because I didn't want anybody around, but then he hit her."

"And instead of saving her, you ended up killing her?"

"Sure. I mean, what was I supposed to do? Tell her that I killed her husband? No, it was a perfect opportunity to just get rid of something I didn't want to deal with." He shrugged. "So I did."

"And why did you have to kill Oscar too?" Doreen asked.

Jesse shook his head. "He was threatening me too, all in the name of his good buddy Edwin. They were both accusing me of killing his parents. So I killed Edwin, laid him out in the park—right where Oscar runs every day. That should have been a warning to the kid, but not Oscar. What did he do? He called me, threatening me, saying that if I was the one who killed Edwin, Oscar would be coming for me. But when I threatened to kill his girlfriend and then blame Oscar for both Edwin's and her deaths? Yeah, suddenly Oscar was all for hiding Edwin's body instead. What a wimp."

She nodded. "Yeah, but you still didn't get a chance to move Edwin's body, not before it was found in the park. ... So now what?" she asked, bringing the conversation back to him and his gun in her kitchen.

"Won't you try to waste more time so your boyfriend can come and save the day?" he asked in a mocking tone.

"No, because you'll probably shoot him too, and I don't want that."

He stared at her in disgust. "What's with all these love-sick people who are looking after others?" he asked. "I never had anybody in my life, all the years I was growing up. Nobody cared."

"I'm sorry, but maybe they already knew what you were like," she murmured. "You're not the kind to help anybody else out, are you? Look what you did to poor Zeus's wife."

He snorted. "Doesn't make a bit of difference," he snapped. "Look at your dog out there. What kind of a watchdog is that?"

"One who's tired," she said, with a note of humor. "I can't say we've been sleeping all that well."

"You won't have to worry about it anymore now," Jesse quipped.

At that, Thaddeus walked into the kitchen. "Thaddeus is here. Thaddeus is here."

He stared at the bird. "Good God, a talking bird."

"Yeah and a character too," she noted, with a smile. "One full of love, so I would appreciate it if you don't hurt him or the other animals."

He looked at her. "I got no reason to kill a bird. What do you think I am?"

She just stared at him, not sure she should tell him. She looked past Jesse over at the fry pan, a big cast-iron thing that was Mack's favored pan whenever he was here to cook. It was the only weapon close enough that she saw, and, even then, she wasn't sure how much of a weapon it would be. She got up.

Jesse said, "Hey, hey, hey, sit down."

"This pan is too close to the edge, and, if it falls, it'll hurt the animals."

He stared at her. "You do know I'm holding a gun on you, right?"

"Sure. How can I mistake that?"

"I'm just wondering." Jesse frowned at her. "You sure don't act like I'll kill you."

"I know I'm not acting like a victim," she replied. "People tend to get upset over that."

"You act like this is a commonplace occurrence."

"It is, kinda," she confirmed. "It's getting a little boring, like too much, too often."

"What are you talking about?"

"I've had many people attack me. So there's cameras all

over the place, but you won't really care about that after you've taken me down."

"No, I won't, but thanks for the warning."

She shrugged. "It's not as if I can do anything to stop you."

"No, you got that right." Jesse gave her an eye roll. "God, you're weird."

"Hey, be nice," she muttered.

He stared at her. "Why?"

"Why not?" she asked. "It won't hurt you to be nice for a change. You obviously have won. Got their money, got rid of Zeus, Rosalina, then Edwin, Oscar, and now maybe me."

She grabbed the cast-iron fry pan and pushed it little bit farther onto the stove.

He stepped up and said, "Don't try anything funny."

"I won't."

Thaddeus hopped up onto the table and squawked, "Police. Police."

Jesse turned, startled, and she whipped up the cast-iron pan and smacked him hard on the side of the head. He dropped like a rock.

In the distance she heard Mack screaming, "Doreen, Doreen, are you there? Doreen?"

And she turned to face him, as he barreled into the kitchen and stared, coming to a skittering stop, noting Jesse was out cold.

"About time you got here," she snapped, with feeling.

He opened his arms, and she raced into them. Mack muttered, "At least you called me."

"If you'd been a little bit faster," she said, "you would have saved me, but, on the other hand, I have to say, that cast-iron pan was a great buy."

Chapter 29

DOREEN'S KITCHEN WAS full. Her deck and patio areas were full. It seemed as if people were everywhere. And animals! Not only had Mugs been taking advantage of the extra visitors to con some additional ear scratches and pets but Thaddeus was holding court on Mack's shoulder and stealing bits of pizza when he could. Goliath, well, he was sitting disdainfully off to the side, watching. Still, he was close and hadn't disappeared, so Doreen would take that as a good sign.

As for Jesse, he gave up the location of the vehicle where he'd left poor Zeus and Rosalina, and the police had promptly taken him away. Search and rescue had been dispatched to Merrit and had already confirmed they'd found the missing vehicle. Recovery operations were in progress. Doreen had managed a quick phone call to Bessie, before the crowd grew bigger, especially after the beer and pizza had arrived. Bessie had broken down into tears and gratitude to have the mystery of her missing family finally solved. All in all it was a great day.

Mack handed her a piece of pepperoni pizza and said, "It's got pineapple on it."

She stared at him, looked at the combination, and shuddered. "You forced ham and pineapple on me before," she muttered, "and I managed that, but I don't know about pepperoni and pineapple."

"Try it," he suggested.

She opened her mouth, and he popped in the corner of the slice, and she bit down. She contemplated it and then grimaced. "Nope, ham and pineapple maybe. I don't think I can do this one though."

He smiled, nodded, patted her hand. "You want more coffee?"

She shook her head. "I am fine, you know," she muttered, as she looked around at everybody. "I get that you're all here to make sure I'm okay."

"We're all here because it seemed like a good idea, and it just happened," he muttered. "Besides, everybody's more than happy when two murders are solved."

"Four," she corrected.

He nodded. "I get it, four, and now we have an area that we can focus our search on."

Just then her phone rang. She answered, "Hello?"

"Hey. This is Doreen, right?"

Everybody around her calmed down.

"Yep, this is Doreen."

"We followed the information you gave us last time about searching closer to Merritt," her caller explained, "and I think we found the car." There was a note of excitement in his voice.

"Excellent," Doreen cried out. "I've got a roomful of cops here right now. We can send search and rescue down to check it out. Do you have locations for us?"

He replied, "I've got GPS, and I've got navigational directions, latitude and longitude. So I'll put that into an email, and you'll let us know what you find, right?"

"Absolutely," she said, "and thank you so much."

She turned and beamed at Mack. "Hopefully this will clinch it. We have a possible location for Zeus and Rosalina's vehicle."

"Let's hope so." He turned to his captain.

The captain pulled out his phone and declared, "I'll call search and rescue." And, with that, he headed toward the river for some quiet and talked to them. When he came back, he said, "A vehicle is taking a look right now. A couple guys were on the original search team way back then, and they want to have a look themselves."

She nodded. "Good news either way. I hope it's the right vehicle, but if not …"

Mack gripped her hand and said, "Then we'll keep looking. Don't you worry."

She sighed. "That one turned out very odd."

Almost as soon as she got the words out, Richard popped his head over the fence.

"What is this? A party?"

And, sure enough, another chair was slammed against the fence, and Roscoe's head popped over the top. He stared at Doreen. "Jesse?"

She nodded slowly. "I'm so sorry."

His face worked, as he realized whatever he'd already heard was now true. "Good God." He looked over at the crowd of people gathered here and said, "Wow, you really do get a lot of support, don't you?"

She nodded. "I do." She slowly walked over to the fence, Mack at her side. "I'm really sorry about your friends. Both of them."

Roscoe nodded.

She told him what Jesse had told her about not wanting to go into business with Zeus and how it all came down.

"I can't believe it." Roscoe rubbed his face. "All this time I wondered how he'd been so lucky that he was doing so well, and I wasn't," he muttered. "And, sure enough, he'd gone into business, stealing the stake my friend had stolen, going into business for himself." Roscoe shook his head. "You just never really know people, do you?" He looked at her sadly.

"I'm so sorry," she said again. She looked back at the food and drinks and asked the two brothers, "You want some beer and pizza?"

Roscoe's face lit up. "Absolutely."

"You have to take the cops along with it though," she teased.

Roscoe looked around at the yard. "Are they all cops?" he asked in a low voice.

She nodded. "All of them."

He winced. At that, Mack turned and snagged a box that had half a pizza in it, grabbed two cans of beer, and returned to the fence. "Here. Have it on your side of the fence, and then you can at least eat in peace."

At that, Richard grabbed the box, Roscoe grabbed the beers, and they mumbled their thanks. Then both heads disappeared behind the fence.

She looked at Mack and raised her eyebrows.

He wrapped an arm around her shoulders and said, "Hey, it's all good."

She smiled. "No, it's better than good. It's great."

And he bent down and kissed her.

Epilogue

Mid-October, Sunday ...

DOREEN WAS WATCHING a video on the internet the next day, with Mack stretched out on the patio beside her. "Do you guys have drones at work?" she asked.

He looked over at her. "We don't own any at the police department."

She nodded. "I always thought they would be kinda cool."

"They're more of a headache for us. You know that people take pictures they're not supposed to with that stuff."

"Oh, I never thought about that." Doreen looked up at the sky. "That would be awfully irritating."

"Yeah. I keep expecting somebody to start taking pictures of you, now that you're so famous."

"Oh, that would be terrible," she murmured, with an eye roll. "Somebody local has bought one, and he's put his videos up on the internet. I don't even know how I got this video," she noted, "but it was recommended to me, and it's going over some local properties, and the view is really cool."

"In what way?" he asked, as he sat up and faced her.

"Look at this area."

"Oh, that's Southeast Kelowna," he noted. "I remember that area. It's really beautiful up there."

"Do they have water problems?"

"Yeah, too much water."

She stared at him. "Seriously? Because this garden is xeri-scaped."

He frowned at her and asked, "What the heck does that mean?"

"It's low-water gardening, so everything is done with desert plants, and you don't really need to water it at all. There's no grass. There's no greenery. It's just desert gardening."

"Interesting," he muttered. "Still, people don't necessarily want to water a garden. Plus lots of people out there have orchards and other kinds of water necessities. However, we do have droughts too."

She nodded and then pointed. "Look at this snapshot." The drone captured a really wide view of the garden. "It's beautiful."

"Of course that whole look is very specific," Mack noted. "I can't say it's my taste."

"Maybe not," she agreed.

He frowned, as he studied it. "Let me see that." He leaned in closer. "I know that property. I was up there a couple years back. The owner of the property just up and disappeared."

"What do you mean, *up and disappeared*?" she asked.

"He went to work but never showed up there or else-where again. His vehicle was found down the road nearby, but no sign of him was ever discovered. No bank accounts were touched. No credit cards used. He was just gone."

"You think he booked it, maybe getting away from the

wife and kids?"

Mack shrugged. "He's a missing person, but still it's possible."

She eyed him, raised one eyebrow, and gave him a fat smile.

He shook his head. "No, don't say it."

"Why not?" she protested. "Just think. I've got the perfect title for it."

"No, no, and no," Mack declared. "What title could you even come up with for that scenario?"

She proudly said, "X'd, … as in *X'd in the Xeriscape*."

He closed his eyes slowly and moaned. "Okay, now that's a groaner."

"Yep, but it works, doesn't it? So that's next." She patted his hand and added, "Just think. It's a cold case, so I won't have to interfere in your life or your work at all."

He shook his head. "And it would be just my luck that it will turn out to be the exact opposite, and you'll trample all over one of my cases again."

"Nope, you don't have anything to do with this one. You already were there to investigate. You did your thing. It's a cold case. Now it's my turn. *X'd in the Xeriscape*'s mine."

He groaned, and she burst out laughing.

This concludes Book 23 of Lovely Lethal Gardens:
Whispers in the Wisteria.
Read about X'd in the Xeriscape: Lovely Lethal Gardens,
Book 24

Lovely Lethal Gardens: X'd in the Xeriscape (Book #24)

Riches to rags. ... Some people make plans. ... Some people change themt, ... and it's chaos in the end!

Doreen loves gardens, all kinds of them. In the Okanagan, situated at the tip of the desert, water-frugal gardening makes sense. When Doreen sees a lovely xeriscaped garden from a drone video, she's fascinated. When Mack mentions a mystery surrounding the property, she is mesmerized.

Getting the details, however, is no easy feat. That's because there aren't many. But digging in and asking questions is something Doreen and her clan are good at, and it doesn't take long to delve into the mystery in a big way, ... much to Corporal Mack Moreau's disgust.

Making a nuisance of herself might work sometimes, but too often it backfires. This time is no exception, ... and no way, once Doreen is on this case, can she ever let go …

Find Book 24 here!
To find out more visit Dale Mayer's website.
https://geni.us/DMSXeriscape

Author's Note

Thank you for reading Whispers in the Wisteria: Lovely Lethal Gardens, Book 23! If you enjoyed the book, please take a moment and leave a short review.

Dear reader,

I love to hear from readers, and you can contact me at my website: www.dalemayer.com or at my Facebook author page. To be informed of new releases and special offers, sign up for my newsletter or follow me on BookBub. And if you are interested in joining Dale Mayer's Reader Group, here is the Facebook sign up page.
http://geni.us/DaleMayerFBGroup

Cheers,
Dale Mayer

About the Author

Dale Mayer is a *USA Today* best-selling author, best known for her SEALs military romances, her Psychic Visions series, and her Lovely Lethal Garden cozy series. Her contemporary romances are raw and full of passion and emotion (Broken But … Mending, Hathaway House series). Her thrillers will keep you guessing (Kate Morgan, By Death series), and her romantic comedies will keep you giggling (*It's a Dog's Life*, a stand-alone novella; and the Broken Protocols series, starring Charming Marvin, the cat).

Dale honors the stories that come to her—and some of them are crazy, break all the rules and cross multiple genres!

To go with her fiction, she also writes nonfiction in many different fields, with books available on résumé writing, companion gardening, and the US mortgage system. All her books are available in print and ebook format.

Connect with Dale Mayer Online

Dale's Website – www.dalemayer.com
Twitter – @DaleMayer
Facebook Page – geni.us/DaleMayerFBFanPage
Facebook Group – geni.us/DaleMayerFBGroup
BookBub – geni.us/DaleMayerBookbub
Instagram – geni.us/DaleMayerInstagram
Goodreads – geni.us/DaleMayerGoodreads
Newsletter – geni.us/DaleNews

Also by Dale Mayer

Published Adult Books:

Shadow Recon

Magnus, Book 1
Rogan, Book 2
Egan, Book 3
Barret, Book 4
Whalen, Book 5
Nikolai, Book 6

Bullard's Battle

Ryland's Reach, Book 1
Cain's Cross, Book 2
Eton's Escape, Book 3
Garret's Gambit, Book 4
Kano's Keep, Book 5
Fallon's Flaw, Book 6
Quinn's Quest, Book 7
Bullard's Beauty, Book 8
Bullard's Best, Book 9
Bullard's Battle, Books 1–2
Bullard's Battle, Books 3–4
Bullard's Battle, Books 5–6
Bullard's Battle, Books 7–8

Terkel's Team
Damon's Deal, Book 1
Wade's War, Book 2
Gage's Goal, Book 3
Calum's Contact, Book 4
Rick's Road, Book 5
Scott's Summit, Book 6
Brody's Beast, Book 7
Terkel's Twist, Book 8
Terkel's Triumph, Book 9

Terk's Guardians
Radar, Book 1
Legend, Book 2
Bojan, Book 3
Langdon, Book 4

Kate Morgan
Simon Says... Hide, Book 1
Simon Says... Jump, Book 2
Simon Says... Ride, Book 3
Simon Says... Scream, Book 4
Simon Says... Run, Book 5
Simon Says... Walk, Book 6
Simon Says... Forgive, Book 7
Simon Says... Swim, Book 8

Hathaway House
Aaron, Book 1
Brock, Book 2
Cole, Book 3
Denton, Book 4

The K9 Files

Rowan, Book 10
Caleb, Book 11
Kurt, Book 12
Tucker, Book 13
Harley, Book 14
Kyron, Book 15
Jenner, Book 16
Rhys, Book 17
Landon, Book 18
Harper, Book 19
Kascius, Book 20
Declan, Book 21
Bauer, Book 22
Delta, Book 23
The K9 Files, Books 1–2
The K9 Files, Books 3–4
The K9 Files, Books 5–6
The K9 Files, Books 7–8
The K9 Files, Books 9–10
The K9 Files, Books 11–12

Lovely Lethal Gardens

Arsenic in the Azaleas, Book 1
Bones in the Begonias, Book 2
Corpse in the Carnations, Book 3
Daggers in the Dahlias, Book 4
Evidence in the Echinacea, Book 5
Footprints in the Ferns, Book 6
Gun in the Gardenias, Book 7
Handcuffs in the Heather, Book 8
Ice Pick in the Ivy, Book 9
Jewels in the Juniper, Book 10

Killer in the Kiwis, Book 11
Lifeless in the Lilies, Book 12
Murder in the Marigolds, Book 13
Nabbed in the Nasturtiums, Book 14
Offed in the Orchids, Book 15
Poison in the Pansies, Book 16
Quarry in the Quince, Book 17
Revenge in the Roses, Book 18
Silenced in the Sunflowers, Book 19
Toes up in the Tulips, Book 20
Uzi in the Urn, Book 21
Victim in the Violets, Book 22
Whispers in the Wisteria, Book 23
X'd in the Xeriscape, Book 24
Lovely Lethal Gardens, Books 1–2
Lovely Lethal Gardens, Books 3–4
Lovely Lethal Gardens, Books 5–6
Lovely Lethal Gardens, Books 7–8
Lovely Lethal Gardens, Books 9–10

Psychic Visions Series
Tuesday's Child
Hide 'n Go Seek
Maddy's Floor
Garden of Sorrow
Knock Knock...
Rare Find
Eyes to the Soul
Now You See Her
Shattered
Into the Abyss
Seeds of Malice

Eye of the Falcon
Itsy-Bitsy Spider
Unmasked
Deep Beneath
From the Ashes
Stroke of Death
Ice Maiden
Snap, Crackle…
What If…
Talking Bones
String of Tears
Inked Forever
Insanity
Psychic Visions Books 1–3
Psychic Visions Books 4–6
Psychic Visions Books 7–9

By Death Series
Touched by Death
Haunted by Death
Chilled by Death
By Death Books 1–3

Broken Protocols – Romantic Comedy Series
Cat's Meow
Cat's Pajamas
Cat's Cradle
Cat's Claus
Broken Protocols 1-4

Broken and… Mending
Skin

Scars

Scales (of Justice)

Broken but… Mending 1-3

Glory

Genesis

Tori

Celeste

Glory Trilogy

Biker Blues

Morgan: Biker Blues, Volume 1

Cash: Biker Blues, Volume 2

SEALs of Honor

Mason: SEALs of Honor, Book 1

Hawk: SEALs of Honor, Book 2

Dane: SEALs of Honor, Book 3

Swede: SEALs of Honor, Book 4

Shadow: SEALs of Honor, Book 5

Cooper: SEALs of Honor, Book 6

Markus: SEALs of Honor, Book 7

Evan: SEALs of Honor, Book 8

Mason's Wish: SEALs of Honor, Book 9

Chase: SEALs of Honor, Book 10

Brett: SEALs of Honor, Book 11

Devlin: SEALs of Honor, Book 12

Easton: SEALs of Honor, Book 13

Ryder: SEALs of Honor, Book 14

Macklin: SEALs of Honor, Book 15

Corey: SEALs of Honor, Book 16

Warrick: SEALs of Honor, Book 17

Tanner: SEALs of Honor, Book 18
Jackson: SEALs of Honor, Book 19
Kanen: SEALs of Honor, Book 20
Nelson: SEALs of Honor, Book 21
Taylor: SEALs of Honor, Book 22
Colton: SEALs of Honor, Book 23
Troy: SEALs of Honor, Book 24
Axel: SEALs of Honor, Book 25
Baylor: SEALs of Honor, Book 26
Hudson: SEALs of Honor, Book 27
Lachlan: SEALs of Honor, Book 28
Paxton: SEALs of Honor, Book 29
Bronson: SEALs of Honor, Book 30
Hale: SEALs of Honor, Book 31
SEALs of Honor, Books 1–3
SEALs of Honor, Books 4–6
SEALs of Honor, Books 7–10
SEALs of Honor, Books 11–13
SEALs of Honor, Books 14–16
SEALs of Honor, Books 17–19
SEALs of Honor, Books 20–22
SEALs of Honor, Books 23–25

Heroes for Hire
Levi's Legend: Heroes for Hire, Book 1
Stone's Surrender: Heroes for Hire, Book 2
Merk's Mistake: Heroes for Hire, Book 3
Rhodes's Reward: Heroes for Hire, Book 4
Flynn's Firecracker: Heroes for Hire, Book 5
Logan's Light: Heroes for Hire, Book 6
Harrison's Heart: Heroes for Hire, Book 7
Saul's Sweetheart: Heroes for Hire, Book 8

Dakota's Delight: Heroes for Hire, Book 9

Tyson's Treasure: Heroes for Hire, Book 10

Jace's Jewel: Heroes for Hire, Book 11

Rory's Rose: Heroes for Hire, Book 12

Brandon's Bliss: Heroes for Hire, Book 13

Liam's Lily: Heroes for Hire, Book 14

North's Nikki: Heroes for Hire, Book 15

Anders's Angel: Heroes for Hire, Book 16

Reyes's Raina: Heroes for Hire, Book 17

Dezi's Diamond: Heroes for Hire, Book 18

Vince's Vixen: Heroes for Hire, Book 19

Ice's Icing: Heroes for Hire, Book 20

Johan's Joy: Heroes for Hire, Book 21

Galen's Gemma: Heroes for Hire, Book 22

Zack's Zest: Heroes for Hire, Book 23

Bonaparte's Belle: Heroes for Hire, Book 24

Noah's Nemesis: Heroes for Hire, Book 25

Tomas's Trials: Heroes for Hire, Book 26

Carson's Choice: Heroes for Hire, Book 27

Dante's Decision: Heroes for Hire, Book 28

Steven's Solace: Heroes for Hire, Book 29

Heroes for Hire, Books 1–3

Heroes for Hire, Books 4–6

Heroes for Hire, Books 7–9

Heroes for Hire, Books 10–12

Heroes for Hire, Books 13–15

Heroes for Hire, Books 16–18

Heroes for Hire, Books 19–21

Heroes for Hire, Books 22–24

SEALs of Steel
Badger: SEALs of Steel, Book 1

Erick: SEALs of Steel, Book 2
Cade: SEALs of Steel, Book 3
Talon: SEALs of Steel, Book 4
Laszlo: SEALs of Steel, Book 5
Geir: SEALs of Steel, Book 6
Jager: SEALs of Steel, Book 7
The Final Reveal: SEALs of Steel, Book 8
SEALs of Steel, Books 1–4
SEALs of Steel, Books 5–8
SEALs of Steel, Books 1–8

The Mavericks

Kerrick, Book 1
Griffin, Book 2
Jax, Book 3
Beau, Book 4
Asher, Book 5
Ryker, Book 6
Miles, Book 7
Nico, Book 8
Keane, Book 9
Lennox, Book 10
Gavin, Book 11
Shane, Book 12
Diesel, Book 13
Jerricho, Book 14
Killian, Book 15
Hatch, Book 16
Corbin, Book 17
Aiden, Book 18
The Mavericks, Books 1–2
The Mavericks, Books 3–4

The Mavericks, Books 5–6
The Mavericks, Books 7–8
The Mavericks, Books 9–10
The Mavericks, Books 11–12

Standalone Novellas
It's a Dog's Life
Riana's Revenge
Second Chances

Published Young Adult Books:

Family Blood Ties Series
Vampire in Denial
Vampire in Distress
Vampire in Design
Vampire in Deceit
Vampire in Defiance
Vampire in Conflict
Vampire in Chaos
Vampire in Crisis
Vampire in Control
Vampire in Charge
Family Blood Ties Set 1–3
Family Blood Ties Set 1–5
Family Blood Ties Set 4–6
Family Blood Ties Set 7–9
Sian's Solution, A Family Blood Ties Series Prequel
    Novelette

Design series
Dangerous Designs

Deadly Designs
Darkest Designs
Design Series Trilogy

Standalone
In Cassie's Corner
Gem Stone (a Gemma Stone Mystery)
Time Thieves

Published Non-Fiction Books:

Career Essentials
Career Essentials: The Résumé
Career Essentials: The Cover Letter
Career Essentials: The Interview
Career Essentials: 3 in 1